MURDER CAN KILL THE APPETITE

There aren't many amusements in little Delphi, South Dakota—and that suits Tory Bauer just fine. Widowed, over forty, and somewhat exceeding the surgeon general's weight guidelines, she's content to sling hash at the locals in the Delphi Cafe and craves no additional excitement. Her oversexed fellow waitress and trailer-mate, Delphine, however, is always hungry for a new thrill. So when young, good-looking Mormon missionary Charles Winston brings his soul-saving fervor to the Cafe's table, Del's all over him like ketchup on fries, totally unconcerned about how her boyfriend—the dangerously short-tempered county deputy, Big Dick Albrecht—will react.

And it's Tory who has to clean up the sloppy mess left behind—because it's she who discovers Winston's corpse stuffed in a mop closet several days later. Tory's large appetite for answers and natural talent for deduction are dumping her into a crockpot of lethal, long-simmering small town secrets. And if she's not careful, she'll wind up in the missionary's position: flat-out, stone-cold dead.

KATHLEEN TAYLOR

FUNERAL FOOD

A TORY BAUER MYSTERY

AVON BOOKS ◆ NEW YORK

A version of *Funeral Food* has been previously published under the title *The Missionary Position* by Aegina Press in 1993.

AVON BOOKS
A division of
The Hearst Corporation
1350 Avenue of the Americas
New York, New York 10019

Copyright © 1998 by Kathleen Taylor
Published by arrangement with the author
Visit our website at http://www.AvonBooks.com
Library of Congress Catalog Card Number: 97-94073
ISBN: 0-380-79380-6

First Avon Books Printing: February 1998

AVON TRADEMARK REG. U.S. PAT. OFF. AND IN OTHER COUNTRIES, MARCA REGISTRADA, HECHO EN U.S.A.

Printed in the U.S.A.

WCD   10 9 8 7 6 5 4 3 2 1

To Terry, and the Dianes, whose love and impatience prodded this book, finally, into being. And to Boob, who surely wishes it had taken longer.

....

Acknowledgments

I'd like to thank the following people for their help in researching and writing this book: Spink County Sheriff Gary Newman, for his suggestions on official procedure; Betty Baloun at the library, for keeping the copier warmed up; Curtis and Matthew Taylor, for the vernacular; and Kris Hansen, Jane Stimson, and Jody Weisflock, whose chapter-by-chapter enthusiasm kept me going.

And I would like to thank my agent, Jane Dystel, and my editor, Carrie Feron, for helping to put the revision into shape.

Author's Note

In the beginning, there was Delphi.

Before I became intimately acquainted with its citizens, before I knew I had a mystery on my hands, before I had any notion of whether I should, much less could, write a novel, I knew Delphi.

Though the story that follows came to me in bits and pieces, as I struggled for the courage to face what seemed the impossible task of writing a murder mystery, the little town of Delphi, South Dakota, sprang, fully formed, into my head.

Delphi's streets and buildings, the heat and dust, the flat prairie and open sky, the joy and sadness, and the rhythms of small town life were presented to me intact—a gift that even an as an aspiring writer, I knew enough to treasure.

Tory, Stu and Neil, Del and Presley, Rhonda, Ron Adler and the rest, all came later, some as I wrote this story. After finishing three novels set in Delphi, I now know these people as well as I know myself—they live and breathe. Their lives are their own, their stories belong to them.

But when I started the first draft of *Funeral Food*, all I knew for sure was the town, and that knowledge kept me going through the very difficult process of writing a first novel. Even after the manuscript was finished, various complications prevented this book from being released nationally until after two more Tory Bauer mysteries, *Sex And Salmonella* and *The Hotel South Dakota* had been published.

But I knew that the story really started earlier. And so did the folks in Delphi. Here, now, are the people and the town, as I first knew them.

Kathleen Taylor

Prologue

I'm not the first to observe that funerals are for the living, not the dead. Whether Uncle John is stuck forever in a pine box, on his way to a better world, or somewhere in between, is beyond our knowledge, and our control. And since the deceased is pretty well beyond caring about the ceremonies and rituals that commemorate the end of life as we know it, it's safe to assume that survivors are the ones who demand a proper send-off.

Personal belief systems notwithstanding, the ceremonies we choose to honor the dead are remarkably similar to each other. Relatives and friends gather. They speak and they cry. They accompany the dear departed to a final resting place. They speak and cry some more. And then they come back and eat.

The words are the same. The tears are the same. And the food is the same.

At least that's how it works in Delphi, South Dakota. No self-respecting funeral would be caught without a hearty meal dutifully prepared by the church ladies, spread out buffet style in the reception hall, CCD center, or auditorium.

Mourners know the drill. They talk and cry, and sometimes even laugh, as they pile their Styrofoam plates with a casserole hot dish and red Jell-O salad, carrot sticks, buttered buns, and bar cookies. They sit together, drink coffee and punch, tell old stories and invent new ones, surrounding each other with comfort and continuity.

Our preference for routine and conformity goes a long way toward explaining why we are the way we are. Mired in routine, we don't need a funeral, or funeral food, to carry on, doing exactly the same things in exactly the same way.

That sort of near-ceremonial gathering, minus the crying and dead bodies, occurs every day in Aphrodite Ferguson's Delphi Cafe.

We gather, we talk, and we eat bad food.

And on the cusp of a hectic, hot and sticky noon hour, on a day that started out like all others, unfortunately unaware that my own routine was about to become permanently altered, I tried to maintain continuity for the rest of the locals by ignoring an earnest, freshly scrubbed, young man dressed in a long sleeved white shirt and dark tie.

An out-of-towner, not much more than a boy really, who had no way of knowing that noon special he'd ordered would be nearly identical to the food that would be served at his own memorial service.

Or that I would be the one to find his body.

1

....

Old Men at Breakfast

JUNE 23

Without a doubt, a humorless Christian Conservatism is the ideological default setting here. While friends and neighbors will not scurry across the road to avoid you if you come out of the Liberal Closet, resisting adoption by one of the mainstream churches is simply beyond the experience of most natives.

In a region where Wednesday evenings are left free of school activities for confirmation classes and football games begin with a prayer—refusal to teach Sunday School and chair bake sales is treated with a disbelief bordering on horror.

Though I never set out to be a rebel, the fact that I prefer to address Heaven alone and in private, produces a fair amount of over-reaction from the local mainstream.

A while back, my name appeared in ''The Un-Churched,'' an irregularly mailed, home-published bulletin that listed, by address and telephone number, the Plains States Unsaved.

It was another salvo in my Aunt Juanita Doreen Engebretson's never ending cycle of hope that I'd be tempted
back into The Fold. Any fold. Even one usually viewed
askance by the religious mainstream.

Every couple of years, the Latter-day Saints assign another pair of young missionaries to our area. Arriving
happy and hopeful, charged with True Religion and fired
by youth and inexperience, they do their level best to show
us The Way.

Unfortunately, since they looked as though they had just
completed an Up With People Tour, it was difficult for
Delphi's female population to remember that celibacy is
required for the duration of a young Mormon's mission.
And not just the younger females either.

"Jesus," Del whispered with no apparent irony, stealth-
ily watching Charles Winston from the far end of the
counter, "he really is serious about that Mormon stuff."

A sporadic and cynical Catholic, she was honestly
amazed. Delphine Bauer's religious observations consist of
biannual confessions and a bone-deep skepticism of anyone
else's piety.

"Charles," I said, blowing a clump of damp hair out of
my eyes and carrying an armload of #2s to a table full of
out-of towners just behind him, "I appreciate your concern,
but I just don't have time for this right now."

"I think you're afraid to hear me, Tory," he said in a
soft drawl, swiveling around on his stool at the counter, to
continue talking while I worked. "You don't want to admit
how empty your life has been the last couple of years. Honestly, we can help, if you'd just let us."

This conversation was a variation of the same one I'd
been having with Charles Winston, and his partner Donald
Garrett, for the past few weeks. They were sweet, gentle,
persistent boys who usually stopped in for meals, and a late
afternoon break, before returning to their mission homes in
Aberdeen, some twenty-five miles north, which held a small
but thriving Mormon community. Blond Donald Garrett
was a heartstopper with a heretofore undiscovered sensitiv-
ity to the dust and spores with which South Dakota

abounds. On low pollen days, high school girls would appear in the cafe, interrupting summer tanning schedules to accommodate a purely intellectual interest in Other People's Religions.

They would sit across from him in the booth, sipping decaffeinated Coke, making great cow eyes, and nodding seriously. He would testify earnestly with a clogged voice and runny eyes. Unconscious, apparently, of the effect blue eyes and broad shoulders had on teenage girls, Donald sniffled, and thought the gigglers were truly intrigued by his message.

Donald had occasionally been incapacitated to the point of barricading himself in the dust-free room thoughtfully provided by his Mission Mom, while Charles ran down ecumenical hot prospects alone.

"And what is Donald doing today?" I asked a while later, trying to change the subject as I measured coffee grounds into fluted paper filters during a brief lull.

"Sneezin'," Charles said with a grin. He had curling brown hair, dark sparkling eyes, and a sense of humor rare in the seriously religious. It's no wonder that Del, who found most men attractive, flirted outrageously with him, especially on days when Donald stayed behind.

"You can come and talk to me anytime," she said, leaning over just enough to breathe softly on his cheek as she passed by carrying a plate of fresh strawberry pie for the Old Farts. "My life is bleak and empty too," she said, lying through her teeth.

Charles pulled back a little, not a recoil, just a tightening of the defenses. I could see that he was not immune to Del's ample charms. Few males are. But he was serious about his calling and willing to undergo a trial or two in the South Dakota wilderness if need be, even if the trial included resisting the none-too-subtle invitations of a plush, if slightly shopworn, temptress.

Del is not thin and she is not beautiful, and she is more or less my age, which is not exactly young. But no one seems to notice. With a toss of her tousled red hair and a flash of her astonishing cleavage, she reduces men of all ages to jelly, and loves every minute of it.

"How're they hanging today, gents?" she asked the Old Farts, a group of elderly and cantankerous regulars. She winked theatrically, knowing that Charles was watching her out of the corner of his eye. The men in the booth hemmed and hawed and leered in response to a question that would have produced apoplexy if any other woman had asked it.

Bound by mutual antagonism and the steady stimulant of continuing arguments, the Old Farts, mostly retired farmers, met every day at the same gray booth at the Delphi Cafe. They rehashed old conflicts, dreamed up new ones, and caught up on the latest gossip.

If the awful truth were known, the only real difference between them and the rest of us is a certain fashion sense. That and the fact we make sure to use a bathroom elsewhere because the Old Farts always monopolize the one at the cafe.

As a group they were slow to warm to outsiders, but both young missionaries were pretty well accepted by everyone else, once they learned the important cafe rules of behavior, such as: Don't sit in the Old Farts' booth (the one closest to the bathroom, considered their own private property); and Do laugh at Ron Adler's Ole and Lena jokes even though they're rarely funny, and usually obscene.

Though their steadfastly Mormon designs on local souls didn't exactly endear the boys to the cafe crowd, their cheerful willingness to play one of Delphi's favorite games, was encouraging.

The game is simple: You name all your relatives and friends, and all their relatives and friends, tell us what they do and where they live, and we'll cross-check the information with all our friends and relatives to see if we come up with a match.

Points are awarded for similar occupations, affiliations, and vacations, and for living in the same state.

Sometimes we hit the jackpot—it's amazing how often a second cousin's ex-husband lives a block away from a Michigan family of four on their way through to Denver, who only stopped at the cafe to change the baby.

So far the only discovered link with our missionaries has been Del's pilgrimages to Memphis, the final resting place of her hero Elvis, and hometown of dark-haired Charles Winston. We have all heard more than enough about Memphis (and Elvis) from Del, but Charles enjoyed map tracing, and Del certainly enjoyed Charles.

"God, Tory, will you look at that," she said, lasciviously peering through the streaked window as the retreating Charles bent over to retrieve a piece of paper. "Makes my mouth water just to think of it."

I didn't ask her exactly which "it" she had in mind, though she would have been more than happy to specify. I was mostly willing to let her enjoy her own fantasies since Del had rescued me shortly after Nicky's death, by insisting that I move into the trailer she shared with her son, Presley.

"What's the problem?" she had asked when I hesitated. "Pres loves you, I love you. We'll take your mind off Nicky and find a nice married boyfriend to occupy you during my shift so you'll always be home evenings."

To Del, who was Nicky's first cousin and who shared his habit of unexplained nights out, the idea of a Backup Mom for Presley must have carried considerable appeal (and married boyfriends never bothered her conscience).

My reasons for accepting her offer weren't entirely altruistic either. Nicky's insurance settlement had been pitifully small, and I was faced with the dreadful prospect of moving back to the farm with my mother and dotty grandmother.

All in all, it'd been an interesting experiment, relatively uncomplicated since our shifts at the cafe rotate, and my most pressing need is for Diet Coke and buttered popcorn while reading the latest Ed McBain or Tony Hillerman novels.

We settled easily into a routine that suits all of us. I work or read, and take care of Presley. Del spends all her time being Del.

"Ain't she something?" sighed Ron Adler, a married mechanic with no chin, an unrequited crush, and a facial tic that causes him to blink furiously every third word.

"She's a fine"—blink, blink, blink—"figure of a woman."

Nobody defines me as a "fine figure" of anything. Always struggling for control over my own hair and weight, I opt for sensible, easy-to-manage styles. I'm more interested in big pockets than high fashion, and like most large ladies, I'm unwilling to buy clothes that actually fit—the size frightens me.

Del goes for flash, wearing short skirts and heels one day, and jeans and cowboy boots the next.

I have watched her with Charles, leaning toward him when she takes his order, touching his arm lightly, smiling directly into his eyes. It's a well tested routine with a proven track record, and she has bagged a covey of men with it, including her current boyfriend, the well-armed county deputy Big Dick Albrecht.

She claims to be happy with Big Dick and he is obviously skilled in bed, trailer house walls being notoriously thin. But I also saw that Del, who could have any man, wanted this boy too. Badly. Young Charles Winston also saw this, and was unwise enough to let just a little smug amusement show. Charles had probably spent his entire life fending off unwanted females, young and old. His certainty that he was equal to this particular challenge was apparent.

That sort of obstacle, unfortunately for Charles, only served to fuel her fires. That Del nursed a small grudge against men of the cloth complicated and enhanced her determination to have him at all costs. One of her rare misfires was with the Reverend Clay Deibert (son-in-law of my aunt the postmistress, and husband of my cousin Junior the Dreadful).

The cafe was gearing into the dinner rush. Del had thoughtfully watched Charles's asthmatic tan Chevy drive off in a cloud of dust. I'd just finished ringing up a crew of combiners when the reason for Del's attempt at clergy seduction breezed in with her four surgically neat children in tow. Del stabbed out her cigarette, then headed back to sit with an adoring Ron Adler. "You take this one, I'm on break."

Junior (born Juanita Doreen Engebretson II) is a younger, trimmer version of her mother, a dark-haired whirlwind of ambitions and pretensions. Like her mother, she is also possessed of an indomitable will and enormous reserves of energy that are barely tapped managing her picture-book home, husband, and children.

I refilled cups, a pot of decaf in one hand and regular in the other, waiting for Junior and her brood to get settled.

"Hot enough for you?" I asked, swiping the table with a damp rag and setting water glasses in front of Junior and her oldest daughter, Tres. Ninety-three degrees and 84 percent humidity outside, and 80 and 80 percent inside, should be hot enough for anyone, though I have yet to see Junior break a sweat, even in August.

"Actually . . ." She paused to dunk a napkin in her water glass and scrub a spot that I had apparently missed. "Heat and humidity are wonderful for the body. Gives the skin a young, fresh look, and it encourages weight loss. You should get out more." She smiled up at me with innocent good humor. "It would do you a world of good."

As an exercise in goodwill, I put special effort into not hating Junior. It is an ongoing struggle.

"We're on our way to Aberdeen," Junior continued, answering a question I hadn't asked, "and we thought we'd see if Tory had anything good to eat before we left town."

She directed that last comment across the table to her unnaturally well-behaved toddlers. Like three apple-cheeked, red-haired puppets, they nodded in unison back. Triplets Joshua, Jessica, and Jeremy, with their hands folded neatly on the table, smiled up at me too. It was spooky. Eight-year-old Tres (Juanita Doreen III—*Tres* is the Spanish word for *three*, get it?), sat beside her mother, looking out the window. Pretty and dark, Tres used to flash an occasional grin or smother a genuine little-girl giggle. But lately she has been solemn and dignified, as though weighed down with the burden of being Juanita Doreen III.

"What's up today, kiddo?" I asked, her, ignoring Junior.

"Got exciting plans for the big city?" Aberdeen has approximately twenty-three thousand people and a mall. By our standards, it's big.

"Tell Tory your news," said Junior, just as if I had been talking to her.

"Guess what!" Tres said excitedly. "Mom, Grandma, and I figured out what to call my oldest daughter!"

"Did I miss something?" I asked, depressed that this eight-year-old had been pressured, already, into planning her children's names. "I didn't even know you were engaged. Or did you and Presley elope?"

I was hoping for a giggle from Tres.

"Hardly," Junior said in a tone that made me glad that Del was sitting back with Ron, and not eavesdropping.

"You *know* when I have a baby, she has to be named Juanita Doreen, just like Mom and Grandma," Tres said, parroting her mother's and grandmother's insane notion that the world actually needs more Juanita Doreens.

"And you," I added. What with an overbearing mother and grandmother, and three younger siblings, the poor kid could be forgiven for forgetting about herself.

"Yeah, but we can't *call* her Juanita Doreen because that's Grandma's name. So we need a nickname, like Junior and Tres, only with the number four somehow. Last night we finally figured it out!"

"What did you come up with?" I considered and rejected adding that daughters can't be ordered like drapery. The kid already had enough to worry about.

"Ivy," she crowed triumphantly.

I must have looked confused because she adopted the tone that bright children use when explaining the obvious to stupid adults.

"Not ivy like the plant, I-V, like the Roman numeral!"

"She thought of it all by herself." Junior beamed. "Isn't that wonderful?"

"Marvelous," I said dryly. "I can't wait for number six. What would you like?"

While I got carrot sticks and orange juice for the triplets, which they ate and drank without making a mess or spilling a drop, and yogurt and mineral water for Tres and her Mom (tap water was good only for washing tables), Junior continued to tick off her day's itinerary, just in case anyone was interested.

"First we go to the dentist, then we shop for shoes, then we talk to my district manager for a minute."

In her spare time Junior coordinated parties for the sale of a line of household decorations consisting mainly of overpriced bisque woodland figurines and wrought-iron festooned with plastic greenery. A representative displays and sells the goods, in a Tupperware-party-like setting, to women with disposable income and dubious taste.

Junior makes pretty fair money selling this stuff, which she in turn donates to charities whose main function is telling the rest of us what to do. The antipornographers, the music censors, and the GOP love her. On the local level, there are some who wish she would get hit by a truck. "Finally we go to the Aberdeen library," she said.

"What's the matter with Neil's?" I asked. My friend Neil Pascoe runs a private library out of his own home here in Delphi. In '86 he won twelve million in the Iowa lottery, and he has since devoted his money and time to his passions: old car restoration, music, and books. He is perfectly willing to find and lend any book to anyone. In fact his personal library is more extensive than most city libraries, filling the first floor of the three-story Victorian house he shares with his two cats. Books arrive by mail and UPS daily, and I usually look over the new ones with him on the way home after work.

"I want the children to go to a real library, dear," Junior said on the way out. "I simply can't imagine why an unmarried man would want to lend books to unsupervised children," imputing shady motives to one of the nicest men I know.

Not for the first time I was sorry that Del hadn't succeeded with Clay. It was never a case of attraction to the man, though Clay is a mature honey-blond version of our Mormon missionaries—almost unbearably cheerful, studiously pious, and seriously dedicated to his Lutheran pulpit and family. In fact, I like and respect Clay, though I wish he had chosen a different lifetime companion.

No, it was sheer exasperation with Junior, who manages to insult and aggravate everyone around her, that decided Del to take her down a peg or two, via Clay.

"I am going to fuck her husband," Del had said slowly and deliberately, with a chilling smile, after Junior had again said something condescending about the Bauers in general and Nicky in particular. "And I am going to videotape it, and I am going to send it to her afterward."

Del was serious about the threat. She had an impressive collection of audio and video recordings of just such encounters. It was a hobby of hers. Unfortunately (or fortunately, depending on your attitude toward marital fidelity in clergymen married to impossible women), Clay wouldn't cooperate. Del went to him, pleading for private counseling, which he gladly granted. She wasted no time with preliminaries, and he wasted no time in getting the hell out of there. A rejection Del could have tolerated; it was his look of abject horror that offended her.

In the aftermath Del and I rightly assumed that Clay was too honorable and sensible to tell anyone (especially Junior) about the unfortunate incident. We had truly hoped to keep it quiet, for everyone's sake. But secrets have a way of leaking out by osmosis, of infiltrating the prairie air we breathe. And it was soon obvious that everyone knew. Conversation in the cafe would slow in tense, if hopeful, expectation whenever either Junior or Clay walked in during Del's shift, as if everyone were waiting for a confrontation.

Junior is my first cousin and I know her. Whatever her inner turmoil, she is publicly unflappable. She would never subject herself to the kind of spectacle everyone seemed to want. Nevertheless, she ceased to be any more than formally civil to Del, though this civility didn't preclude the occasional nasty remark.

Opinion, freely aired when none of the above was in the cafe, was fairly evenly divided along the lines of sex. The women blamed Del for trying, and the men were disgusted with Clay for resisting. No one gave Junior a second thought. Except maybe Del, who mixed a dash of malice for both into her unsavory intentions for Charles.

Long ago I made my peace with Del's gleeful insistence on having her own way with men, her total lack of restraint, the absence of taboos. I don't pretend to understand how she avoids dealing with the sometimes irreparably mangled lives that result.

But I didn't understand how Nicky did it either. And I loved him too.

At least Charles is not married.

Neither is Big Dick Albrecht, though he perhaps is a different species from Del's other men, who seem content to vie for whatever attention she deigns to give. Big Dick wants her exclusively and is grimly determined to achieve that improbable goal.

Nicknames in Delphi are awarded for any number of reasons. Like Native American warrior names, some are chosen to commemorate watershed moments. For example, Chainlink Harris could well have gone through life known as Clyde, if he had not believed the ninth graders who assured him that his tongue wouldn't stick to the flagpole on a bitterly cold winter day, as long as he said the magic word first.

Obviously, the magic word was Teflon. All in all, a hunk of tongue was a fair trade for a dreadful name like Clyde, and Chainlink seems satisfied.

Big Dick (whose ID tag reads ALBRECHT, GERALD R.) has a legacy name. His father, Richard, a massive six-two and 230 pounds, was known, by inescapable South Dakota logic, as Little Dick. As soon as it was apparent that young Gerald would bypass his father in height and girth, he became, permanently, Big Dick.

"Huge," Del said, when I finally worked up the nerve to ask. Deputy Albrecht was due soon for dinner, and then he and Del were leaving for the Cities (Minneapolis and St. Paul in South Dakota parlance). They had planned a cozy, romantic visit with all the trimmings: tickets to see the Twins lose, a pocketful of crisp twenties, and a motel suite with a Jacuzzi.

Del had arranged for Rhonda Saunders, our nineteen-year-old relief, to take her supper shift. At home her overnight bags were ready and waiting by the door.

"What do you think of this?" she had asked me yesterday while packing, holding up a wisp of white silk and lace that was probably supposed to be underwear, though it had loops and spaces where most of the cloth should have been. "It's the latest thing in user-friendly lingerie." Del had hummed and sorted flavored body oils, genuinely excited about this trip with Big Dick.

Big Dick always took time to joke with the Old Farts or the other guys, and went out of his way to charm my mother and the ladies, before sitting at the counter with Del. He told suitably raunchy stories and laughed loudly.

He would smile broadly. But the smile never reached his eyes, which had a dark reptilian glitter.

And though he would turn sideways if I had to pass him in the aisle, he would always brush his body against mine. He would plant his heavy hands on my shoulders, chest pressing against my back, while he gabbed over my head with whomever I was serving. I could feel that pressure hours afterward. When he wanted a refill, he would seize a wrist and squeeze just slightly harder and longer than necessary to get my attention.

There are large, gentle men. Men who are almost apologetic about their size, who move and speak softly, and who always take the seat next to the window, so as not to be in the way.

And there are men like Big Dick, who use their size as a weapon, a tool for intimidation. Men who never forget their own power, and who never let you forget it either.

Del enjoyed the hint of danger his strength implied, and their relationship went smoothly for about the first six months, until Del, being Del, segued off into a short fling with a Combined Insurance salesman. Big Dick seemed indifferent, which reassured Del enough to accompany the salesman into Jackson's Hole, Delphi's only bar. The pair stayed late, drinking heavily, dancing to the jukebox music, and smooching sloppily. The official report read that Deputy Albrecht had come upon an inebriated man stumbling along the highway that same night. The official report stated that the man had been attacked and beaten by unknown assailants and that he had been transported to an Aberdeen hospital at the request of Deputy Albrecht. The salesman corroborated the story, and the unknown assailants were never identified.

The next night, as I lay in my bed, I could hear faint sounds echoing through the house like soft thuds, from Del's bedroom, and a soft moaning that could have been either pain or pleasure.

When it was finally quiet, I padded softly from my room through the moonlit kitchen and living room, down past Presley's room, into the trailer's only bathroom, which could also be entered from Del's room at the end of the hall.

Not wanting to disturb anyone, I left the light off, and bumped into Big Dick, who stood silent and naked in the middle of the bathroom, bathed in moonlight.

Involuntarily I flicked my eyes down his body. The glance took less time than a blink but he saw it and smiled. He stepped toward me.

I fumbled with the door and tried to back out of the bathroom, to twist out of his way, but he pinned me to the door with his body. His chest pressed against mine, making it hard to breathe.

He leaned down, whispering confidentially as though we had a secret to share, a desire to keep this just between us.

"Want some, sweetie?"

Through the thin nightshirt I wore, I could feel him twitching against my leg.

"Anytime," he breathed, shifting slightly, increasing the pressure of his body against mine. His breath was hot and damp on my neck. I tried to slide down the door, to make myself smaller, but that only raised my nightshirt. He shifted again, this time bare skin against skin.

"Just say the word." He chuckled softly in my ear. Then, abruptly, he turned and went back into Del's bedroom.

I have no idea how long I stood against the door, trembling. But I know that it was hours before I slept because the noises, not soft or echoing this time, began again. And I know I was supposed to hear his triumphant, shattering cry at the end.

Though I avoid Big Dick whenever possible now, he smiles and winks, implying a jolly conspiracy of which I do not want to be a part.

And Del continues to enjoy a theoretically all-encompassing affair with Big Dick, and circumspectly entertains occasional lovers in private.

It is a precarious, and perhaps dangerous, balance.

2

···························

After Dinner Rush

The English/South Dakotan Dictionary defines *coffee*, strong and black, as the daytime drink of choice among natives, who would have ordered a cup of cream and sugar if that's what they had wanted. *Coffee* is also the term used for a workday break, a chance to sit with a cigarette and a cup, to shoot the shit with whoever else happens to be in the cafe. Coffee is what you meet your friends for in the afternoon, even if you order pie and Diet Coke.

Though traditionally observed in midmorning and mid-afternoon, when the gossip is juicy or the weather is bad, coffee often overlaps and absorbs South Dakota's official midday meal, which is "dinner."

In our recent pioneer past, farmers toiled an exhausting number of hours under relentless suns and in howling bliz-zards. Survival was a full-time occupation that could only be accomplished by ingesting several thousand calories each day. We have preserved that tradition, even though today most farmers accomplish their backbreaking toil in an air conditioned, luxuriously appointed tractor cab.

An average farm dinner might consist of fried chicken and mashed potatoes with thick white gravy, homemade buns, chokecherry jelly, green beans from the garden, fruit sauce (another South Dakotan phrase, meaning sliced fruit in heavy syrup), and dessert. The dessert would depend on the season: strawberry, rhubarb, apple and squash pies; cobblers and crisps; egg-heavy cakes; bread or rice puddings, or home-cranked ice cream.

We are a round folk, we South Dakotans.

Dinner specials at the cafe, while not the repast enjoyed on the old homestead, are traditional high-calorie, fat-laden, and salt-drenched meals, served in generous portions at a reasonable price.

Like Ron Adler says, "We gotta harden them arteries somehow." Blink, blink.

As owner and chief cook at the Delphi Cafe, Aphrodite Ferguson begins her morning at five-thirty. A short powerhouse of a woman, she wears a spattered apron that reads "Kiss the Cook," smokes continuously at the grill, and speaks in monosyllables, if at all.

Her meatloaf had been hot and ready since eleven-thirty; the mashed potatoes, gravy, and creamed corn were steaming. Squares of cherry Jell-O, served on a single lettuce leaf, embedded with marshmallows and topped with Cool Whip, sat on individual plates in the salad cooler. And the cafe was hopping already.

The bulk of our customers are regulars, locals whose names and faces and life histories are as familiar as our own. But our location, just a half-mile off, and visible from, Highway 281, on the edge of Delphi, ensures steady drop-in traffic.

Just now, all five booths along the south wall, including the Old Farts' domain, were filled by a small noisy Air Stream caravan from upstate New York who had hardly decided to brave quaint Midwest scowls from ancient retired farmers, and eat quaint Midwest food in an authentic quaint Midwest diner.

They gabbled, pointing out the sights to each other,

laughing and exclaiming in loud, nasal voices, like visitors to a third world country who assume the natives don't speak the mother tongue.

Maybe they'd never seen a rifle on a gun rack in the back window of a pickup before.

I raided the walk-in cooler for more club soda, doubting that the brave New Yorkers would be hardy enough to survive our quaint Midwest tap water, which can cause a certain delayed digestive unpleasantness.

"Is that actually Bach?" one old duck asked another, incredulous, apparently, that civilization had reached this far inland.

I happen to like the Brandenburg Concertos, which were tootling from the crusty portable tape player on the counter under the air conditioner.

The shift captain, a whimsical title that means me in the morning and Del in the late afternoon, selects the music that is played all day in the cafe except when the radio is switched on for the weather, livestock reports, and Paul Harvey.

Del's obsession with Elvis, and her fondness for all music in the country-western mode is more to the local taste, and would probably not raise the eyebrows of outsiders, who seemed to expect cowboys on horseback to mosey in for meals after the roundup.

"We'd like to order now, miss, if you don't mind," a heavyset man with three chins, a florid complexion, and an enormous Rolex, said brusquely. "We're in a hurry here. Bring each of us the specialty of the house. If it's edible, that is."

He did not smile when he said that.

"Well," I said, resisting the urge to add a drawl and drop some final consonants, "The meatloaf is nice and hot, and we made it only last Tuesday."

Customers like this bring out the worst in me.

They bring out the worst in Del too, who told a woman dressed in a mustard color designer jumpsuit that "red" was the salad flavor "doo-joor."

"I heartily recommend Delphi's own spring water,

drawn from an artesian well sunk fourteen hundred feet below the Earth's surface,'' Del said, with a wink at the jumpsuit's companion, setting glasses in front of them.

I was juggling three specials and one tuna on whole wheat (water packed, no mayonnaise) when Big Dick finally pulled up to the cafe. He was still armed and in uniform, and obviously unready to leave for Minnesota. There was a figure slumped in the shadowy backseat of his patrol car.

Del's welcoming smile died when she saw his expression.

Though I tried to move out of his way, Big Dick's hands grazed my waist on his way toward Del. He waited impatiently while she delivered an armload of specials, and then cornered her at the small table along the cafe's west wall.

Though the caravaners kept me too busy to spy outright, I could see that their conversation was heated. With his back to the rest of the cafe, Big Dick pounded the table softly in emphasis. Del's eyes narrowed and shifted to the wall as she lit a cigarette and dragged on it furiously, ignoring customers and Aphrodite's inquiring glance.

Big Dick's voice rose in muted anger. Del glared back and muttered something short and sharp. With no warning, he stood and grabbed Del's shoulders and shook her violently. The cigarette fell from her hand and down the aisle, leaving a trail of ash.

Then he stormed out of the cafe and drove off leaving a rooster tail of dust and spattered gravel.

The New Yorkers, who now had another quaint story to add to their repertoire, buzzed among themselves.

Del sat at the table with unfocused eyes, smoking unsteadily.

"Can I help you, miss?" the jumpsuit's companion turned and asked quietly.

"You can fuck yourself," Del said precisely, and served her remaining orders with a mechanical smile.

Abashed, the New Yorkers paid their bills.

While Aphrodite does not approve of recommending anatomically impossible sexual stunts to patrons, she views outsiders existentially, real only while they are seated in the cafe. Once they leave, they're like figments of our imagination, though these figments add considerably to the financial security of the establishment. She shrugged philosophically as the Air Streams drove off.

Shaking her hair back, Del walked the length of the cafe to the pay phone, fished in her pocket for a quarter, and dialed, drumming her fingers on the wall while she waited.

"Rhonda," she said, "listen, don't worry about coming in for me this afternoon. I'll be here."

Del closed her eyes and said into the phone, "No, he has to escort a prisoner to Fargo." Pause. "The shits, ain't it?"

I didn't need to hear any more. It was obvious that Big Dick had to cancel their trip, and obviously Del was disappointed. Still, I didn't think the vehemence of their argument was caused solely by not being able to have soggy sex in a Minneapolis whirlpool.

I was relieved that Del had not met with any success on the Charles front. That poor boy would never survive a confrontation with Big Dick.

Del's grim expression and flat eyes precluded any questioning, so I went back to work.

"My nose is starting to wheeze, Tory," announced my Uncle Albert Engebretson, a man of daily water-pack tuna sandwiches and various unsettling medical symptoms. "Do you think it means anything?"

I couldn't remember any life-threatening diseases heralded by wheezy noses. "Nah," I said. "It's probably just a little hay fever."

He didn't look relieved.

"You think it could be a polyp?" he asked holding his cup at a goofy angle, trying to use the coffee's smooth surface as a mirror to look up his own nose.

Uncle Albert is a soft, round, insurance salesman with a small independent office next to the grocery store. Mild and balding, he strives mightily to live up to his wife's and daughter's expectations, though his paperwork would be unreadably sloppy and his deadlines amiably missed were it not for Mrs. Beiber, a secretary/receptionist so terrifying that none dared to use her first name.

His grandchildren adored him. But his wife and daughter fussed constantly: tucking shirts, spit-cleaning, and correcting grammar. He bore it all with amazing composure.

I admired his restraint. If I were constantly surrounded by Juanita Doreens, I would probably have resorted to murder by now. Uncle Albert's retreat into hypochondria seemed a reasonable survival strategy. And the fact that the combined force of his women's indomitable wills has not yet molded him into their image proves Uncle Albert's inner (albeit hidden) steel core.

"Just the same"—he nodded to himself—"I think I'll make an appointment."

I refilled his cup, looking fondly at the sparse hairs glued in precise formation over the top of his shiny head. I leaned over and smooched his forehead noisily.

"What's that for?" He looked up with genuine surprise, blushing a little.

"Just because," I said.

Dinner rush was mostly over, the crowd had thinned considerably, and Del had regained a brittle, though nonconversational, poise.

I got myself the last brownie (stashed behind the salad dressing so no one else would find it) and sat sipping a Diet Coke on the stool closest to the till. With tired, aching shoulders, I closed my eyes and rolled my head, wincing at the grinding crunch.

Warm hands massaged my neck and between the shoulder blades. Thumbs kneaded expert, exquisite circles in sore muscles.

Thinking it was Del, or maybe even Aphrodite, who occasionally leaves her kitchen sanctuary, I leaned into the massage, eyes still closed, and murmured, "God, that's even better than sex."

"Someone hasn't been doing it right, then," a masculine voice said with more than a hint of amusement.

I whirled around, startled, embarrassed, and blushing furiously, and looked straight into Stuart McKee's impossibly beautiful green eyes.

My heart stopped.

I had been a sophomore in high school when my lamentably late husband Nicky first noticed me, though I had been there, lumpy and ungainly, hiding out in the library and sneaking candy bars in the bathroom all along.

I'd once asked why he had absorbed me into his group, an assortment of goofballs and hoods that included his wild red-haired first cousin, Delphine Bauer.

"Hon," he said, slipping his fingers under my nightgown—we were in bed, we were always in bed when I asked those questions—"you needed me."

That was the only explanation I ever got from him.

My mother, needless to say, had been horrified. Though not a snob of Junior and Aunt Juanita's caliber, she considered Bauers a species lower on the human evolutionary scale than our Osgood/Engebretson/Atwood branch (notwithstanding the fact that my own father had disappeared many years earlier, after it was discovered that he had a wife and three children in Sioux City, Iowa, to whom, I daresay, he also neglected to mention us).

"They're awfully fond of their own cousins, dear," Mother'd said, dredging up an old rumor about Oscar Bauer, late grandfather to the present clan, and a woman of reported ill-repute who also happened to be a daughter from Oscar's father's brother-in-law's first marriage.

In South Dakota, a cousin is anyone to whom you might possibly be related.

Luckily for me, I was not Nicky's cousin, and so a pregnancy scare, compounded by our own ignorance, hurried us into a civil ceremony. Would Nicky have married me if he had known then that pregnancy was never to be a threat? I honestly don't know.

For a long time I thought the problems in our marriage were caused by my inability to bear children, and that Nicky was looking for something in other women that I could not give him.

I was wrong, of course. Nicky was looking for the same

thing that I gave him, enthusiastically, all the time.

I willfully ignored Junior's first hint that Nicky was cheating on me. The next, with Aunt Juanita as a backup announcer, I furiously denied.

Sometime after the three hundredth, I came home from work early and discovered Lila Pankratz tied naked to my bed. With my pantyhose.

I have actually spit in Lila Pankratz's coffee.

Nicky really outdid himself the last time.

The newspapers reported that Nick and an unknown female (later identified as a Northern State University cheerleader) died from the injuries incurred in a one-car rollover on a gravel road, sometime in the early morning hours. The papers, thank God, omitted that she was found without underwear of any sort, and that his pants had been pushed down around his ankles.

I suppose it was impossible to drive safely that way.

Delphi, being what it is, knew all the sordid details immediately, but at least I was spared the acid pity of total strangers, on whose kindness it is never wise to rely.

The resident armchair psychiatrists thought that my father's disappearance had made me desperate for male acceptance and fearful of further abandonment, willing to settle for an irresponsible charmer rather than go it alone. And in a limited way, they were right, though giving Nicky every freedom did not, in the end, keep him from that final departure.

And even if I had known all the drawbacks in this particular deal with the devil, I would still have signed on the dotted line, though I have a hard time suppressing the nasty wish that Lila Pankratz had lost the lottery instead of a nineteen-year-old coed.

Everyday survival with Nicky took most of my energy before his death. And simple survival took all my energy afterward. I was not looking for a replacement.

Then Stu McKee moved back to Delphi and into my dreams.

With slightly receding sandy-brown hair, the spare beginnings of a paunch, and deep laugh lines around his astonishing eyes, Stu is Midwest handsome, but no one's definition of gorgeous.

In the way that we all know everything about each other, I knew that Stu had moved from Delphi and South Dakota, in disgust. His father Eldon, owner of McKee's Feed right across the street from the cafe, had reneged on a promise to retire and turn the store over to Stu. After a decade of patient waiting, a hale and ornery Eldon (definitely an Old Fart) still refused to leave the helm, so Stu had left for Minnesota.

Last winter Eldon had suffered a minor stroke that slowed him enough to summon his son. Stu reluctantly returned to take charge, though the old man could not resist sticking his nose into the business and his fingers into the till. As much to keep Eldon occupied as for any other reason, he and Stu also worked as handymen. Though they were both officially available for small jobs involving easy carpentry and household repair, it was usually Eldon who made the house calls, and Stu who hunted up jobs for him. Eldon had, just lately, been taking his own sweet time tearing down an old chicken coop at my mother's place.

At first Stu was just a pleasant addition to the regulars. Always smiling, joshing the ladies gently, and reminiscing with the Old Farts, he never complained about the food or the weather. He was well liked, and he left generous tips.

But he had a disconcerting way of smiling directly into my eyes when he ordered, of asking how I was, and then actually listening to the reply. He would touch me lightly when he wanted more coffee, broad fingers gently grazing the inner surface of my arm.

At first I assumed that was his way with waitresses. It was more than a month before I noticed that he never touched Rhonda, and that he kept a cool distance from Del.

"Watch out for him," Del had said, nodding in Stu's direction, not seriously believing that there was a need for warning. "He's a tricky one."

I doubt I would have taken any special notice of Stu or his small attentions if not for the dreams.

Always identical, they start innocuously enough, with the

cafe crowd transplanted to Jackson's Hole. The Old Farts are grousing in the corner over a pitcher of beer. Del is tending bar with a frozen smile. The lighting is dim, the smoke is heavy, and couples are slow-dancing to something torchy by the Eagles.

I am thin and beautiful and dressed in satin. Even my hair looks good. Without a word, Stu takes my hand and we begin to dance. His arm tightens across my back, pulling me against him. He breathes softly on my neck. I am trembling, and when our thighs graze, I can feel a throbbing through his jeans.

With a diamond sparkle in his emerald eyes, he quietly, gently promises, "Any time."

Then Jackson's melts away and we are naked in my bedroom, and I am tied to my bed and he is smiling at me and I know we are going to make love. I want to make love. I am so ready that I will explode with just a touch.

If he doesn't hurry, I will untie myself and finish the job alone.

It is always then, with a pounding heart, that I wake up, gasping and savagely disappointed.

It's tough to serve a man breakfast with equanimity after a dream like that. After a dozen of them it was becoming impossible.

With just one (count 'em) boyfriend/lover/husband on my record, I am not adept at flirting. And I'm even less adept at figuring out whether Stu is really coming on to me, or if he is just being kind, with a little body contact thrown in for good measure.

My marriage to Nicky had, so far, kept me from finding out. Besides a pitifully small insurance settlement, Nicky left me with a permanent empathy for the families of philanderers.

Stu did not reluctantly move back to Delphi with only a longstanding resentment against his father. He also brought his wife and son.

Delphi didn't know Renee McKee, and she was happy to keep it that way. An intimidatingly elegant Minnesota native, Renee took one look at South Dakota and closed her mind.

She had a job as a legal secretary in Aberdeen, and with five-year-old Walton in a day care center close to her office, only rarely were either seen in town.

It was reported that she hated South Dakota in general, and Delphi specifically, and that she was beginning to hate Stu for bringing her here.

My own feelings for Stu were decidedly confused. He's married, I thought firmly, as he turned to greet someone in a booth.

I made myself remember Nicky's betrayals, the hurt, the pantyhose. Lila Pankratz. Unfortunately I could still feel the delicious pressure of Stu's warm hands on my shoulders.

Calling myself a fool, I stood and stretched, waiting for Stu to get settled with a couple of regulars. With his back to me, I noticed the firm set of his shoulders and his soft hair, just long enough to curl below his cap, a variation of which nearly every man in the state wears.

"Thanks for the back rub," I said, ignoring that he was in one of Del's booths, forgetting that my shift was nearly over. I filled his cup and placed one hand lightly, deliberately, on his shoulder and gave it a small squeeze. Definitely not a caress. I firmly resisted the urge to run a finger along his neck, at the hairline.

I wanted to bury my hand in his hair. I wanted to lean over and kiss his neck. I wanted to lock myself in the bathroom and scream.

"Any time," he said with a smile.

I nearly dropped the pot.

Recognizing every single component of that infernal dream didn't stop it from recurring.

And it didn't stop my heart from fluttering each time Stu walked into the cafe. And reminding myself that I was short, fat, and funny-looking didn't keep me from being almost certain that he was interested.

I was in deep trouble.

Aphrodite, whose carrot-red beehive is sternly supported

by direct order and copious amounts of hair spray, pushed
my last two Delphi Burgers (double patty, cheese, bacon,
lettuce, tomato, and fries) through the space over the stain-
less steel countertop that divides the kitchen from the rest
of the cafe.

I filled Mountain Dews to go with the burgers, served
them with a smile, then sat to wait out the rest of my shift,
hoping no last-minute caravans would arrive.

Del, with a freshly minted smile, was bustling around
efficiently.

"I'll take this one. You can take off if you want," she
said to me as Charles slumped into one of my booths, leaning his forehead on the heel of his hand.

Though usually buoyant, with the joy of his mission
sparkling in his brown eyes. and a good word (from at least
one of the Good Books) in his soft drawl for everyone,
Charles was subdued, quiet and pale.

His eyes were red-rimmed, and I thought perhaps he'd
been crying.

Had Big Dick heard of Del's infatuation? Had he threatened this boy? Was that the source of their fight? I well
knew how unsettling the deputy could be.

I groped under the counter for my purse and glanced
back at Del and Charles on the way out the door.

She slid close to him on the same side of the booth, her
arm looped loosely around his shoulders, one breast pressed
to his side. False commiseration glittered in her eyes.

He closed his eyes and leaned his head back on her arm.

Charles looked very young and vulnerable and I was,
suddenly and irrationally, frightened for him.

Across the cafe, Del shot me a look of pure triumph.

3

....

Delphi's Oracle

Average Americans, when asked to visualize a small prairie town, searching their memory banks for old movies and fifties sitcoms, would probably be able to describe Delphi perfectly: a wide dusty main street, dotted on either side with mom-and-pop businesses, nary a franchise in sight (unless you counted Iva Hausvik's Amway distributorship in her home beauty shop); dilapidated buildings, some made even uglier by the addition of vinyl siding and sheets of artificial brick; quiet residential blocks, each house with a small square of lawn, a vegetable garden out back, and flower beds lining the sidewalks.

Our imaginers might even see tree-lined streets, though in this they would be wrong, since few trees survive the combined forces of temperature extremes and wind damage, and those that do usually contract some kind of disease, like the elms that were planted everywhere in the fifties, and are still in the process of being decimated by Dutch elm disease.

People would expect a preponderance of pickup trucks, a scattering of dogs, and a passel of kids running and laughing, churches on every corner, and a tavern with a brisk business. And since this is the prairie, the relentless sun would not be a surprise, nor the constant wind.

The summer humidity, though, astonishing in a state whose nearest ocean is many millions of years ago, can be a shocker, even to natives. South winds push warm, moisture-laden air up from the Gulf of Mexico to produce a crushing pressure that makes breathing hard work, and air-conditioner repairmen smile in their sleep.

In January, when the water pipes have frozen solid and the car won't start even after being plugged in all night, we are warmed by the memory of enveloping heat.

In June, when the average humidity is 88 percent, with a sticky waistband, the beginnings of heat rash (never mind where), and squinting into the fierce sunlight, I wonder why assorted Great White Fathers went to such trouble to steal this god-awful state from the original owners.

Humidity makes me crabby. Having no car, and having to walk home through the dust and humidity, makes me even crabbier.

Across the wide street from the cafe, Stu's new Chevy half-ton pickup was diagonally parked in front of the feed store, with Eldon's beat-up maroon Ford beside it. The building's narrow white siding and black trim were in need of fresh paint and the large MCKEE'S FEED sign hung slightly askew. Faded herbicide and seed posters lined the streaked front windows.

In the narrow grassy lot between the feed store and the new brick post office stood a battered pickup with a camper topper, thoughtfully parked nose in, which allowed everyone to keep track of Rhonda, who officially lived on a farm with her family, but who spent most nights, and many interesting afternoons, there with her large biker boyfriend, Michael. Michael rides an extremely loud, extremely large Harley, sometimes delivering Rhonda to work on it, from across the street, before roaring off in a cloud of dust.

We have come to appreciate the entertainment value of

the truck's low shocks. And thanks to Aunt Juanita, we know the truck is sitting squarely on feed store property because she tried to drum up a permanent ban on vehicles parked between buildings. After that failed, she brought in surveyors to make sure that no immorality was taking place on post office property.

As if we needed any confirmation, the spotless exterior of the new brick post office testified to the efficiency of a postmistress who ruled with an iron fist in a stainless-steel glove.

One-hundred-year-old St. John's Lutheran, at the end of that block, on the same side of the street, is a perfect small-town church. Severely decorated and maintained, the dark wood interior is always cool and serene. From the cafe doorway I could see Clay hunched over his desk through the window of his church office.

In the next block, Adler's busy, tidy gas station and garage was nestled by the bar. Faint strains of country-western music drifted from the open door of Jackson's Hole. Inside, shadowy figures played pool and drank beer at scattered small tables.

On my side of the street the cafe, flat-roofed and rectangular, sits at the end of the block. Faded plywood DELPHI CAFE signs, one facing the highway and the other the street, creaked slightly in the wind.

A tall white plank fence stretched between the brown cafe and the white, two-story Delphi Grocery next door, blocking the cafe side entrance and alley from the street. A small addition housing Uncle Albert's Delphi Insurance, tacked to the other side of the store, completed the block.

All three businesses shared a hard-packed dirt parking lot in back. In front, the sidewalk was shaded by large awnings. A pair of Eldon McKee's rickety brown wooden benches sat between the cafe and grocery entrances.

Neither Aunt Juanita nor Mrs. Beiber wished to encourage the idle, or Uncle Albert, by placing a bench near the insurance agency.

More to get out of the sun than to purchase anything, I ducked through the screen door and into the grocery store, though it was nearly as hot and sticky inside as out. A ceiling fan rotated in large lazy circles but did not seem to move any air.

I sniffed tentatively. Once or twice I've caught the scent of marijuana underlying the sweet strawberry incense that usually burned in a small brass pot by the till. Rhonda had noticed it too.

"Hey," she had said to me one day, grinning and drawing the syllable out. "Nice air freshener."

This afternoon I noted only the assorted ordinary odors of a small grocery: produce, laundry soap, lollipops, and dust.

"Tory, I knew you'd stop," Crystal Singman said from behind the old oak counter, in a deeply melodious voice. "Would you like a cup of tea?"

Crystal and her husband, Jasper, were relatively new to Delphi, having bought the store less than a year ago. Many of the natives still eyed them warily, and some were downright hostile.

Tie-dyed and bell-bottomed, Crystal and Jasper were aged flower children with enough gray in their leather-bound braids and sparkle in their wire-rimmed bifocals to authenticate stories of the Summer of Love.

"No tea, thanks," I said, "but I'll take some lemonade." She always kept a pot of tea and a pitcher of freshly mixed lemonade for customers. As far as I know, no other herbal refreshment was ever offered to the buying public.

Crystal and Jasper tried very hard to please the local establishment. Unfortunately, the harder they tried to please, the less they fit in.

"We were led to Delphi, and for what reason?" Crystal used to ask every customer who came in. "God has blessed me with the Sight," she would continue, answering her own question. "And it is my duty to use that gift to guide others." She always concluded that speech with a small bow and a generous "At your service."

"Just what we need," Mother said to me later. "More flakes in Delphi."

Crystal and Jasper, their van putting along on fumes, had

turned from the highway into Delphi on a whim, intrigued by a prairie town named after the Greek oracle. Delighted to find the grocery store for sale, the unusually well-bankrolled pair bought the establishment on the spot and confidently awaited whatever adventure heaven had ordained.

In the meantime they ran the store competently, taking care to stock each regular's preferences, earning a grudging profit from grumbling natives.

They delighted the Methodists by joining their church. And then they delighted the Lutherans by joining their congregation. Then they delighted the Baptists by signing up for adult bible study.

When word got around, the assorted churches, having a somewhat proprietary view as regards parishioners, ceased to be delighted by the Singmans.

"God wears many faces, and speaks in many languages," Jasper said gently to angry membership committees, "all of them holy."

The churches were genuinely baffled, never having met Polydenominationals.

The Singmans attended a different service every week, donating generously to each. They were never turned away, but they were not made to feel entirely welcome either.

Del, who is more seriously Catholic than she realizes, was horrified. "What is the matter with them?" she sputtered. "Don't they know what they are?"

I found the whole situation amusing, though Jasper and Crystal were as saddened as the mainstreamers at my lack of commitment to an organized Higher Power.

It was inevitable that the pair would make our missionaries welcome in their home. They had already spent several enlightening evenings together, though Mormons generally take a dim view of psychic powers, except as manifested by their own prophets.

"Come, Tory, I need to speak with you privately." Crystal beckoned mysteriously toward the back room, although there was no one else in the store to overhear us.

She handed me a sweating glass and I followed her am-

ple form behind the counter, noticing that she jiggled pretty
freely beneath her caftan. Crystal is one of the few women
who makes me feel petite.

She arranged herself regally in an overstuffed chair next
to a stack of boxes.

I perched on the boxes, curious.

"First, you must tell your Goddess to change the hiding
place for the cafe keys," she said in a theatrically large
whisper.

By "Goddess," Crystal meant Aphrodite. It was her
small joke.

"The gutter support is not secure enough," she said.

I had never taken her claims of psychic prowess seriously, but I was impressed. Aphrodite, Del, and I were
supposed to be the only ones who knew that an extra set
of cafe keys was hidden on a small ledge behind the downspout.

"How did you know we kept them there? A vision?" I
asked. Exactly how does a psychic revelation manifest itself?

"Yes, a vision," she said with a small smile, "but not
the kind you mean. Not long ago, I was getting ready for
bed and I happened to glance out my bedroom window to
see our esteemed county deputy reach for the keys and let
himself into the cafe."

Crystal and Jasper lived in the cramped apartment above
the store, and their bedroom overlooked the cafe's side entrance.

"He was in there a long while," Crystal said, "and when
he emerged, he was eating a sandwich. This has happened
more than once. Tell your Goddess for me, please. She
should know that the armed authorities are exceeding their
bounds."

Crystal still harbored the hippies' mistrust of the police.

"Second, and perhaps more important," Crystal said,
leaning toward me, "I have been having dreams, portents
about your friend, the Redhead."

This time she meant Del.

"The dream images are vague, but I have been told that

she is playing in dangerous waters that could well bring trouble for herself, and tragedy to those around her. She must be warned. Will you do this? It is important for our safety and well-being, as well as hers, that Harmony be restored to the enveloping spirits.''

If I understood correctly, Crystal was asking me to relay her premonition to Del, who had taken an instant dislike to the pair and would not set foot in the store.

''They're spooky,'' was all Del would say in explanation. ''The both of them.''

Though Del would discount immediately any warning coming from our psychic grocer, she never paid attention to anything I said either.

If Crystal's deputy sightings were correct, that would explain why the trailer had been quiet lately. Apparently Del and Big Dick had changed the location of their nocturnal festivities to the cafe. Though Del was certainly not supposed to tell anyone where the spare keys were, I don't suppose it mattered much.

It now seemed likely that Del had entertained other visitors after-hours at the cafe, as well. She often came home flushed and late, especially when Big Dick was out of town. It would certainly appeal to her to serve dinner on the same booth where she had made love the night before. And it would appeal to her to cheat on Big Dick there also.

''I'll give it a shot,'' I said doubtfully. ''But I can't guarantee anything. You know Del.''

Crystal nodded, and then patted me roughly on the shoulder. ''You have been through much, Tory. Something good will happen to you very soon. I feel it.''

I smiled and hoped she was right.

''By the way, your book is in,'' she said as I left. ''It will be at the library when you get there.''

She raised her eyebrows, tapped her forehead, and shrugged.

4

....

The Question

If Del and Presley and the trailer arrangement rescued me physically after Nicky's death, then Neil Pascoe and his books saved my sanity.

Del had installed me in the bedroom off the kitchen the day after the funeral. I burrowed in, refusing to leave the house or to receive any callers. Not generally tidy, I spent hours mechanically cleaning and organizing the trailer—folding towels and arranging the spices alphabetically. The rest of the time I watched TV blankly or stared at the ceiling. Or cried helplessly.

One afternoon the doorbell rang three times in quick succession. I was home alone, and curiosity finally moved me to open the door. There, on top of the chest freezer in the shed, was a small stack of books with a piece of paper taped to the top cover.

"Dear Tory," the typewritten note read.

I know you are not up to company right now, but I thought a few books might help you get through this

*time. These aren't great literature, of course, just
something to pass the hours with.*

*You can help me too—I'd appreciate your opinion
of the series. We're not talking* New York Times
Book Review *here, I just want to know what you
think. I'm starting a library and haven't decided exactly which books to stock yet.*

*I won't bother you in person—you can leave a note
with these. I'll pick them up in a week, same time,
same place. If you have any other books you'd like
to read, make a list and I'll try to find them for you.*

> *Sincerely,*
> *Neil Pascoe*

The paperbacks, old and well worn, had lurid covers:
Cop Hater, The Mugger, The Pusher, The Con Man, and
Killer's Choice. Detective books apparently, most written
more than thirty years ago by an Ed McBain.

I left them on the table, determined not to be sucked into
some kind of scheme by Neil Pascoe, who was much
younger than me, and whom I barely knew.

I tried to ignore the books, but they drew me like a magnet. After a couple of days I picked up the first paperback.
It was okay, a bit dated, a bit too hardboiled for my taste,
but readable.

I zipped through the second and third, enjoying each a
little more. By the time I finished the last in the stack, a
full day before the next installment was due, I realized that
Neil was a wise man.

While I was reading, I was in the 87th Precinct with the
detectives, not in South Dakota, mourning in a trailer
house. And while I was reading, I was not obsessively re-
arranging things or crying (for which Del and Pres were
duly thankful).

I stuck a note to the books, asking for more, and by the
time I finished the second stack, I was hooked. On mysteries in general, on the 87th Precinct in particular, and on

Neil Pascoe's system of Grief Management Through Lite Literature.

He led me from Agatha Christie, through Tony Hillerman, to P. D. James and Ruth Rendell, to Scott Turow. For variety, he threw in *Pride and Prejudice*, *The Hobbit*, and everything by P. G. Wodehouse and Dave Barry. He left history books and classics and science fiction short stories.

It was a species of madness, that obsessive reading. I sometimes read three books a day. But it was a healthful madness, if ever there was such a thing.

Of course, I didn't get over Nicky by distracting myself with literary puzzles. But the books helped, and time helped, and most of all Neil helped.

Any awkwardness I might have felt with him was dispelled at our first meeting.

"Who was the first boy you ever kissed?" he'd asked, initiating the first Question of the Day.

I almost said "Nicky," but that wasn't strictly true. Nicky was the first, last, and only one who mattered, but in the third grade a freckled kid named Conrad Pinkleman used to corner me in the coat room and plant wet kisses on my face.

"Conrad Pinkleman," I said, wondering where he was leading, "but he moved away the next year and I haven't seen him since."

"I knew it," Neil hooted.

"You knew it was Conrad Pinkleman?" I asked, doubtful.

"No. I knew he would have a goofy name. I have a theory that everyone's first kiss came from someone with a goofy name."

"Oh? And who was yours, then?" I asked.

"Letitia Trickle," he roared. And that was that.

By the time Neil had collected enough books to open his library, I was able to leave the trailer. By the time he had finished filling an entire room with mysteries and thrillers, I had gone back to work. By the time I gave up refolding Presley's underwear, I was stopping in to talk every afternoon, and we were comfortable enough not to talk if that was the mood. We were friends.

I closed the gate behind me and walked up the sidewalk. I suppose any well kept twenty-two-room lemon-yellow house would look imposing. This one, with porches and towers and gables and dormers and lintels and gingerbread and stained glass and hanging plants and wicker porch furniture, all painstakingly restored to original condition and color, was overwhelming. And magnificent.

A large wooden sign, placed prominently near the oak front door, read in florid, old-fashioned script: "Pascoe's Lending Library—Please Come In and Browse Amongst the Many Fine Volumes Contained Herein. This Establishment Is Open Every Day and During Reasonable Evening Hours."

Another smaller sign, on the other side of the door, painted in the same style, read: "Library Patrons are Kindly Asked to Ring the Bell Twice on Entering."

I pushed the button three times, my signal, and entered the dark, cool foyer. A gleaming oak staircase curved gracefully up to my right. On the left, a hall tree and coat rack flanked a chintz-trimmed window seat. I stooped to greet Elizabeth Bennet and Mr. Darcy, Neil's cats, curled together on the cushion.

I continued through to the library, which took up the entire first floor of the house. Each of the odd-shaped rooms was lined with glass-doored bookshelves arranged according to subject and Neil's whim. The whole was decorated in high Victorian overabundance, with tables and leather chairs and couches in convenient corners.

Humming to myself, I turned into the tower room, where Neil was usually to be found in the afternoon. He was leaning carelessly against a huge oak desk that was strewn with unopened packages, comfortably laughing and talking with Stu McKee, who carried a stack of paperback books tucked under one arm.

Neil beckoned, shaking hands with Stu, who turned to leave. The pair were almost the same height, though that was their only similarity. Stu, fair with a medium build, was slightly older than Nicky. Neil was broader and heavier than Stu, and a good ten years younger. His coarse black hair was already shot with gray, his hands wide and callused, and his dark eyes sparkled with intelligence behind heavy glasses.

"We really do have to stop meeting like this," Stu leaned over and said confidentially as we passed, his fingers cupping my elbow fleetingly. "People will talk."

Seeing him unexpectedly had set my heart thudding and scrambled my thought processes. I just winked and grinned, like an idiot.

"Who's your favorite blind singer?" Neil, who didn't notice my confusion, asked. This was a Question of the Day.

The Question is a sort of IQ test of quick wit. I win when I make him laugh. I figured he was expecting me to pick someone obvious like Stevie Wonder or Ray Charles. At one time I probably would have said Roy Orbison— those dark glasses fooled me for years.

"Diane Schuur," I said smugly. "Building a Blind Singer Collection?"

"Maybe," he said, grinning mysteriously as he sat in the chair behind his desk.

Neil often asked questions about my preference in books and music, and I would find those selections on the shelves a week later. Because he's insatiably curious (Del thinks he's snoopy), the Question is sometimes just an information-gathering tool.

"Listen to this, Tory," he said, aiming a remote in the general direction of his state-of-the-art stereo system. "I know it's out of season, but this stuff is absolutely marvelous."

Music had been playing quietly in the background the whole time, though I hadn't noticed it while Stu was in the room. Amazingly enough, it was Christmas music.

But it was Christmas music like I had never heard before.

"Mannheim Steamroller," Neil explained. "Great, huh?"

We listened, entranced, to the blend of medieval and synthesizer music, old carols and new compositions. I forgot heat and humidity for a while, and remembered snow and packages and candy canes.

Neil broke in suddenly. "What's your favorite eye color?"

That caught me off guard. "Green," I said, too quickly I guess, because he looked at me searchingly for a second before nodding to himself.

"Why?"

"Never mind, it's a surprise. Oh!" he said, suddenly changing the subject. "I think the new McBain came in."

"I know already. You can't tell Crystal your surprises if you want them to stay secret." I pointed a finger at my forehead and intoned what I hoped was an eerie imitation of Crystal's voice. "It came to me in a dream. Your book, it is already on the best-seller list."

"I haven't talked to Crystal today," he said without looking up, using a pocket knife to slit the tape on the boxes that littered his desk. "Besides, Jess brought these just before you got here. Ah, here it is."

Jess was our UPS delivery man.

He lifted the book out of the box and handed it to me with a huge grin. "You know, I think I created a monster."

"It's all your fault." I laughed, clutching the book, anxious now to get home and read.

He also gave me a copy of the Mannheim Steamroller tape we had just been listening to. Though he'd switched to CDs long ago, he regularly made taped copies for me. I'd never get any new music if he didn't.

"I figured you'd want one," he said with a smile. "If you like it, be sure to take the little tab out, so no one can record over it."

He reminded to do that all the time, and I usually forgot.

On the way out, I paused. "By the way, what kind of books does Stu McKee read?" I tried to keep my tone casual. "I don't think I've ever seen him in here before."

"Sorry," Neil said archly, crossing his heart with a forefinger. "It's against the Librarian's Oath to discuss one patron's literary taste with another."

This was patently false. We talked about other people's taste in books all the time. We particularly found Aunt Juanita's fetish for Harlequin Romances funny.

His attitude confused me, but I didn't want to seem overly interested. Though I discussed most of my life with Neil, I was reluctant to have him know that I was lusting after a married man. I knew he'd disapprove.

Hell, I disapprove.

5

....

Blasphemy and Orgasms

Our trailer, all twelve by forty-eight blue-and-white shabby feet, is parked by itself at the end of the main drag, on the far edge of Delphi. To the north is the grain elevator, the tallest structure in any prairie town. To the east are widely scattered farms bordered by fields and pastures. Across the street is Neil's library, and on the west is an entire block of empty lots.

At one time Nick had planned to establish a trailer park on the property.

Of course when Aunt Juanita heard about it, she ramrodded an ordinance through the town council that barred the setting of any more mobile homes inside the city limits.

"We cannot allow the ambiance of our community to be sullied by an enterprise of this nature," she declared. Aunt Juanita is a powerfully convincing speaker, though how the ambiance of a small dusty town could be adversely affected by a few rusty trailer houses is beyond me.

Since Del's trailer was already in place, the ordinance

didn't affect it, though Aunt Juanita strove vainly to have the law made retroactive.

So now, by the strangest of coincidences, I live out on the edge of town, buffered from the Delphi version of commerce by Nicky's last Get Rich Quick Scheme. And if the truth be known, I prefer it that way.

Presley certainly enjoys the privacy. If we had close neighbors, he wouldn't be able to crank his music up full blast, as he does every time Del and I are gone.

The beating rhythm of the bass vibrated through the walls of the small lean-to shed sheltering the west door of the trailer.

A crashing wall of pure noise hit me as I went in. I couldn't make out the lyrics, though I'm sure it was the kind of devil-worshipping, rebellious, in-your-face song that upsets Junior so.

I am of the opinion that Bad Boys purposely write music to upset the grown-ups. Somehow, the grown-ups always forget how they once musically upset their own parents. Remember scandalous "Light My Fire" and "Hey Jude"? I have lately heard bouncy string arrangements of both tunes wafting gently overhead in Aberdeen's Kmart.

"Blatantly sexual, anti-Christian rock music," Junior, playing Minister's Wife, said to me one day, "makes our young people focus on perversions. It creates obsessions that warp their minds. It leads them to blasphemy."

Now you might think murder would be considered the worst sin in the Christian litany, but you'd be wrong. It's blasphemy, the failure to take Christians as seriously as they take themselves, that makes them livid.

Blasphemy and orgasms.

"All these new songs are about sex," Junior continued, "And the poor teenagers are surrounded, bombarded with unhealthy stimuli. It's taken away all the innocence. The old music was much less dangerous." Junior often sounds like a pamphlet.

I suggested she listen to "Shake, Rattle, and Roll," an innocent oldie with none of that nasty stuff. No siree.

Not that I actually *like* most of the new music. I prefer

old sex and drug tunes myself. But I like to argue with Junior. Especially when she's wrong.

However, pleading for the right of adolescents to rot their minds with bad music didn't mean that I wanted to be deafened by it.

Presley and Chainlink Harris were on their stomachs in front of the TV, playing Nintendo. They didn't know I had come in until I turned the stereo down.

"Hey," they whined together, "we were listening to that."

Both were wearing T-shirts depicting their current favorite superhero, Boogerman, a particularly obnoxious role model chosen for just that reason. Boogerman's motto was "The Best Defense Is a Good Snotball." With his sidekick, a congested dog called Phlegm, he made the world safer through mucus.

"Are you two ready yet?" I asked. They were supposed to be packing for an overnight birthday party at an Aberdeen motel.

"Yup," Pres said. "Say, Tory, do you have a couple of bucks I can borrow? Mom forgot my allowance."

Mom always forgot his allowance. I dug out five in bills and change from the day's tips and handed it to him.

Though I firmly believe that only pederasts have any practical use for twelve-year-old boys, Presley was a pretty good example of a perfectly awful age group. Especially considering that he's Elvis Presley's illegitimate son.

Of course I don't really believe that. No one in Delphi believes it. But from the minute her pregnancy was obvious, Del swore that she was carrying the King's child, and she never once veered from that story.

We'd have an easier time believing her if the human gestation period was something like five or six years, though Del has an explanation to cover the fact that Elvis died long before Pres's arrival.

"The first time was so fast, we forgot about being careful. But the second time we did it, I saved the rubber, you see, and stuck it in the freezer. Then I bought this turkey baster . . ."

Del does have an actual photograph of herself with Elvis standing in what she claims is an upstairs Graceland bedroom (it could well be, the decor is Early Bordello). Nicky and I spent a lot of time with Del in those days, and I remember asking him what he thought of the whole thing.

"Babe," he'd said, "with Del, anything is possible."

Probably because we couldn't have children of our own, Nicky doted on Pres. He would hold him up to the mirror and play games with him, searching Presley's tiny face intently. "He's talking to me," Nick would say in all seriousness. "He's trying to communicate something."

In general, Delphi has given up trying to puzzle out Del's motive in the Elvis story. We accept her lie, though we don't believe it, a fine, small-town distinction.

The notoriety was a little tough on Pres of course, though he weathered it pretty well. Even in the prairie, it's no more a social liability to have Elvis for a father than to have been abducted by space aliens, or to possess the ability to channel the spirits of ancient Atlanteans.

A small-boned, extraordinarily handsome boy with dark curly hair and a wicked smile, Pres seems to have gotten most of his genes from the Bauer, rather than the rock and roll side of his family.

Agile and thoughtful, he's tolerable, except when he's being a pain in the ass.

I carried my small sack of groceries into the kitchen, sighing at the mess. Though I had served Presley a huge dinner at the cafe, he had apparently fixed himself a small afternoon snack, remnants of which lay all over the kitchen.

The bread, butter, peanut butter, and jelly were all out on the countertop. The lids were piled, and sticky knives stood in the jars. A large blob of jelly dripped to the floor. An open bag of potato chips had spilled, and several were smashed into the carpet.

An upper cabinet door swung freely from one bent hinge. The other hinge appeared to have been pulled from the face frame. It was laid neatly on the windowsill over the sink.

"*Boys!*" I shouted. They apparently noted the tone of my voice because both appeared immediately.

I looked significantly at the mess. They took the hint and set to cleaning as quickly and efficiently as twelve-year-old boys are able. Which is not much.

"Either of you want to tell me about the door?" I asked.

They looked at each other, and then at the floor. Presley spoke up.

"It must be a really cheap door, Tory," he said sheepishly. "We were just trying to do a few chin-ups."

I waited for him to continue. Chainlink skillfully avoided meeting my eyes.

"We'll fix it ourselves," Pres said, batting his lashes at me. That trick never worked when Nick tried it either. "Honest. You just have to show us how—and wait until tomorrow because we're leaving in a few minutes." He smiled hopefully.

Presley knew that I knew that any attempt they might make to repair the damage would result in an even bigger mess. I gave up and changed the subject. "Whose birthday are you celebrating anyway?"

"John Adler's," he said.

John Adler, a miniature of his father, had recently embarrassed Presley and Chainlink by secretly recording a campout farting contest and later playing it to some older girls at the park.

The last I heard, Pres had sworn to kill him. Or at least set his shoes on fire.

"I thought you didn't like John Adler."

"We don't," they said in unison.

"He's a monkey dick," Pres said.

"He's butt snot," Chainlink said.

"He's a dingle dork," Pres shouted.

"He's a penis wrinkle," Chainlink roared and they both collapsed against each other, laughing.

"Then why," I wanted to know, "are you going to his birthday party?"

They both looked at me as though I had come from another planet.

"Because we get to swim at the motel." They both nodded soberly, amazed that something so obvious needed explanation. Delphi had no municipal pool, the nearest one was fifteen miles south, in Redfield.

Outside, a horn tooted. Their driver, Gina Adler, deserved a medal (or institutionalization) for taking ten twelve-year-olds for an overnight.

The boys grabbed their sleeping bags and stormed out, leaving the door open behind them.

The house had seemed cool at first, but a South Dakota June can baffle even a good air conditioner, and trailers never have good air conditioners.

I turned off the Nintendo, picked up crumpled paper plates and cups, and took Del's overnight case back to her room, since she wouldn't be needing it. Then I sank wearily in the old green recliner, enjoying the quiet.

I willfully ignored the hanging cabinet door. It would keep; the McBain wouldn't. The logical part of my brain remembers that the guys from the 87th are figments of an author's imagination, but the rest of me thinks that they're real.

For the same reason that I can't bring myself to read Agatha Christie's *Curtain* (because I don't want Hercule Poirot to die), I can't wait to read an 87th Precinct novel. I'm certain, that somewhere, these men really exist, and I want to know what they're up to now.

Before I read even three pages, the phone rang.

I sighed, let it ring twice more, wishing I had the willpower to ignore it, then crossed the room to the avocado wall phone in the kitchen.

"Hello," I said with resignation, hoping it would be a wrong number.

"Tory? Tory Bauer?" an extremely loud, high-pitched voice asked. "This is Lottie. Lottie Kendall. From the farm, you know, north of your Mother's?"

"Yes." I sat down at the kitchen table. This was apt to take some time. In addition to being gabby, Lottie was also nearly deaf. I held the phone away from my ear.

"Well, hello Tory," Lottie shouted. "What do you think of this heat? Though you aren't apt to be as hot, sheltered in town, as we are out on the farm, are you now?"

I squinted through the kitchen window at the sunlight baking the flat treeless expanse to the east and wondered what shelter she had in mind.

"It's pretty hot everywhere, Lottie. What can I do for you?" It frequently took a little prodding to persuade Lottie to come to the point. Any point.

"Well, you know it's your dear mother's day to go to Aberdeen. She works so hard, you know, your mother, taking care of Nillie, without any help at all."

Nillie was my grandmother. Mother did indeed work hard caring for Grandma, but she had no help because she wanted no help. It was a sore spot with the rest of the family. Aunt Juanita had even offered to hire a live-in maid, and Mother refused. For once in my life, I agreed with Aunt Juanita.

Except for her weekly trip to Aberdeen, Mother either cared for her at the farm or took Grandma along on errands and outings. At least she took her along until the Sunday Junior spotted a live chicken poking its head out of Grandma's purse.

Lottie is a goodhearted, talkative soul, a few bricks shy of a full load. She is perfectly happy to sit with a slightly loony old woman one afternoon a week. She and my grandmother get along fine.

"I'm here at the farm," Lottie continued loudly, "like I always am on your mother's afternoons out. I enjoy getting away from my own house sometimes, even for an afternoon. Don't you find that getting out of your house is a relief sometimes?"

If I had known I would have to decipher a call from Lottie, I'd have offered to work overtime.

"Your grandma, she's feeling poorly these days, you know. Her mind is wandering a bit."

That was an understatement. The death of her first six infant daughters had unhinged her to the point where she could never quite remember that the seventh and eighth were alive and well.

"We have to go to the chicken coop," Grandma had said, bundling me up in the dead of night when I was about eight, "And dig up Fernice and Juanita and put them in the cemetery."

Since Fernice was my mother, and she had awakened and was standing in the doorway, I wasn't frightened. I was already used to Grandma, though her chicken obsession was wearying.

One time she moved the poultry into the garage, because the coop smelled funny to her. As far as I was concerned, all chicken coops smelled funny.

There were times when Grandma was nearly normal, baking cookies and reading stories. But regularly she'd trek into the uncharted wilderness of her own mind. She spends most of her time there these days. Mother just keeps the doors locked and watches her carefully.

"You know how that goes, right Tory?"

I'd been daydreaming and missed some of what Lottie had been saying, but it didn't really matter. She was nowhere near to making her point yet.

"We all have days when we put our bras on backwards." She chuckled. "Anyway, today your grandma is pretty quiet, and we are just sitting, watching the stories on TV. Your mother has such a nice TV, bigger than the one we have at our farm. I told Hubert a hundred times that we should get a TV like your mother's. Of course Hubert's a poop. He says we can't afford it. What brand of TV is your Mother's anyway?"

Thinking that this was the reason for the call, I answered, "Sony."

"Oh dear, I thought it was American. Hubert will never buy a Japanese television. Pearl Harbor, you know. Anyway, there we were, enjoying our stories. The color on that set is awfully good, don't you think?"

"Yes, Lottie." I think I sounded a little weary.

"Then the phone rings, and who do you think it was?"

Nearly all of Lottie's questions were rhetorical, so I just listened and drummed my fingers on the table.

"Well, it was Hubert," she said. "My husband you know," as though we knew dozens of Huberts and had trouble differentiating. "I was so surprised, Hubert never calls me when I am sitting with your grandma. He knows how much I enjoy a quiet afternoon with her. He knows I hate talking on the telephone.''

I was beginning to hate it pretty thoroughly myself.

"So Hubert says that he is having trouble with the microwave oven, that he fooled with it for almost an hour and couldn't get it to work, and can I run back home and fix his dinner? Now I left him written instructions on how to use the dang thing, but you know men. Useless in a kitchen.'' She chortled.

"I tell Hubert that I can't leave Nillie alone, because your mother, she never wants your grandma left alone, even for a minute. She makes sure to tell me so each time I come. So the only thing I can think to do is bundle Nillie up and drive her over and heat up Hubert's food and be back before Fernice even knows we've gone. But what do you think happened?''

"I honestly couldn't guess, Lottie,'' I said truthfully.

"Well, dear, I was walking Nillie out the door, and she's real upset. The sweet old thing doesn't want to go for a ride and she keeps talking about that chicken coop. Good thing your mother is having it torn down.'' Lottie dashed down another conversational alleyway. "A menace, I say. Nearly ready to fall over on its own. Someone could get hurt.

"Anyway, up drives that nice young man with the car that sounds like it's about to die any minute. You know, Charles Winston, the one with the accent and the odd religion. He gets out and offers to sit here with your grandma while I run over and heat up my idiot husband's dinner.''

I smile, picturing earnest Charles delivering his spiel to a wacky old lady with a chicken fixation.

"Such a handsome boy. Reminds me of my second oldest boy, Roger, except for the accent, of course. Both of them so tall and with curly hair, though Roger is a normal Methodist, not one of those people with lots of wives. 'One wife is all I can handle,' Hubert always says—''

"Lottie,'' I interrupted, too tired and crabby to follow her anymore. "Does this story have a point?''

"Oh yes. Anyway, I am only gone about twenty minutes but when I get back, the nice young man seemed bothered. Upset. He's in an awful hurry to go. Here it was only about one-thirty or so, but he couldn't even take time to sit and visit with me." She sounded aggrieved.

I could understand. After twenty minutes alone with my grandmother, a chat with Lottie would seem like duty above and beyond his calling.

"As he goes out the door," she continued, "up drives Deputy Albrecht in his police car. That young Charles stood at the edge of the driveway, talking to him through the window for I don't know how long. You know sometimes when the wind blows just right, I can't hear very well outside, but it seems like they might even have been shouting. That doesn't seem very likely, does it? What in the world would they argue about?"

She veered off on another tangent, "Deputy Albrecht had a very red face, though. Do you think he could have high blood pressure? As young as he is?"

Back on the track again. "But your grandma, she needed to go to the bathroom so I went back into the house and helped her with her business. When she got done they were both gone."

Lottie paused, winded.

I waited some, and she was still quiet. "Is that what you called to tell me?" I asked, thinking she'd finally got to the meat of her story.

"Good heavens, no." Lottie laughed. "While I was home helping poor Hubert with the microwave, I noticed that my kitchen light was burned out and we are clean out of sixty-watt bulbs. If your mother stops in town to see you before driving back out to the farm, will you ask her to pick some up for me at the store? Save me a trip, you know. Thank you, dear."

I hung up, rubbed my aching ear, and took some aspirin.

6

....

AKA Desire McClain

I don't know if it was the furnace of the Great Depression or the heady excitement of World War II or a simple product of latitude and longitude, but the Midwest forge has produced several totally distinct types of Women of a Certain Age.

The Sweethearts waited patiently for their best friends' older brothers to come home from wars or universities, and until after the wedding ceremonies, before shyly surrendering themselves. Of course they didn't all wait (it's every generation's conceit to claim the invention of sex), but whether they waited or didn't, their priorities centered on the kitchen, rather than the bedroom.

They raised their children and tended their husbands in neatly ordered houses, content to be the last of the Red-Hot Housewives. Now that they are grandmothers, a hug is legal tender and cookie jars are full by constitutional mandate. They have a core of tempered sternness wrapped in a sweet, soft optimism.

Sweethearts never were much aware of the larger world around them, being fully occupied with weeding, cooking, and caring for anyone who lingered long enough to be caught by their gravitational pull.

Lottie Kendall, of course, is a Sweetheart.

The Party Gals were the toast of the USO. They dated, married, sometimes divorced, and often outlived the handsome young soldiers who dashed off to save the world for freedom.

These were pretty girls, good dancers with long slim legs and enough native intelligence to calculate the actual value, in lifetime benefits, of a quickie in the backseat of a Ford.

Party Gals smoked, laughed loudly, and drank. They often worked as shopgirls and waitresses, but did not aspire to any career beyond the adoration of doomed, desperate boys who pleaded in hoarse whispers, "Just this once."

They still smoke, laugh, drink, and dance whenever possible. With makeup and hair coloring that looks harsh anywhere except in a smoky room, they have preserved an aura of brittle sexuality. Most are still slim-hipped, their flat rear ends and compact bellies encased in tight polyester slacks, and their evenings are much too busy for watching grandkids. They steal each others' men and expect doors and chairs to be held for them.

Iva Hausvik eyes her clientele at the beauty parlor carefully, sometimes winding a perm just a bit too tight, or applying color a shade off if she catches one of them flirting with her man.

Willard Hausvik, who still cocks his hat at the jaunty angle popular in the forties, entertains quiet fantasies about the Gals now and then. But his Iva can still hold her own on the dance floor, under the covers, and with a baseball bat. He knows to leave well enough alone.

The Tough Broads are Rosies who never stopped riveting. They may have men, they may be alone, but either way, they can take care of themselves. With solid biceps and rock-hard opinions, they live in firmly and efficiently ordered worlds. Aphrodite has a sign tacked up over the deep fat fryer that reads: PISS, SHIT, OR GET OFF THE POT! You'd better believe she means it.

The Matrons are well educated, well dressed, and well preserved, and have their lives well in hand. These are the women who run the show. They juggle careers, housework, families, and causes with ease, leaving exhausted husbands and obedient children in their wake.

Matrons know their duty, and they do not shirk, whine, or look back. They ask no quarter, nor do they give any. They are harder than hell to live with.

I should know, I'm surrounded by them.

Someone told Aunt Juanita that she should cultivate her speaking voice, as it was her best feature. Unfortunately Aunt Juanita took that advice to heart. A motivated woman with a powerful means of expression, Aunt Juanita has absolutely no qualms about imposing her will on others.

I remember hearing, long ago, the barest wisp of a rumor about Aunt Juanita and a married man, before the advent of Uncle Albert. If there is any truth to this story (Mother snorted disdainfully when I asked her), it has been put firmly behind her. Auntie is steadfastly treading the path to glory, and she is determined to take us with her.

As a Matron-in-Training, Junior upholds all her mother's ideals, though I think Clay is proving more difficult to handle than Uncle Albert.

And of course there's Mother.

"Really, Tory," she said, examining the cupboard hinge barely on tiptoe. Mother is tall and firm. I am short and round. "That boy should be sent to a military school. What will he do when he's sixteen, accidentally burn down the trailer?" A small smile played around her mouth. Evidently that was not such a bad idea, I'd probably have to move back to the farm.

Though she would never admit it, Mother finds Presley charming. The Bauer charm has always been dangerously appealing, and Pres inherited more than his share. He grins shyly and answers her nosy questions about homework, friends, and future plans, and against her better judgment—

he is a Bauer after all—Mother likes him. She does not
extend her grudging approval to Del.

"I suppose his mother is on her way to the Cities by
now." She never refers to Del by name, an indication of
her dislike.

"Nope," I said. "Big Dick had to cancel, something
about escorting a prisoner to Fargo. They had quite a dustup
in the cafe this morning about it. Or at least I think that's
what the fight was about."

"Oh?" Mother raised an elegant eyebrow and sipped the
rest of her iced tea at the kitchen table. She pretends not
to enjoy gossip, but she's a Delphi native. It's in her blood.

"I think he might have heard that Del's been flirting with
Charles Winston." Mother knows about Del's proclivities.
Who doesn't?

"I can try and get the details for you," I teased. "It'd
make a good plot line, you know—the waitress and the
missionary."

Most people assume that my grandfather left a sizable
bank account as well as a mortgage-free farm operation to
his wife and surviving daughters. They are wrong. With
most of the land cash-rented to Clay, who combines farm-
ing with his ministerial duties, even in years with good
harvests, there is still not enough money left over to support
Mother and my grandmother.

Federal subsidies and supports notwithstanding, very few
farmers around here can afford just to farm. The wives, and
often the men, are forced to take part- or full-time jobs to
make ends meet. My mother is no different; she feeds herself and her mother by writing pornography.

Well, it's not actually pornography, at least not hardcore.
Under the name Desire McClain, Mother has written a series of popular paperback romance novels—the kind of
books you find in racks at the checkout counter, with a
partially undressed heroine swooning in the arms of a glis-
tening hero with sculpted biceps and cast-iron thighs on the
cover.

Her stories are always about beautiful, repressed women
and forceful, virile men whose real function, regardless of

occupation or historical era, is to teach Orgasm 101 to these hopeless females. It is a function they thoroughly and frequently exercise. While I enjoy reading about sex as much as the next lonely lady, her books are too full of ''throbbing organs'' and ''quivering mounds'' for my taste. Still, considering the genre, the novels are well written, and Mother has a solid following and a five-book contract.

Of course the incongruity of my tall, proper, and (I'd bet the farm on it) celibate mother writing torrid, sweaty sex scenes is not lost on me. It wouldn't be lost on the rest of Delphi either, if Delphi only knew. Mother has pulled off one of the greatest coups in the history of small towns—she has a secret that stayed secret.

I wouldn't know myself, if she hadn't left a contract copy right on the table, in its envelope, when I popped in for an unannounced visit. Even so, it took some serious badgering and a solemn promise not to tell before I learned any of the details.

''For heaven's sake, Tory,'' Mother said, plainly disgusted with me, ''I would never snoop through your mail.'' This was a slight untruth on her part. She did it all the time when I was sixteen, and she'd do it now, if I was ever foolish enough to leave any sitting out.

I often wonder what life would have been like for Mother if my father had not been quite so generous with his marriage vows. I have only vague memories of him; all evidence of his existence disappeared when he did, and Mother refuses to discuss him.

Would she have been content running his life, as Aunt Juanita does with Uncle Albert? I have no grand illusions about my father's character, he probably left Delphi and continued to marry assorted women and beget assorted children, and abandon them all in an orderly fashion. I have no desire for contact with him, and I doubt Mother does either.

Personally, I see no reason for keeping the writing a secret. Of course, Delphi would be publicly proud of its semifamous citizen and privately aghast at the sexiness of the books. It all seems ripely amusing to me, but Mother is an extremely private person; her failures and successes are her own. I respect her wishes.

So far, that strategy has worked. The general assumption is that she makes weekly trips to Aberdeen to buy groceries and to meet a man.

Mother is strong, physically and emotionally. She cares alone for my difficult grandmother, organizes the repair work around the farmstead, writes steamy successful novels, and interferes in my life. She is content.

"I suppose you'll have to call Eldon McKee about that hinge," she said on the way out, organizing the repair work around the trailer too. "But tell him that I will not tolerate any more delays with that chicken coop. He's no more than half-done with the demolition, and if I have to finish it myself, he will not be paid."

She was certainly capable of dismantling a building, if so inclined. I remember watching her chop down a diseased elm in the yard with a fury that was frightening to a small girl.

I walked her to her car through the blazing late afternoon sun in proper South Dakota fashion, and leaned in the window to say good-bye. On the front seat beside her were several large manila envelopes. Her weekly travels include a visit to the post office box she rents for Desire McClain's correspondence—a key ingredient to keeping her career a secret in Delphi involves not allowing her sister, the postmistress, to see her mail.

On top of the envelopes lay a pry bar, two feet long, painted a gleaming blue, with the business end honed to a razor-sharp steel edge.

"Going into construction?" I asked, pointing at the bar.

She shook her head resignedly. "No, just doing more of Eldon's work for him. He asked me to pick this up in Aberdeen today. I don't know what's wrong with his old one, but he says this one is absolutely necessary in order to finish tearing down the chicken coop." She handed it through the window to me. "And Lord knows, he can find enough reasons to delay as it is."

The pry bar certainly looked efficient. It was perfectly

balanced and lightweight. I took a swipe through the air and experimentally smacked the palm of my hand with the flat side.

"Sometimes it's just easier to run errands for everyone and ask questions later," she said as I handed the bar back in to her.

"That reminds me," I said. "Lottie called a couple of hours ago. She wants you to pick up a package of sixty-watt light bulbs in town before you go home. Says the kitchen light is out."

Mother frowned, "My kitchen light?"

"No, hers." I told her the story, expecting a smile, and some speculation about the argument between Charles Winston and Big Dick. It certainly intrigued me.

Her response was a surprise. I could see by the flat, tight line of her lips that she was angry.

"Alone. I've told her over and over," she said, speaking in incomplete sentences to the windshield. She turned to me, "I only left her because I trusted Lottie to understand." She sighed. "Well, I guess that takes care of that, doesn't it?"

I understood why Mother was upset—my Grandmother was likely to convert to Mormonism (and donate all their worldly belongings) just because a handsome young man convinced her that it was a good idea.

I also realized that Mother would no longer be able to leave Grandma in Lottie's unreliable care. And since she wouldn't allow any of the family to help, tending her own mother would truly be a twenty-four-hour-a-day burden, assumable immediately.

But ol' Desire McClain is made of stern stuff. As she drove off, she leaned her head out the car window—not with a parting farewell, or a plea for assistance, or even an endearment—but with the admonition, "Don't forget to call Eldon. Get that door fixed before Presley does any more damage."

7

....

The Church of James Taylor

I was a good girl. At least until I met Nicky and discovered that being bad can be pretty good too. What I mean, is, I almost always did what I was told. I minded my teachers. Within reason, I minded my loony grandma. I minded my mother.

And within reason, I still do.

Mother had suggested calling Eldon McKee. Certainly he was a competent, though notoriously slow handyman. A small job like this would take only an hour or so, which meant it wouldn't interfere much with Mother's chicken coop removal.

I reached for the phone and then hesitated. Chewing the inside of my cheek, I poked experimentally at the broken cupboard door, trying to decide what to do. Del and I could probably jury-rig the hinge so it would function, though its chin-up days were plainly over. Presley had probably learned his lesson about gymnastics in the kitchen, so there was little danger of further damage.

But Mother would ask, either tomorrow or the next day, if I had called Eldon. And demand an explanation of why I hadn't.

I could not tell her that I was terminally attracted to the dithering handyman's married son, and that calling the Feed and Seed Store, for any reason, seemed dangerous.

And I didn't want to tell her that I ignored her reasonable advice.

But I wasn't all that interested in trying to fix the door myself.

All my waffling was for show anyway. With a sinking heart, and a complete loss of self-respect, I knew that I would call the feed store and pay Eldon to do a job I could do myself, just on the off chance that Stu might answer the phone.

Talk about your hopeless females.

I didn't need to look up the phone number. Long ago I'd memorized the number for McKee's Feed. And for McKee, Stuart and Renee, though I've never had reason (or the courage) to call either.

My fingers didn't want to punch in the correct sequence. I got two wrong numbers before ringing through. My heart was echoing so loudly in my ears that I barely heard the answer.

"McKee's Feed. This is Stuart McKee, how can I help you?"

My mind went totally blank. I nearly dropped the phone.

"Hello?" Stu said, "Is anyone there?"

Hang up, my better judgment said. This is crazy.

"Hi, Stu," I said, ignoring my better judgment, trying to sound normal. "This is Tory Bauer. Would your father happen to be around? I have a small job here at the trailer for him."

"Well, Tory, hello," he said slowly, sounding pleased. I could hear him grinning. "I'd recognize your voice anywhere. I'm sorry though, Dad is pretty busy right now. There seems to be a sudden rash of small emergency jobs around town. He's booked solid."

I didn't care. The point of this phone conversation was

not to hire Eldon. The point was to have a legitimate excuse to call Stu.

"Is there anything *I* can do for you?" Stu asked. It was an offhand question, a polite question.

Anything, I wanted to shout. You can come over here and do everything for me.

"Well," I said, trying not to gulp. "I have a kitchen cupboard door that is hanging from a lower hinge. The upper was pulled from the frame. Presley and a friend were a little rambunctious here today. It's probably not too hard to fix. In fact, I'm sure I can do it myself, you don't need to bother. Never mind."

I was babbling.

"Well, let me come over and at least look at it." He laughed. He rustled some papers in the background. "Let's see, I'm busy tomorrow morning, but how about in the afternoon? What time do you get off work?"

"Two," I said, barely breathing.

"And Del will still be working then, right?" Stu asked. "How about the rambunctious kid, will he be home?"

There were a million possible reasons for wanting that information, all of them innocent.

"Yes, no, and why?" I asked stupidly.

"Carpentry is a messy business." He chuckled. "The fewer people I have to work around, the easier it is. Especially in a trailer."

"Oh," I said, embarrassed. He must think I'm an idiot. "You want me to stay away too?"

"Of course not," he said. "I need someone to show me where everything is." He paused for a second, and then continued lightly, "Besides, I bet you could use another back rub."

We said good-bye and I slowly put the phone back in place and sank down on one of the cracked vinyl kitchen chairs.

For an hour and a half.

Did this mean anything? Did this mean everything? Did I want it to mean anything? Was I going crazy?

That last was the only question I could answer.

What was that old caution, be careful what you wish for? Problem was, right then, I had no idea what I actually wished for.

I realized that I'd better regain some composure before Del came home. I didn't want her to be a part of this at all. She'd hoot. She'd chortle. She'd want all the sordid details.

And sordid the details would be. Tory, I moaned, what have you gotten yourself into? Stu McKee is a married man. At the very least, I had woven an obsession out of thin air. At the worst, I would be compounding a betrayal.

But it wouldn't just hurt Stu's wife and son.

It would also betray the person who stayed up nights, worried, angry, and frightened. The one who sat stoically disbelieving while Big Dick Albrecht explained just how, and with whom, her husband had died.

The person I would most betray by having an affair with Stu McKee, would be myself.

The whole internal debate was probably moot. Stu would come over, fix the hinge, present a bill, and be absolutely horrified if he had an inkling of my real longings.

I plugged *James Taylor's Greatest Hits* into the stereo and fixed myself a large Tupperware glass of gin and Diet Squirt with a dash of grenadine (my amateur approximation of a sweet Tom Collins), pulled the drapes, and sat in the recliner.

When I'm down and troubled, and I need a helping hand, I go to the church of James Taylor. In the quiet dark I close my eyes and listen to him. I let his sweet nasal voice soothe my soul. He brightens up even my darkest night.

A couple hours of good old JT and several drinks later, I was surprisingly calm, ready to face Del, and the future, hinges and all, with equanimity.

A few more drinks, a tape rewind or two, and I might even be able to face the past.

I heard Del stomping and talking in the entryway. It was nearly eight-thirty, much later than usual. I hadn't noticed the time passing.

She poked her head in the door. "Tory?" she called

softly, and then spotted me in the chair. "Why are you sitting in the dark?" She didn't wait for an answer, and I didn't have one for her anyway.

Del was flushed and in high good humor, with an almost manic grin. I was curious. Last time I saw her, Charles's head was leaning on her arm. I remembered her look of triumph.

Who are you to judge? I reminded myself. Think of Stu McKee. No, don't think of Stu McKee.

"Open the drapes, get some light in here," Del said with a wink. "We have company."

She stepped aside and Junior Deibert came through the doorway.

If it had been the Pope himself, followed by the Ringling Brothers Circus, I wouldn't have been more surprised. Andrew Dice Clay and Gloria Steinem were more likely to hang out together. Elizabeth Taylor and Debbie Reynolds.

It would be an understatement to say that I was amazed.

"You just won't believe it," Junior said cheerily as she pulled the living room curtains open.

The sun blinded me momentarily. I had forgotten that it was still daylight.

"I did the absolute goofiest thing." She peered around, then said absently, "Mother met us in Aberdeen for supper, and then she treated the children to a movie. So I drove home alone."

That didn't seem so goofy to me, but since Junior rarely requires acknowledgment of her statements, I waited quietly and watched her. She had never set foot inside our trailer before (probably any trailer, ever) and here she was, opening curtains and chirping just as though she had been invited.

Maybe she had been. I raised an inquisitive eyebrow at Del, who shrugged and grinned.

Only Junior could spend a whole day shopping with four children in a heat wave and still look neatly pressed. She was wearing the same clothes as in the cafe earlier, and evidently had not yet been home. As minister of St. John's Lutheran in Delphi, Clay was entitled to the use of the parsonage in town. But he preferred living on the farm next to my mother's, a couple of miles south and east of town. In this, if nothing else, Junior humors him.

She bustled around the living room, looking at pictures, examining book titles, storing up information for a report to Aunt Juanita, no doubt. She suppressed a small shudder at Del's velvet Elvis wall hanging.

I agreed with her; it gave me the creeps too.

"I stopped at the grocery to pick up milk, bread, and eggs. And *what* do you think I did?" she continued, finally.

Short of shooting Crystal Singman, I couldn't think of a single thing that would surprise me now.

"I locked the keys in the car."

I tried to look properly exasperated for her, since in Junior's well-ordered world, this was obviously a major screwup.

"Clay has the extra set, but he's tied up in a counseling session." Junior shot a quick look at Del, who smiled in return. "And he simply cannot be disturbed while he's counseling."

"I found her wandering the streets aimlessly," Del broke in, trying to speed up the narrative, "and brought her here to wait for Clay."

"Couldn't your dad take you home?" I asked, hoping to get rid of her quickly. "You could get your car tomorrow." The idea of making small talk with Junior all evening was disheartening.

"Dad's at an insurance meeting and won't be home until late."

Uncle Albert had insurance meetings about twice a month. He usually came home in the wee hours, slightly tipsy, with a pocketful of loose change. He used to hide the deck of cards in his briefcase, but Mrs. Beiber told on him. Now he stashes them under the front seat of his car.

"I just didn't know what to do. No one I knew was home. There was absolutely nowhere else I could go while I waited for Clay. I thought about walking home, but these just aren't the proper shoes." She held out a foot to illustrate her point. The small-heeled, expensive pumps were sadly inadequate for a long hike, some of it along gravel roads. Their driveway alone was a half mile long.

"Then I spotted Delphine locking the front door of the cafe, and she convinced me to come along here and wait. We left a note on Clay's desk so he'll know where to find me."

So Del locked up late. Had she been at the cafe the whole time? Alone? Why was she playing good Samaritan? And *why* was she smirking?

Those were all weighty questions. In the meantime, I needed another drink. Since we were stuck with her for the duration, I asked, "Can I get something for you, Junior?"

"Here, you sit and let me do it." Del, unusually helpful, snatched the empty glass from my hand. She sniffed at it and nodded. "I'll get one of these for you too, Junior."

"That'd be fine," Junior said distractedly, hastily rolling up Presley's new poster, the one with Boogerman's latest slogan: "You Might Think This Is Funny, but It's Snot." The illustration was even more disgusting than you'd expect.

Out of the corner of my eye, I could see Del mixing drinks on the counter, being overgenerous with my gin in Junior's glass.

She brought our drinks and poured herself a Coors in a frozen mug. A couple of green olives bobbed lazily up and down in the beer. A South Dakota Martini.

Junior does not believe in awkward pauses. She chatted continuously about the new line of home decorating products, the trouble she was having deciding which curtains to put up in Tres's bedroom, the bake sale she chaired for the Luther League, and the fact that thunderstorms were predicted for that night. None of which interested us in the least, though it relieved us of the necessity of paying attention. Junior didn't converse, she discoursed. All we had to do was sip and nod occasionally.

And we seemed to be doing quite a bit of sipping. Del jumped up to mix refills even before we needed them. Gin and Diet Squirt is a perfect drink for hot weather, tart and refreshing. Powerful as hell though, with a tendency to sneak up on you. Especially the way Del was mixing them.

If Del's strategy was to get Junior drunk, I figured she was in for a disappointment. Junior doesn't get drunk, she just gets more talkative.

I headed carefully toward the bathroom and wobbled a bit at the weak spot in the living room floor. Mobile homes are notorious for that. I once heard a story about a romantic couple sharing a bath (a small romantic couple, since trailer bathtubs are both shorter and narrower than standard) where the bathroom floor gave way and they fell to the ground, killing or embarrassing them both. I couldn't remember which.

I'd ask Stu to look at the floor, if he had time to look at anything else besides me. Dangerous thought. I giggled a bit. From the couch, Del eyed me strangely.

When I got back, Junior was sitting in the recliner, with a full glass in her hand, talking and gesticulating, sloshing the drink in her lap a little. She didn't seem to notice.

Wow, I thought, maybe she does get drunk.

I sat on the couch, hugging a throw pillow in my lap—a time-honored Fat Lady trick. As practical camouflage, a pillow is pretty useless, but it made me feel better. Especially with slim, trim, perfect Junior droning away.

Somewhere along the line, someone had turned on the TV, a lulling audio backfill.

I must have closed my eyes, because it took a minute or so to realize that Junior was talking to me.

"Huh?"

"I said," she said, with just a pear-shaped hint of exasperation, "that you look more and more like Grandma Nillie all the time."

Trust Junior to notice.

My mother, Aunt Juanita, and Junior all resemble my late Grandpa Paulus Osgood, who wore a freshly pressed long-sleeved white shirt with his clean faded overalls every day of the year. Tall, strong, and stern, Grandpa had an inner strength that lit his face with an intelligent glow.

Grandma Nillie Mae Obermeier Osgood, on the other hand, is, and always has been, short and round, and for as long as I can remember, totally loony. With a poultry fixation.

"I've been thinking about putting up a brooder house," I said, exasperated, but Junior just smiled. She doesn't get irony.

Somewhere along the line, Del had changed into tight shorts and a bright tank top. She sat calmly at the other end of the couch.

As a rule Junior's pronouncements produce a controlled fury in her, even when they contain a modicum of truth. I had already noted the marked resemblance between my grandmother and myself, and was not especially thrilled to be reminded. Del accepted Junior's commentary with uncharacteristic grace and seemed amusedly content.

As an excuse to leave the room while Junior continued to ramble, I decided to change into something more comfortable too. As I rooted around in my closet for a pair of shorts with enough elastic in the waistband to handle the latest weight gain, I heard the deep-throated rumble of a large motorcycle outside.

8

....

Junior's Lesson

Though we live on the edge of the Great Prairie, with nothing but the curvature of the Earth to limit our view, the scene outside my bedroom was still pretty dismal. Especially in the dark. Through the windows over the bed, I could see the upper story of Neil's house across the street.

Another large window overlooked our driveway to the east. The view there usually consisted of weeds and the rear end of Del's Plymouth jutting beyond the shed.

Just now this view also included Rhonda Saunders, resplendent in neon spandex and black leather, dismounting from a Harley.

We have a small staff at the cafe, making do with part-time Summer Girls for relief. Totally interchangeable, the girls can usually manage to make coffee and clear tables without much muddle. But generally, as waitresses, they make pretty good gum chewers.

Every once in a while, a Summer Girl shows a flair for waitressing (a mixed blessing, to be sure) and is promoted to Regular Relief. That's how we got Rhonda.

At work Rhonda favors unlaced tennies, tube tops, and electric-colored biker tights. Shiny earrings that resemble fishing lures dangle to her shoulders, and her upswept blonde hair spews from the top of her head like a lopsided, neon-wrapped fountain. She stores tips and tickets in a low-slung leather pouch strapped around her hips.

Though she is a good waitress, she scares the hell out of the Old Farts, who are much more comfortable with Del's obvious, and mature, sexuality.

Rhonda's juvenile sexuality was also fairly obvious. Illuminated by the porch light, she and her large leather-clad companion engaged in an extraordinary series of kisses, which I watched, fascinated, from behind the sheer curtains.

Pulling apart finally, Michael smacked Rhonda playfully on the rear, then roared off toward town. She turned and bounded gracefully up the steps leading into the shed, a large, full shoulder bag tucked neatly under one arm.

It was turning into quite a party.

She knocked and came in without waiting.

"Hey, ladies," her greeting lengthened into a drawl, "are we all havin' some fun tonight?" She dropped her purse and folded herself into an improbable position on the rug with effortless ease, and stifled girlish giggles.

Her pupils were dilated and I wondered if she had been smoking pot, but it was hard to tell. Teenage girls, even ones on the cusp of their twenties, all giggle constantly, talk incoherently, and eat like horses.

"What is there to eat in this here establishment?" She leaned forward, trying to eye Del seriously. It didn't work, she started giggling again.

I decided we should get some food into her.

"I can make popcorn," I offered, "or would you like Fig Newtons?" That was generous, offering cookies from my private stash.

"Sure," she said, "sounds great. I knew Tory'd come up with something delicious."

The inference was obvious—fat people always have the best munchies. But coming from Rhonda, the comment didn't rankle. Besides, though she was slim and pretty in a corn-fed way, I could see the traces of her mother's heavy ankles and saddlebag thighs. Genetics is sometimes the best revenge.

"I'm bartender," Del said, gathering glasses. "You want anything to drink, Rhonda?"

I know it's illegal to serve alcohol to minors, but if Rhonda is old enough to have noisy sex in a pickup topper on main street, ride stoned on the back of a Harley, and support herself waiting tables, she's old enough to drink.

"I'll have lime vodka and root beer, if you've got it," she said.

Thank God, we didn't. Del mixed her a very weak Gin and Squirt while I drizzled melted butter over bowls of popcorn on the island that separated the living room from the kitchen.

I stole a peek at Junior, who was absently sipping her drink, wondering how she would react to Rhonda's alcohol consumption. I assumed she would not correlate the giggles and voracious appetite. Like most Americans who obsess about drugs, she was unable to detect them right under her nose. I realized that Junior, who rarely drank at all, had already downed three tumblers of gin and was working on a fourth. At this stage, she wouldn't detect an earthquake.

Rhonda rooted in her purse and pulled out a new cassette tape, still in the long plastic anti-shoplifting shield.

"Michael got this for me," she said, removing the tags, and cutting the plastic carrier. "Wait till you hear this band, it's great!"

Even in the hinterlands, music store clerks remove of the tags and anti-shoplifting devices from cassettes at the checkout counter. Michael must have an interesting method of "getting" music for Rhonda.

The band was absolutely awful, each song had a pounding beat with no melody and unintelligible lyrics, which was just as well with Junior sitting in the same room.

As I munched, I thought about Rhonda and Michael kissing in the driveway. I was reminded of Neil's First Smooch Theory.

"Say," I said, mostly so Rhonda would have to turn down the stereo, "I want to ask a question. What was the name of the first boy you ever kissed?"

"I can't even remember the name of the first one I ever fucked," Del said, though a slight grimace wrinkled her features, labeling that a lie.

"Just a second," Rhonda interrupted, scrunching one eye in concentration, stuffing popcorn continuously into her mouth. "This stuff is great," she said contemplating her empty bowl.

"Oh!" She looked up suddenly, "I remember. Boomer Dufloth!" She beamed at me like a student who has just gotten the right answer to a really tough question.

Boomer, whose real name was Virgil Eugene, qualified on both counts.

"Come on, Del," I pleaded, intent, for some reason, on proving Neil's theory. "You can remember."

"Oh, for Christ's sake," she said and tilted her head back to concentrate at the ceiling. "Conrad Pinkleman," she said after a while. "There, are you happy? Then I caught the little shit kissing Lila Eisenbiesz in the church basement. So I tripped her during First Communion."

Apparently, Lila Pankratz nee Eisenbiesz got an early start.

I was surprised to know that Del and I had Conrad Pinkleman in common, but it still proved Neil's point.

"What about you, Junior?" I asked, charitably including her in the conversation.

"Jimmy Smith," she said dreamily. "Boy was he cute." Of course.

"May I ask why you're dredging up all these wonderful memories?" Del was less than amused.

"Neil Pascoe has a theory," I said, finishing my drink, "that everyone's first kiss came from someone with a goofy name." Exasperated with Junior, I continued, "It mostly works that way."

"I like Neil," said Rhonda, still on the floor with her arms looped around her legs and her chin resting on one pointed knee. "He always leaves a good tip and never complains about mixups."

Del snorted. "He's a real winner all right."

"No kidding," chimed Junior.

My amazement at Del and Junior in agreement was overshadowed by a sudden irritation. "What do you mean by that?" I asked sharply.

"Oh come on, Tory," Del said, trying to smile away my anger. "The guy is obviously a fag."

"I agree," parroted the newly amenable Junior.

"No he isn't," I said firmly.

"And how would you know?" Del asked. "In all your book chats, has he ever once made a pass at you?"

"What difference does that make?"

"That's what I thought," she continued. "How about you, Rhonda? Any action from the eminent librarian?"

"Well, no," she said slowly, "but the older guys hardly ever get frisky, except for Eldon McKee." She shuddered slightly.

Neil was barely ten years Rhonda's senior and she considered him an "older guy?"

"Junior?" Del was determined to beat this to a pulp.

"Good Lord, no."

"Me neither," she said, obviously the telling point in her argument. "I'd call this"—she swept the room in a grand gesture—"a fair representation of the women Delphi has to offer. We have old and young, married and single, country-western and rock and roll."

If she said "thin and fat," I'd deck her, so help me.

"And he isn't interested in any of us. That spells fag to me."

"He's rich enough," I said, reminding them of Neil's millions, "and probably discriminating enough, not to be bound by geographical limitations."

"Listen, honey," Del said, trying to be conciliatory, "rich, poor, married, single, young, old. It just doesn't matter. They all come to me sooner or later."

I thought Junior might finally disagree, but she was busy studying her empty glass.

Mine was empty too. I grabbed Junior's and went for refills. I had no concrete proof that Neil was not gay, just a bone-deep conviction that he was not.

I wondered why I was upset by the notion. Neil was my friend. It wouldn't matter to me what he was. Still, I was certain.

"He watches too." This was Del's parting shot.

"What in the fuck is that supposed to mean?" I think I was getting ready to duke it out with her.

"He has a telescope," she said, "and he spies on the town with it. I bet he's doing it right now."

I knew Neil had a telescope; he used it for amateur astronomy.

"All right, let's just check," I said, marching into my room and kneeling on the bed. Del and Rhonda followed.

"Well?" I asked.

There were no telescopes pointing from any of the windows in Neil's house.

"Well?" I said more pointedly, maybe even threateningly.

"Okay, okay," Del put her hands up in front of her face in mock terror. "Sorry, I didn't know the idea would bug you so much."

Neither did I. I would have to think about it. A little later, when my head wasn't so fuzzy.

Junior still sat in the recliner, rocking gently. Her eyes were open, but slack. I thought she would probably not feel very well in the morning.

The silence was a little awkward. Del and I rarely argue, and it caught both of us off-guard. We tried to smooth it over with chatter about mascara and blush and feminine hygiene deodorant spray.

Rhonda stretched out the floor on her back, with her feet casually propped up on the arm of the couch. She balanced a full glass on her flat stomach. I hadn't noticed her mixing another.

But then I hadn't noticed mixing myself another either, and my glass was also full.

"Can I ask you guys something?" Rhonda held the glass

up and rolled neatly over on her stomach. "I mean, something really personal?"

We nodded, curious. Junior rocked.

"What is the big deal about sex?"

More learned minds than ours had wrestled with that one to no avail. I motioned to Del to take the floor. It was her area of expertise, anyway. I was definitely out of practice.

"I mean, it's nice and all," she went on before Del had a chance to say anything, "but I'd rather go shopping."

Del opened her mouth, but Rhonda continued.

"Michael, you know, he's great. But it's all he thinks about. We never talk, we just ride the Harley and smoke." She shot a sideways glance at Junior, who did not seem to be paying attention. "And screw. Day and night. All the time. Every day. Don't they ever," meaning men, I guess, "think about anything else?"

"Unfortunately, hon," Del said with a grin, "they stop thinking about it just about the time you start."

"That can't be true," Rhonda said, looking at me sadly. "I mean, your Nicky, he, uh, well, you know. It's not a secret, is it?"

No, it wasn't a secret.

"I mean, he didn't stop thinking about it, did he?"

"No, he never stopped thinking about it, right until the very end." Funny, it didn't hurt as much as I expected, saying it out loud.

"And you *like* sex, don't you? I mean it's not a chore, right?"

She was asking me, not Del. I blew out all of my air, trying to organize my answer.

"I did," I said, slowly, "but it's been a long time. I expect it's different with every relationship. Nicky was good"—I shrugged—"but I think that had more to do with his sense of fun than any specific technique."

I pictured Stu McKee. Would he have the right technique? Would he be fun? Would Nicky's shadow always loom?

"Let's not dismiss technique here," Del interrupted. "To learn the proper technique, it takes experience and the right teacher." She preened a little. "Once a guy learns the right moves, he could be Godzilla and you'd still enjoy it."

"But what other moves are there," Rhonda asked, "besides in and out?"

In a way, it was too bad Nicky was gone. He could have answered that one for her. Then again, it's just as well. His answer would probably have included a demonstration.

Del grinned hugely; she was getting ready to convene a seminar. It would be worth listening to; my moves were sadly out of practice.

But before Del could begin, Rhonda, aimlessly tapping a long fingernail on her glass, said, "I do kinda sorta enjoy it." She looked directly at me, "At least it doesn't hurt."

Had it ever hurt with Nicky? Physically I mean. I suppose it did the first time, but I mostly remember a marvelous sense of well-being, of being loved and wanted. I remember laughing. I remember being thrilled when he wanted me again, and I remember learning to want him too. I never had to ask anyone what was the big deal about sex. Poor Rhonda.

"It would be better," she said, "if he didn't always holler at the end. Do they all do that?"

Do I look like Dr. Ruth too? Dr. Ruth and my grandmother, what a combination.

"Some do," Del said, "some don't." She would know.

Come to think of it, so did I. I had overheard enough of Del's men, including Big Dick Albrecht, to compile a random sampling.

"But don't let them tell you that they can't help it," Del continued. "They can be quiet enough when they want a blow job under the table."

Under a cafe table? An interesting notion.

"That's another thing," Rhonda said, looking at the floor. "Sometimes Michael, he wants me to . . ." She paused and picked at a carpet thread. "Uh, you know. Do that for him. I honestly wouldn't mind," she continued, "but my jaws get so tired, and it's hard to breathe and my neck hurts." She rooted for words, "And the taste . . ." Her face contorted and she shuddered.

"Just get used to it, sweetie," Del said, a little bitterly. "As far as I'm concerned, semen has all the taste, temperature, and texture advantages of snot. If you want a throat full of gunk, catch a cold, it's more fun. But if you want to keep a man, you'd better learn to do it gracefully."

I myself had never properly mastered the necessary techniques, but Nicky didn't seem to mind. Then again, I hadn't kept him very well either.

"This is pitiful."

We had forgotten that Junior was dazed in the recliner. Here we go, I thought, a lecture about evil and sex and perversions. I considered the pillow on my lap. Maybe I should smother her with it before she starts.

"Absolutely pitiful," she said, fixing each of us in turn, with a baleful eye.

Rhonda squirmed like a child caught stealing cookies. Even Del seemed a little abashed. Was it illegal to describe sexual activities to a minor? Would Junior report us? She had wasted no time telling Aunt Juanita when she discovered Donnie Adler (Ron's brother—more chin, no tic) and me playing doctor behind the barn. Of course we were only eight at the time, but old habits die hard. If there was a toll-free number to report illegal sex talk, Junior would know it.

"Just a second here," I said, intending to protect Rhonda from undiluted Junior outrage.

She ignored my interruption. "With all your experience"—she emphasized the *all* with a disbelieving shake of her head—"and the two of you still can't help this girl with a simple problem."

She glanced at Del and me, waiting for some kind of response. We had none. With an aggrieved air, she turned to Rhonda.

"There are only four things you have to remember," she said like a teacher drilling irregular verb conjugations to underachievers. "First, make sure you are comfortable. His position doesn't matter. Do this right and he won't notice if he's hanging upside down from the ceiling. Just see to it that you don't have to support yourself on your elbows—

kneel on pillows, have him stand on a ladder, or sit on the kitchen cupboard. Don't try it lying down, you can't manage at all, and your neck will cramp.''

Rhonda nodded solemnly. For the second time in one evening, I was dumbfounded. Del sat with her mouth hanging open in astonishment.

''Second,'' she went on, ''don't feel like you have to put the whole thing inside your mouth. There's absolutely no need to gag yourself, it's only the head that matters, anyway. If you're in the right position, you can control just how far in it goes.

''Third, have some music with a strong rhythm going, and keep time with it. You know what really works?'' she asked.

For the life of me, I couldn't think of a single applicable tune.

''Old Herb Alpert and the Tijuana Brass albums. That Latin tempo is perfect.''

Would John Phillip Sousa work too?

''Fourth, and most important,'' she continued, ''is keep your thumb on that long vein running up the underside of, ah, it.'' Junior, explaining Blow Job How-To's, could not say the word *penis* out loud.

''When you feel that vein starting to pulse,'' she said, leaning forward to emphasize this point, ''just swallow and keep swallowing until the vein stops throbbing.''

She leaned back and smiled, ''You'll never taste a thing, your jaws won't seize, and he'll love you for it. Then he can return the favor.''

There was a full beat of total silence, in which I tried to picture Junior carrying out her own advice on Clay. My mind rebelled at the thought.

Apparently so did Del's because she burst into infectious laughter that caught us all, including Junior. For the first time in my life, I actually thought of Junior as a human. I would never again see her in quite the same light.

We were still laughing when Clay arrived. The sight of him set off another wave of laughter. On the kitchen cupboard? Standing on a ladder? Returning the favor?

Oh, please.

He smiled heartily, if a little confusedly, waiting to be let in on the joke. We'd let Junior do that for us.

"Thank you for entertaining my wife until I finished," he said formally. "I appreciate . . ." His voice trailed off.

Junior got to her feet unsteadily and swayed a bit. Her voice had not lost any of its clarity, so I had forgotten her gin intake.

Clay's eyes narrowed. "I think we'll pick your car up tomorrow morning. You can ride home with me," he said to Junior, eyeing Del suspiciously over her head.

Del shrugged and smiled, as if to say, Hey, it's not my fault. Suddenly I felt a little ashamed. Yes, it was our fault.

"Sure, whatever you say, dear," Junior said, mustering her dignity ineffectively.

"Can I get a ride with you?" Rhonda piped in. It was only three blocks to Michael's camper, but Rhonda never walked anywhere.

She ejected her tape from the stereo, popped it into her bag, and stood attentively, apparently much sobered and probably itching to put Junior's lessons to the test.

The three piled into Clay's car, Junior waving gaily out the passenger window, and drove off.

To the west, distant thunder rumbled. The land surrounding Delphi is so flat that we can watch thunderstorms brewing over the Missouri River, one hundred miles away. In a couple of hours this storm would reach us. It looked to be a doozy, with constant lightning flashes illuminating the flat underside of the thunderheads.

"That was fucking amazing," Del said mostly to herself, back inside as we stacked the glasses and bowls and put things away. "Didn't you think that was simply fucking amazing? Who would have guessed?" she asked the air.

Not me, that's for sure. I had my own questions.

"Why were you so late getting home tonight?"

"Aha," she said with a smug smile, "that's a long story, better left for another time. Looks like you have a story to tell me too."

For a second I panicked. I was more drunk than I had

realized. Had I babbled on about Stu McKee during all the talk about sex?

She pointed at the hanging cupboard door. "Things get a little wild here this afternoon?"

"Oh, that," I said, relieved. "Nope, it's all taken care of. I called McKee's to get it fixed. He's coming tomorrow afternoon." I figured that was all she really wanted to know.

"Keep a close eye on him, then," she said darkly.

I knew she didn't particularly like Stu, but I didn't think she would want him kept under surveillance. "Why?"

"Because I've heard the old fart drinks on the job."

She thought Eldon was coming to fix the door. I considered that for a moment, then clamped my jaws shut and nodded.

"You'd better get to bed, missy," Del said, pointing me in the direction of my bedroom with a gentle shove. "In case you forgot, morning comes around mighty early in these here parts."

It was a little after midnight. Suddenly I felt exhausted and woozy, grateful to be going to bed. I knew I'd have a hell of a headache when I woke up, but right then I didn't care.

I fell into an immediate, deep sleep.

I was dancing with Stu, he was warm and strong and smelled like a fresh shower after a hard day. James Taylor was singing "Steamroller Blues" in the background.

Junior was droning to Rhonda in the corner, "And then you squirt whipped cream all over it, like so."

Del was behind the bar, pouring a glassful of straight gin. "It's a South Dakota Martini," she said, "the vermouth is in New York where it belongs."

Then I was tied to my bed, naked. Stu stood over me and smiled. He slowly reached into his pocket and pulled out a pistol. He leveled it at my head, shrugged wistfully, and pulled the trigger.

The explosion was deafening, a crash that shook the trailer to its very foundations, rattling the windows and dishes, scaring the absolute bejesus out of me.

I jumped out of bed, noting that I was neither naked nor tied down. That damn dream again.

A blinding flash of light was followed by another incredible roar. I ducked and covered my head instinctively. A trailer is not the safest place to be in a severe thunderstorm. This one had arrived seemingly minutes after I lay down, though the clock in the corner blinked an incredible three-thirty in red.

I looked out the west window to see if any of the buildings in town had been hit by lightning, a not infrequent occurrence.

I didn't see the patrol cruiser sitting in the driveway until the next flash. The bolt after that revealed a person in the front seat of the car.

I peeked through the sheer curtains, reflecting that spying was getting to be a habit.

Inside, Big Dick leaned against the driver's side door, one arm resting on the steering wheel, the other looped carelessly across the back of the front seat. His head was tilted back and his eyes were closed.

At first I thought he was sleeping. In our driveway?

Then I noticed a dark shape next to him on the seat, hunched over so that it was barely visible. Another person? Yes, it had to be another person, bent over next to him.

He took his hand from the steering wheel and laid it on the person's head, smoothing and caressing and then suddenly burying his hand in the hair. Red hair.

Del's hair.

I should have gone back to bed right then. This was none of my business. But I stared out the window, hypnotized.

Big Dick's hand clenched in the hair, becoming a fist. He pulled Del's head up, looked at her face, and laughed. Still gripping her hair, he forced her head back down. Her hand beat a tattoo against the steering wheel, and still he laughed.

I knew what was happening now, and I felt suddenly sick. Junior's gentle tricks would never control Big Dick.

A sudden lightning flash lit my window and he saw me.

I tried to duck, to turn, but his eyes locked me in place, frozen, unable to move.

While one hand pumped Del's head in an increasing tempo, he pointed the other at me, like a small boy playing at guns.

He narrowed his hooded eyes and smiled as he deliberately aimed his index finger like a loaded pistol and mimed pulling the trigger. I could clearly see his lips form the word *BANG*. He pushed Del's head all the way down, and threw his head back and roared laughter.

I turned and stumbled through the living room, down the hallway to the bathroom, and was violently ill. Again and again, until there was nothing left inside me but self-loathing. I crawled back to bed without looking out the window and, amazingly, slept.

9

....

Burglar Bait

Morning is generally my favorite time of day, especially in the summer. I enjoy being up and out before temperatures spiral toward the unbearable, while the wind still resembles a gentle breeze and the humidity has not yet gained the suffocating weight of a Volkswagen parked on your chest.

I don't mind waking early to riotous birdsong and the distant rumble of semis on the highway. Padding quietly around the trailer before Presley turns on cartoons, and Del plugs Elvis tapes into the stereo, I sip my first Diet Coke, treasuring the brief privacy, the last quiet moments each day.

Every morning my alarm rings at five. I lie in bed for a few more luxurious minutes, shower and dress and try vainly to think of something interesting and attractive to do with my hair, give up on that, inhale some caffeine, and walk to work. By five-forty-five I am pouring coffee for the first of the early breakfast crowd who know that even though the cafe doesn't officially open until six, Aphrodite will unlock the front door for them anyway.

At least it works that way on mornings when my stomach isn't rolling, when the early sun doesn't drill needles into my eyes, and I get out of bed on time. This morning I had barely enough time to brush my teeth, sigh at my bleary reflection while trying to fluff some life into my hair, and gulp a few aspirin on the way out the door, thankful that the sun would be at my back for the three-block walk.

With a pounding head and uncertain stomach, I vowed the old vow. Never again, I said to myself. Dump it out, smash the bottle.

It was still relatively cool, though the thermometer would read in the middle 90s by noon. The short rain that accompanied last night's storm had settled the dust, leaving the air fresh, with a crystal sparkle. Too bad I was too miserable to enjoy the stark beauty of the flat countryside bathed in early morning sunshine.

I walked my usual route, turning north at the corner by Uncle Albert's insurance agency, cutting across the back parking lot that his agency, the grocery, and the cafe share. This was the shortest route, since Aphrodite would not have unlocked the front door yet, and the fence spanning the alley between the two buildings blocked the side entrance from Main Street. Otherwise I'd have to walk past the front door, down to the other end of the cafe, around the side, through the sticky muck made by the steady drip of the air conditioner runoff, and back around to the side door. This way was shorter and would save me the trouble of scraping mud off my shoes at the door.

Aphrodite's black van, with lurid desert scenes airbrushed on the sides, was already parked behind the cafe, and I could hear the echo of the game but ancient air conditioner already rattling away on the far side of the building.

I paused a thankful second or two inside the shed doorway to allow my eyes to adjust to the dark. The shed itself, built mostly to keep drifting snow out of the back hallway, was a small addition tacked onto the original building. To my left was an old metal cupboard crammed with tools, extra light bulbs, and assorted unclaimed lost and found items. To the right was a tall, deep mop closet, with brooms, buckets, and cleaning supplies.

Nightly mopping was theoretically the job of the Summer Girls. Faint Lysol fumes meant that Jolene Bartelheimer had at least made an effort last night, though brown swirls and muddy shoe tracks were still visible on the cracked linoleum floor.

Girls these days just don't know how to clean, I thought, doing an excellent imitation of my mother. I'd have to remind Del to remind Jolene to be more thorough. Neither Aphrodite nor the health inspectors looked kindly on dirty floors.

The inner door of the shed led directly into a dimly lit narrow passage that spans the width of the cafe. A walk-in freezer at one end is mirrored by a nearly identical walk-in cooler at the other. In between, against the outer wall, are floor-to-ceiling shelves, storage for canned goods, five-gallon buckets of pickles, barrels of dry pancake mix, and other restaurant essentials.

A swinging door separates the back room from the kitchen proper. I pushed through, steeling myself against the bright light, the steam and noise of the dishwasher, and the greasy odor of frying bacon, ham, and sausage.

Aphrodite, smoke wreathed about her head like a halo, was bent over, pulling a large sheet of hot baking powder biscuits from one of the ovens below the big gas stove burners. She was wearing bright red polyester knit slacks and a snug orange T-shirt with "Where in the Hell Is Zell?" splashed across the back.

"Morning," I mumbled, trying to hurry through the kitchen, away from the pop and sizzle of frying pork.

"You look like shit," she said on my way past.

There was no point denying the obvious. I just shrugged in agreement. She shook her head and turned back to the bubbling vat of white gravy to which she was adding browned sausage. The whole mess would be generously ladled over hot biscuits.

It was one of the few truly delicious meals Aphrodite served. This morning the very thought made me shudder.

There was a mound of damp white rags on the stainless-steel countertop that divided the kitchen from the seating area, Aphrodite's hint that things could use a bit of neatening. I stashed my purse under the till and looked around to see what needed cleaning before we opened.

The room wasn't dirty, exactly, just out of whack a little. The chrome napkin holders were not centered neatly on a couple of the tables, the salt and pepper shakers were half-filled and sloppily arranged, and some of the chairs were pulled out of place. Along the bar, the condiments were supposed to be spaced neatly between the five stools, but nothing lined up properly, and the gold-flecked Formica was circled with streaks.

Jolene's chances of continued gainful employment were lessening by the minute.

I tilted a glass under the Diet Coke spigot, wondering if I had enough time to put things to right before anyone showed up wanting breakfast. I wondered if I would get through the morning without being sick. I wondered how I had ever talked myself into drinking gin and Diet Squirt and if a bowl of cereal would help settle my stomach. I hoped Del had left some interesting cassettes, since Bach did not seem the proper music to fuel a hangover recovery.

In the far corner of the counter, on our side of the bar, under the air conditioner, I rooted through the box of tapes Del and I usually leave at the cafe, rejecting the Brandenburg Concertos 4–6, and the Mamas and the Papas. Bonnie Raitt looked promising—hard-living music for a hard-living woman. Me.

I punched the eject button on the player, expecting to find Del's perennial favorite, *Blue Hawaii* in the slot. I was surprised to see my Brandenburg Concertos 1–3, the copy Neil had made for me. I was confused. This was the tape I'd played yesterday, and Del would certainly have switched to her music as soon as I left. She detested classical. Too tired to puzzle over it, I tossed the Brandenburg tape at the box; it missed and skittered to rest behind the tape player.

Twenty minutes later, Bonnie crooning, with the chairs straightened and the counter gleaming, and Willard Hausvik tapping at the door, we were off to the races.

It was a normal morning, noisy and busy, with no time to consider my own misery. Heidi, Jolene's morning counterpart, breezed in fifteen minutes late and set to pouring coffee and ringing up tickets.

I was taking plates of biscuits and gravy, which still looked and smelled awful, to some out-of-towners when Heidi tapped me lightly on the shoulder.

"I found this, like, under the change tray in the till. It's, like, addressed to you. Do you want it?" she asked through her gum. My stomach rolled as I recognized the flavor. Watermelon.

She held out a folded slip of paper with my name, "Torie Bower," misspelled in pink felt pen on the outside.

I waited for my eyes to focus and translate the uphill girlish script into something resembling any language I knew. As nearly as I could make out, the note read:

You're mother Fernice Atwood (she spelled it for me), said to tell you that she is leaving a flat bar here at the cafe for E. MacKee (the dad, not the young one) to pick up in the morning. Your suposed to give it to him when he comes in for breakfast 'cuz he needs it in town for a job which is not at the farm where he ought to be. Anyway, the flat bar is under the counter by the empty ketchup bottles, and you're Mom said to be sure to remind you so I am. She would have written this note herself, but she said I could use the practice or something.

Thanx,
Jolene

She had signed the note with a flourish of hearts and a round happy face drawn in a lower corner.

The world was chockful of minor league mysteries this morning. Why would Del, who refused to listen to composers dead longer than Patsy Cline, want to play the Brandenburg Concertos instead of Elvis? Why did Mother leave the new blue flat bar, purchased at Eldon McKee's behest for Eldon McKee's convenience, at the cafe, instead of with Eldon McKee himself? And how did Jolene Bartelheimer, an honor student with a professed intention to teach grade school, pass sophomore English?

I'd have concentrated on these mysteries more thoroughly were it not for the little man who insisted on stabbing the backs of my eyeballs every time I tried to think. Or move. Even he paused at the sight of Del entering the cafe, three full hours before her shift was due to start.

Like most waitresses, Del spent no more off-time at her place of employ than absolutely necessary—it was just too easy to be roped into providing free those services for which she was underpaid during the normal working day. I hoped she intended to relieve me early so I could go home and back to bed. For a week.

I was disabused of that notion soon enough. She headed immediately behind the counter, not even stopping to flirt with Ron Adler, who was anxiously trying to wave her down.

"Elvis," she said desperately, rooting through the tape box, even though she generally kept duplicate copies of all her favorite tapes at home, one of the few favors she grudgingly allowed Neil to perform for her. "I need my Elvis."

Though Del was always meticulous about her appearance, this morning she looked ragged around the edges. Her hair was none too neatly pulled back in a ponytail, she'd applied no makeup, and she was wearing the sloppy sweatshirt usually reserved for washing the car.

She looked as though she had just jumped out of bed and rushed over. If anyone ever formed a chapter of Elvis Anonymous, Del would make the perfect poster photo of a junkie in need of a fix.

"Ah," she said with evident relief, waving a cassette in

the air, "here it is." She stuffed the tape deep into a tight jeans pocket and sauntered over.

"Glad to hear you're finally developing some musical taste," she said, nodding at the Bonnie Raitt while pouring herself a cup of coffee. She peered at me closely. "You look like shit."

I'd heard that one before.

"And whose fault is that, Miss Delphi Bartender?" I asked, perhaps a shade more sharply than I had intended.

"Sorry," she said, laughing. "No one held a gun to your head. Besides, it was worth it to see Junior sloshed."

I had to admit that made this morning's discomfort a little more bearable. I was even prepared to like Junior. I'd try, anyway.

"Say," Del said, quietly, looking at the floor, "has Charles been in yet this morning? I have to talk to him."

"No, come to think of it, I haven't seen him."

That was odd; Charles was a morning person who usually appeared quite early, chipper and cheerful with a sleepy, sniffling Donald Garrett following in his wake.

"I'll catch him later, I guess," she said, sipping her coffee and scanning the cafe. Ron Adler finally caught her eye, and she nodded at him. "It's not important anyway. How about Big Dick?"

"He hasn't been in either," I said, remembering the awful scene I had witnessed last night. "Are you sure you want to see him?"

"Sure," she said, puzzled. "Why not?"

I could think of a hundred reasons why not, but kept quiet.

As Del walked to Ron's booth in the far corner, she slowed down, looked back over her shoulder, and fingered her ear lightly, a signal to do some eavesdropping. Most people foolishly believe that waitresses neither overhear nor repeat, snippets of conversation not directed at them. They are wrong.

It was time for some coffee refilling and PR chatting anyway, so I made the rounds with steaming pots of regular and decaf, working over to the booth Del had indicated, where Clay Deibert was sitting alone.

I raised a questioning eyebrow at Del. Did she want me to hear Clay talking to himself? Del smiled and touched her ear again, so I leaned over a little while pouring coffee for the ladies in the next booth, so I could listen better.

Clay was reading the paper, and humming lightly to himself. A catchy little tune whose title escaped me. One of those sixties ersatz Latin pop things.

Del who was now seated across from Ron, grinned expectantly. I concentrated, ignoring my headache, and then it hit me. "The Spanish Flea." Herb Alpert. Oh my God.

I turned my head and bit my lip in an effort not to laugh out loud. Del didn't even try. She wiped her eyes, ignoring the curious looks, and laughed again because at that moment Junior, wearing a headscarf and sunglasses, came in and sat with Clay.

Vainly trying to squash some truly ridiculous mental images involving Junior, Clay, and a stepladder, I set a cup of coffee in front of Junior.

"Morning," I said in a genuinely friendly voice. "You're out and about pretty early today."

Junior actually growled at me.

Though she had applied makeup carefully, beneath the foundation and blush she was deathly pale, and her hand shook slightly when she reached for the cup. With sunglasses off, her eyes were bloodshot and red-rimmed.

"Would you like anything?" I asked. "Pancakes? Oatmeal? A side order of Maalox?" Just looking at her made my hangover feel better.

"That's a good idea, dear," Clay said brightly, patting Junior's hand. "Some food would help to settle your stomach. You order something, I have to talk to your father a moment. Will you excuse me?" he asked, ever the gentleman, and hummed his way over to the table where Uncle Albert was talking with, or rather listening to, Eldon McKee.

I turned back to Junior, pen and pad in hand to take her order.

"I don't imagine it sounds too appetizing," I said to her, "but a poached egg on dry toast would make you feel better. Should I tell Aphrodite to start one for you?"

Though I didn't regard her with anything like affection, this shared hangover made me feel as though we were comrades in arms, survivors of the same battle. Food would help settle her stomach, and I had made the suggestion in good faith. A peace offering to cement a new type of relationship.

"Was it fun?" she turned and hissed in a low, angry voice. "Did the three of you enjoy yourselves?"

I pulled back a bit, surprised.

"You aren't smart enough to have planned the whole thing," Junior said nastily, "but you sure took advantage of the situation, didn't you? You and your tramp friends."

So much for peace offerings and new relationships.

She clamped her mouth into a tight public smile for Clay, who seated himself at the booth again, still humming the same tune.

"Did you decide on some breakfast?" he asked.

"I couldn't take anything," Junior said in a controlled voice, fixing me with a vile stare, "from you right now. Run along and take care of your other tables."

I doubt that it would have done any good to explain to her that there had been no malice aforethought. There wasn't even any malice afterward. Well, not much, anyhow.

I said to Clay, "What is that song you've been humming?" waggling my eyebrows at Junior. "I know I've heard before, it but the title escapes me."

"It's an oldie, from the Tijuana Brass," he said earnestly as Junior's pale face flushed a deep red, "from one of our favorite albums. I can't remember the title, either, but there are lots of good tunes on the record."

"I'll bet there are," I said, giving his shoulder a squeeze. "A good beat and you can dance to it, right?" I spoke directly to Junior, "Sure I can't get you anything?"

I gave her a Ron Adler triple blink and a bright smile, and turned away, hoping she hadn't lately taken up knife throwing.

I expected Del to have been following that little exchange, since she can lip-read pretty well, but she was deep in conversation with Ron Adler. Her brow furrowed as she looked out the window distractedly.

I poured a cup of decaf for Uncle Albert, who was now sitting alone since Eldon likes to table hop.

"You look a little tough yourself, so the conspiracy theory must be an overreaction," he said confidentially.

Junior had probably phoned Aunt Juanita bright and early with her nausea and accusations.

"Things just sort of got out of hand, I guess. I thought we were having a pretty good time. Evidently," I said, glancing over at Junior, who studiously avoided eye contact, "that's a minority opinion."

He patted my hand. "Don't worry about it, sweetie. The nice thing about the bottle flu is that it doesn't last forever. Now your Aunt Juanita's crabbiness"—he paused with a smile and a shrug—"that's a different story."

Aunt Juanita had been mad at everyone for more than twenty years. We'd survive.

"And how are you?" I asked, giving him a chance to talk about his favorite subject.

"Pretty good, I guess," he said, "except for these shooting pains in my elbow."

Unfortunately I couldn't stay and listen. Eldon was drumming his fingers on the counter at the till, waiting for Heidi, who was too busy checking her hair in the mirror to notice him.

I banged the empty pots on the counter loudly to get Heidi's attention. Unfortunately that also woke up the fellow with the pick behind my eyeballs.

Heidi jumped but misread the hint and started wiping the counter at the end furthest from the till. Sighing, I rang up Eldon's ticket myself.

"Tough night, eh toots?" he said with a leer. Short and wizened, with one eyelid drooping permanently at half-mast, he shared with Stu only his astonishingly bright green eyes and the propensity to wear caps, jackets, and shirts slathered with seed company logos. The old joke about farmers (and feed store owners) not wearing Nike tennis shoes because seed companies don't give them away had the unfortunate ring of truth.

"I hear you got something for me," he said, leaning over the counter confidentially, touching my shoulder.

Hangovers make me too stupid to deal kindly with flirtatious old men. I just looked at him tiredly, resisting the urge to squint.

"Your ma?" he asked pointedly. "Didn't she leave something here for me?"

"Oh, sure," I said, finally realizing that he wanted his flat bar. "Just a second, I'll get it for you."

"Quite a gal, your ma," Eldon said conversationally while I squatted to rummage behind the empty ketchup bottles. My knees popped loudly as I held on to the counter with one hand for balance and worried about the waist button of my jeans. I wasn't built for squatting.

"A bit gruff sometimes," Eldon rattled on, "likes things done just so, easily riled. But I like 'em like that."

"She'll be so pleased to know that you feel that way," I said, still looking under the counter.

The flat bar wasn't there. I checked the shelves over and under and on either side. No flat bar.

"Why aren't you working out at Mother's farm today?" I asked, mostly to keep him talking while I continued to look. It was an unnecessary gesture. Eldon talked nonstop, even without encouragement.

I pulled myself up too quickly, which neither my head nor my stomach appreciated.

"Well, now, it's like this, you see. Stuart's wife, she's from Minnesota and she's another one of those particular gals like your ma. She's got it in her head that she wants one of them sliding glass doors in her dining room wall and she has been raising holy hell with Stuart to get it done."

I turned slowly, looking down at all the shelves. No flat bar.

"And Stuart, he's busy today, says he has something important to do, and asks would I mind getting started with the job? I myself don't see what the rush is, what with all this heat and punching a hole in a wall is apt to be hot work and Renee, she don't like a working man to drink a beer in the middle of the day, even in a heat wave. But Stuart, he says, sly like, 'Dad, I'm never going to get any if we don't get started with this door thing.' And I figure if I can't get any myself, I might just as well fix it for Stuart. Right?''

"Uh-huh," I said, not actually listening to him.

I caught Del's eye and motioned her over.

"And so I called your ma last night and told her I wouldn't be out to the farm for a day or two, and I know she's picked up the flat bar in Aberdeen for me, because your Ma always does what she says she's going to do. She wasn't too happy about the delay, I know, but Fernice, she's a lady and she says since she's coming in anyway, she can leave the flat bar at the cafe for me to pick up in the morning.

"So if you got it, I'll just mosey on and put a smile on my son's face.''

"Just a second," I said to him, still not listening, and turned to Del.

"Did Mother leave a blue flat bar here for Eldon last night? Jolene's note said it was with the empty ketchup bottles. But I can't seem to find it anywhere."

Del squinched her face in thought. "Yeah, your mom did leave a crowbar kind of thing. I remember Jolene taking it.''

"Well, it's not where Jolene said it'd be," I said, exasperated. "It's Eldon's and he needs it now."

Del glanced over at Eldon, who was still mumbling amiably about "particular gals.''

"Jolene wouldn't know which end of her nose to blow without being told. You're sure it's not *behind* the ketchup bottles?''

"Be my guest," I said, welcoming her to check for herself.

Del looked and then stood up, clearly puzzled. Her knees

didn't pop on either trip. "I saw her put it there. Do you suppose Aphrodite moved it?"

"Not likely," I said. Aphrodite considered this side of the cafe our domain. When she did leave the kitchen, it was not to rearrange hardware.

"Hang in there a minute, hon." She beamed at Eldon, who was beginning to shuffle restlessly. "We're experiencing a momentary delay in our transmission."

Eldon beamed in return. Just listening to Del cheers most men, even when she makes no sense.

"I don't know why I'm doing this," she grumbled. "I'm barely going to have enough time to get back home and shower before dinner as it is." She bent over, affording Eldon a view he'd treasure.

After scanning my tables to see that everyone was fully supplied with coffee and silverware, with Heidi securely ensconced behind the till, I began searching the shelves more thoroughly for Eldon's pry bar.

It's amazing the amount of clutter that accumulates in a cafe. Necessary things like cups and coffee filters and utensil bins take up most of the space. But there was plenty of room for the inexplicable too. The pair of men's bikini underwear, for instance, stashed under the box of individual jellies. Or an entire box of unrolled Ace bandages.

The search was starting to catch my interest, rather like a treasure hunt where the point was not only to uncover treasures but to guess their use.

Why in heaven's name would anyone store a set of tuning forks at a cafe?

"Bingo!" Del said, crawling backward, out from under the shelf along the north wall, where Aphrodite keeps a battered green cash box that she calls her Burglar Bait. In it are a hundred or so rumpled dollar bills and a handful of tens and twenties, all randomly but carefully dotted with red fingernail polish. Once a week Aphrodite makes a show of storing bundles of cash in the box, a diversionary tactic to disguise the fact that she stores the real cash from the cafe in her unlocked van.

The ruse works. Several times over the years the Burglar

Bait has been broken into, usually by kids who almost immediately try to spend the marked bills on hamburgers and French fries. The other money, sometimes thousands of dollars, lies unnoticed and unstolen in an old purse under Aphrodite's front seat.

The younger waitresses are not in on the switch. Only Del and I know, and we take the secret seriously. I haven't even told Mother.

Del stood up, brushing herself off with one hand. "We'd better check the box," she said to me quietly. "It looks even more dented than usual and the flat bar was lying right in front of it."

She contemplated the flat bar seriously, and then handed it to Eldon with a smile. She froze in midmotion, staring beyond Eldon, her smile suddenly an open "O" of astonishment.

Hesitant, even a little afraid, I turned around and was struck absolutely dumb by what I saw.

10

....

A Jolly Old Elf

Factory workers eventually learn to tune out the rumble of heavy machinery during their shifts. They gossip, threaten to unionize (at least in right-to-work states like South Dakota), and dawdle over coffee breaks, barely noting the roar.

It's not much different in the cafe. Long ago I stopped hearing the constant clink of silverware and the clank of plates and cups. After the first few days of high summer, the rattle and wheeze of the air conditioner fades into the background. The low buzz of conversation forms a choppy sea of sound that isolates unrelated words and fragments of sentences that are accented by the bell on the till.

Even early in the morning when Aphrodite and I are alone, the fluorescent lights hum and the coolers and freezers and refrigerators all add their own notes to the mix. The hiss and sizzle of the grill and fryer is constant.

I rarely hear the background noise now. I talk and laugh, taking orders, listening for the heavy thunk of loaded plates on the counter and the scrape of chairs signaling the end of a meal. I try not to hear Ron Adler's Ole and Lena jokes, which are hardly ever funny enough to bother listening to.

It's never quiet in the cafe.

And thanks to Ron Adler, it wasn't completely quiet now, though conversation died in midsentence, with forkfuls of egg and pancakes ground to a halt between the plate and the mouth. Matches burned unnoticed near unlit cigarettes.

In the silence Ron, whose back was to the door and who was a little slow on the uptake anyway, said, "And Lena says, 'Ole, don't your ears ever get cold?' " His voice reverberated through the unusual quiet.

Ron always enjoys his own jokes, and he started to guffaw before noticing the uncomfortable silence around him.

He turned in the booth, blinking and embarrassed like a small boy whose mother had caught him swearing. Then he saw what everyone else saw and his jaw hinged open in surprise.

He saw Santa Claus.

In late June, in a sweltering heat wave, in the middle of the morning just inside the door of the Delphi Cafe, Ron Adler saw Santa Claus.

He was a right jolly old elf too. A shade taller than expected, but splendidly dressed in a white-trimmed red fur outfit. His pant legs were tucked into tall black rubber barn boots, and a wide belt buckled snugly over what looked like a fiberfill stomach.

He wore a carefully combed and curled white shoulder length wig under his tasseled cap, and his thick white beard and mustache looked real. His cheeks were powdered apple-red, and gold wire-rimmed glasses balanced low on the bridge of his cherry nose.

One green mittened hand clutched a wide strip of thick leather to which large jingle bells were attached. In the other he held a brown burlap sack.

He was Santa Claus and we were astonished.

I had absolutely no idea who he was, but I laughed when I saw him in spite of myself.

He stood motionless and scanned the cafe. We stared back at him, motionless, except for Aphrodite, who couldn't see the front door from the kitchen.

She trundled through the swinging gate, drying her hands on the dishtowel draped over her shoulder. She took one look at Santa, snorted, and pushed back through the gate.

He gave the leather strip a mighty shake. The silvery jangle was overloud in the quiet. "HO, HO, HO!" he said, in an exaggerated, purposely deepened voice with familiar overtones. "Ho, ho, ho," he laughed again, his voice still disguised, but sounding genuinely amused this time.

He strode across the cafe and stood opposite me, at the other side of the counter.

"Do you know who I am, little girl?" he asked, looking away quickly, before I could establish eye contact.

He walked familiarly and I thought I recognized the set of his shoulders.

"Why you're Santa Claus," I said, deciding to play along.

"You're wrong about that, little girl." He chuckled loudly, sure of the cafe's undivided attention. "Completely wrong."

He walked around the tables, stopped and tapped Uncle Albert, who was smiling broadly, on the shoulder.

"What day is it today, kind sir?" he asked Uncle Albert.

Uncle Albert's brow wrinkled then cleared, "June 24th, I believe," he said.

"Intelligent man! Remarkable man!" Santa, paraphrasing Scrooge, beamed. "And does Santa generally appear on June 24th?"

"Actually," Uncle Albert said, enjoying himself, "Santa traditionally shows up on December 24th."

"What a delightful man!" Santa said, throwing in a few "ho ho's" for good measure. "So if Santa comes on December 24th, with presents for all good little girls and boys, who might appear on June 24th?"

He threw the question to the room and had no takers.

He turned back to me, "How about you, little girl? You look intelligent enough to figure it out."

Junior would probably dispute that statement. It all reminded me of Neil's Question of the Day, but Neil was far too shy for this kind of public display. I drew a blank and shrugged.

He "tched" sadly.

"On June 24th, so says an old German legend, a little-known saint traveled about the countryside, taking burdens from the deserving poor, easing their sorrow. But . . ." He paused theatrically, gazing at each table and booth in turn. "Legend also tells that this saint sometimes made others' burdens lighter by taking privileges and possessions from the undeserving."

His voice swelled to fill the room. In the background, Bonnie Raitt was still singing plaintively, the air conditioner wheezed, and kitchen noises continued unabated, but we were silent. Whoever he was, Santa was having a marvelous time. He smiled at me, and I could not resist grinning in return.

The man in the Santa suit continued, jingling the bells softly all the while, "So, if Santa comes on December 24th bringing gifts, and I come on June 24th taking things away . . ." He turned slowly and pointed at me. "Who am I?"

And suddenly, I knew. I laughed and I knew.

"You're the Anti-Santa," I said.

"Absolutely correct. And I'm going to take something very special from you." He laughed heartily, almost forgetting to disguise his voice.

I was beginning to think that I knew who was inside the costume.

There was a feeling of guarded amusement in the cafe, a realization that a show was being put on for our benefit. In a town where minor incidents are instantly embellished and endlessly repeated, this was a mother lode of story material. People buzzed among themselves, smiling. Even Junior grinned, a white shaky grin, but genuine nonetheless.

Only Del refused to be drawn in. She crossed her arms and leaned one hip against the counter, watching warily.

She raised an inquiring eyebrow at me. I shook my head, lying "no idea" in return.

"But first we'll start with the other boys and girls," Anti-Santa said. He pulled a chair away from the table closest to the door and sat down, with his sack crumpled on the floor beside him.

He hummed a Christmas tune while he fished in a pocket and took out a rolled sheet of parchment paper. He set his elbows on the table, pushed the glasses up on his nose, and squinted at it.

I recognized the melody from the music Neil had played yesterday. And I remembered who else had heard that particular tape. And I remembered who had "something important" to do this morning.

Across the street at the feed store, only Eldon's beatup truck was parked in front. Stu's pickup was nowhere in sight.

My headache had faded and the sudden tightening in my stomach might have been caused by something other than the overconsumption of alcohol.

"The first name on my list is Heidi Helen Halvorson." He twisted around and looked at her expectantly, then patted his knee.

We all looked at Heidi, who was cowering behind the till, shaking her head.

"No way," Heidi said, blushing furiously.

"Oh go on," I whispered. "It'll be okay."

The rest of the cafe was perfectly content to let Heidi, a teenager who was not yet officially One of Us, test these unknown waters.

She shot a desperate glance at me, and I remembered how awful it was to be called on unexpectedly in class, to be the first to give a speech, to be asked a question for which you did not know the answer.

Surprised by these protective feelings, I mustered a stern glare for Anti-Santa. If his purpose was to humiliate this girl, then I would refuse to help.

He patted his knee reassuringly and smiled.

"Go ahead," I said to Heidi, hoping I could trust the red-suited man.

Heidi walked to the middle of the cafe and balanced gingerly on his knee. She looked like a frightened rabbit, ready to bolt.

Anti-Santa reached over and pulled a paper napkin from the chrome holder in the middle of the table. "What flavor gum are you chewing?" he asked kindly.

"Uh, watermelon," Heidi said quietly.

"I thought so," he said with a laugh, holding out the napkin. "Spit it out."

"You gotta be kidding," she said loudly, surprised back into herself.

"Nope, right here in the napkin."

Heidi looked at me again, and I gave her a "go ahead" gesture. She took the napkin and delicately deposited the gum in the middle of it.

He crumpled the wad and dropped it in his sack.

"Do you have any more?" Anti-Santa asked.

"About a half-pack," she said, beginning to smile. She pulled a handful of foil scraps and torn wrappers, and more gum from her pocket, and theatrically sprinkled it like glitter into his outstretched, mittened hand.

"Good," he said, stuffing the gum into his sack as well. "To benefit the entire restaurant, I am removing this odious watermelon scent from the premises."

There was a scattered applause, probably from those who had found the mix of watermelon and bacon unappetizing.

Del nudged me with a frown, so I stopped clapping.

Anti-Santa dismissed Heidi, who was now prepared to enjoy someone else's embarrassment from behind the till.

He consulted the list again, looked up, announced, "Albert Engebretson," and patted the chair next to him. Apparently he wasn't going to ask Uncle Albert to sit on his lap, though I think Uncle Albert would have.

In a life of insurance writing and postmistress placating there is very little room for goofiness. Uncle Albert was ripe for adventure. He sat on the chair, smiling, leaned forward, and absently rubbed his elbow.

"Albert, you're a good man with many tribulations," Anti-Santa said, placing a mittened hand on his shoulder. "I'd like to ease your burdens if I can."

Junior accepted the implication with a wan smile and a sip of coffee. Clay caught my eye, winked, and reached across the table to give his wife's hand a squeeze.

"Look directly into my eyes," Anti-Santa said to Uncle Albert, who did exactly as he was told. He's had lots of practice.

"For today, and for as long as possible," he continued, "you will feel no pain and experience no unsettling medical symptoms."

Anti-Santa stared intently into Uncle Albert's eyes for a beat or two longer, then nodded to himself. Uncle Albert blinked and sat back in the chair.

He rolled his neck experimentally and flexed his arm several times. "Some kind of hypnosis, right?" he asked wonderingly.

"Magic," Anti-Santa said solemnly.

"Well, I'll be damned," Uncle Albert said, mostly to himself, since he never swore in public, and certainly never in front of his daughter. He slid next to Junior at her booth, stretching and flexing and mumbling happily.

The cafe hummed with conversation now, a swirling buzz of amused, curious chatter. We were all having an unexpected good time.

Except for Del.

"I can't believe we're standing around watching this clown do parlor tricks," she said disgustedly.

"Come on," I said, "lighten up a little. What's the harm? We're in such a rut that anything out of the ordinary throws us for a loop. This is fun and no one is going to be hurt."

"I wouldn't be so sure," she said darkly.

Anti-Santa cleared his throat loudly. The conversation halted. "Ron Adler," he said, peering over his glasses at Ron.

I could think of any number of subtractions that would benefit Ron. Though she was not above manipulating it for her own convenience, Del would not miss Ron's life-threatening crush on her. Neither, I imagine, would his wife, Gina.

None of us, including Ron himself, would miss the tic that caused him to blink rapidly every third word.

"Ron Adler, you have many good points," Anti-Santa said after Ron sat down. "You're a good father and an excellent mechanic. You run an honest, efficient garage, and Delphi appreciates you."

Ron's smile faltered briefly, and his eyes flickered back at Del, who frowned in return. The exchange was so quick, I don't think any one else noticed.

"But you have an annoying habit that we would all like eliminated," Anti-Santa continued.

A worried look crossed Ron's face, or maybe it was curiosity. Ron had no chin and that combined with his rapid blinks to make reading his expressions difficult.

"From this day forward," he proclaimed, "for as long as the spell lasts, you will no longer be able to tell Ole and Lena jokes."

The cafe erupted in laughter and sporadic applause. Even Del managed a small smile. Ron's jokes were groaners of the worst kind. And if you did actually laugh, you hated yourself in the morning.

"How you gonna stop me?" Ron asked, laughing.

"Go ahead," Anti-Santa urged. "Tell one now."

"All right, I will." Ron stood up and faced the crowd. He opened his mouth. And closed it. He opened his mouth again, and nothing came out. He looked back at Anti-Santa, who motioned him to go on.

Ron stood there for a full minute, opening and closing his mouth like a fish. "I'll be dipped, I can't remember a single one."

This time the applause was wholehearted, even Aphrodite hooted and whistled from the kitchen.

Ron appreciated a good joke, even if it was on himself, and he took the ribbing, blinking good-naturedly as he walked back to his booth.

I wondered what Anti-Santa would take from me. Forty pounds would be nice.

Junior was next. She surprised everyone by sitting on his knee without hesitation. Clay beamed at her proudly.

"Juanita Doreen Engebretson Deibert," said Anti-Santa, "you have a well-deserved reputation as a perfectionist. Your home is spotless, your children are well behaved. You are good at your job and you give generously to charity. But—"

"Here it comes," Junior said to the ceiling.

"You take life far too seriously. When was the last time you had a day to yourself? When was the last time you really cut loose?"

"The answer to that one might surprise you," Junior said, studiously not looking in my direction.

"I don't think so," he replied. "I know you have a scheduled business meeting in Aberdeen. You will find that your meeting has been canceled, so you now have an unexpected day of freedom. Do something frivolous, go on a spending spree. Enjoy yourself. Take time to rethink some of your recent judgments."

Junior looked at him seriously. He returned her steady gaze. "Okay," she said quietly, and gave him a fleeting kiss on the forehead.

On her way back to Clay, she snagged me with a thoughtful look that held neither affection nor malice, just a cool appraisal. Maybe there was hope for us after all.

If Anti-Santa could work such miracles, maybe he could exorcise Nicky's ghost and free me to get on with life.

"Oh give me a fucking break," Del said disgustedly under her breath.

Anti-Santa took Eldon McKee's Keltgen cap, one of the zillion seed company freebies he constantly wore, and replaced it with a purple one from the Minnesota Vikings.

"Delphine Bauer," Anti-Santa boomed after consulting his list.

Instead of complying, she asked me quietly, "What if I just refuse?"

"Please," I said under my breath. Everyone was watching. "Don't make a scene."

"What's it to you?" Del asked.

I just shrugged.

She sighed, rubbed her face, and then walked around the counter and deliberately sat on the chair next to Anti-Santa, rather than on his lap. Del's brittle sense of humor did not include self-deprecation. She loved being the center of attention, but only when she called the shots.

He just laughed.

"Delphine Bauer, I want your Elvis Presley tape."

The cafe dissolved in laughter and catcalls.

"What Elvis tape? I don't have any Elvis tape," Del lied.

Carried away, I shouted, "It's in her jeans pocket."

Del fixed me with such a look of pure venom that the laughter died suddenly in my throat.

Anti-Santa held out his hand patiently.

"No," Del said quietly.

He waited.

"Oh for Christ's sake." She stood and dug in the pocket of her jeans. She held the tape out but did not let go.

"I want this back," she said levelly.

Anti-Santa nodded, somber.

"Soon," she emphasized, making no attempt to sound amused.

Her mood infected the whole cafe. We remembered that Anti-Santa was just a sweaty man in a red fur suit, not a saint or a magician.

Or a lover.

He sat a second or two longer, his shoulders slumped, then stood up and announced, "I want to thank everyone for their kindness and indulgence today. Before I go, I'd like to relieve you all of the burden of paying for breakfast." He rummaged in the sack among gum wrappers, caps, jackets, Elvis tapes, aches and pains, and bad jokes, and pulled out a single bill.

He handed it to Heidi, who was still at the register.

"Will this take care of the tab?" he asked her.

It was a hundred-dollar bill.

Bewildered, she shrugged. I did some quick mental calculations.

"That'll be plenty," I said, both disappointed and relieved that he hadn't singled me out.

He threw the sack over his shoulder, gave the bells another shake, and headed toward the door, then stopped and hit his forehead with the palm of his hand, Columbo style.

"That's right," he said, turning, and smiling directly at me, "I did forget someone."

I spread my hands on the counter and leaned forward on them slightly. Waiting for God knows what.

What could he take from me? My awful hairstyle? My Monkees tape?

Maybe he'd do everyone a favor and spirit away Del's bad mood.

He marched back to the counter and put his sack down, standing less than a foot from me. I could see strands of white hair stuck damply to his forehead and that his gold glasses had no lenses. I caught the wispy scent of some marvelous cologne.

Confused, embarrassed, hopeful, terrified, I could not look up at him.

He placed his hands directly over mine, cupping them gently. I felt their warm strength through the wool. With a pounding heart, I raised my head and looked into his eyes.

His emerald-green sparkling eyes.

"And what are you going to take away from me, Anti-Santa?" I asked, struggling to sound normal. Bored. Blasé.

"Your breath, I hope," he said softly, leaning over the counter to plant a warm, soft kiss on my lips that lingered a heartbeat too long to be anything but a promise.

He pulled back enough to search my face seriously, perhaps for confirmation. Finding it, he leaned even closer and whispered, "I'll see you later."

And then he was gone.

I think maybe there was a lot of cheering but I couldn't hear very well just then.

Sometime between spying on Del and Big Dick last night, and realizing that Eldon helped to arrange Stu's sex

life with his wife this morning, I had decided against an
affair, if ever the opportunity arose.

It was wrong. Wrong for Stu. Wrong for me.

Wrong.

And then Anti-Santa took my breath away and I was lost.

"Hey there." Del snapped her fingers in my face. "Are
you lost?"

Flustered and trying to cover it, I busied myself with
straightening and arranging and cleaning.

"Of course not," I said, my voice nearly normal.

"Sure, that's why you sound so normal," she snorted.
"Watch it kiddo, you're skating on thin ice."

"I don't know what you're talking about," I said briskly,
taking two full plates from Aphrodite.

"You better work on your moves, dearie," Del said, her
humor much improved. "I can tell you from experience, a
man who goes to that much trouble to stage a seduction
wants something pretty special for his effort. Want to borrow some flavored body oil?"

"Don't be ridiculous." I backed up quickly, with my
hands full, and crashed into Heidi carrying a stack of empty
plates, which cascaded to the floor. Along with the breakfast platters I had been carrying.

Heidi surveyed the mess of porcelain shards and biscuits
and gravy splattered over a large area of the floor, the wall,
and our legs.

"Oh Jeez, I'm sorry," she said, sounding genuinely
sorry, "I'm sorry, I'm sorry. I'll get the mop and clean this
up."

Aphrodite had thoroughly frightened the relief girls with
horror stories about the cost of broken dishes and glasses.
They lived in fear of docked paychecks.

The stories kept the girls as careful and efficient as possible even though Aphrodite had never yet made anyone
pay for breakage.

From the kitchen, Aphrodite looked at Heidi sternly and
meaningfully.

"Oh Jeez," she said again, near tears.

"Hey, don't worry," I said, trying to calm her down.

"It was my fault for not paying attention. You pick up the big stuff and I'll go get a broom and a mop."

Heidi nodded and then with a look of delicate distaste, carefully picked up slippery pieces and deposited them in the wastebasket under the counter.

I pushed through the swinging gate and mouthed "Bully" at Aphrodite, whose wide smile nearly engulfed her cigarette.

The rapid change from the bright light of the kitchen to the dark passageway and back into the shafts of sunlight shining through the shed window had rekindled my headache.

Or maybe it was fryer smells mixed with cigarette smoke. Or maybe it was irritation with myself for causing the breakage. Or maybe it was just more hangover.

Does lust cause headaches?

Whatever the reason, my head pounded dully as I opened the mop closet door and collected rags from an upper shelf and grabbed the broom hanging from its hook. I had to shift the body slightly to get the wheeled bucket. Bits of dried mud crunched beneath the wheels as it rolled.

I remember reading somewhere that if you whacked a brontosaurus solidly on the foot, it would take seven minutes for the message to travel to its tiny saurian brain.

I know for sure if you startle an overweight, hungover, widowed waitress (who has just decided to commence an affair with a married feed and seed dealer) with the dead body of a handsome young Mormon missionary on the floor of a cafe mop closet, it'll take five full heartbeats for the scene to register.

11

····························

Cook's Day Off

In this century we of faint courage and weak stomach can sail through life protected from that which we would prefer to ignore. The few ills that doctors cannot cure are generally caused by excesses of our own choosing.

We are not personally acquainted with supper before it is cut and wrapped in sanitary portions scaled to fit our crockery.

Cemeteries are rest havens, mortuaries are funeral homes, and the dead are whisked away, still warm, by masked and gloved professionals.

We need not bother our pretty little heads about life's ugly realities, unless we're in the mood.

Believe me, I'm never in the mood.

Despite the fact that I am a widow, my only hands-on experience with dead bodies has been literary. I had never, ever, seen an actual human corpse.

While we thought of him as being dead, my father's abandonment long ago actually had all the advantages of mourning while freeing us from the messy reality of coffins and headstones.

In a rare burst of sentimentality, Mother let me play outside on the church swing set during Grandpa Paulus's funeral, less than a year after Father left—a moral lapse Aunt Juanita has never allowed us to forget.

Mother harbored no such protectiveness after Nicky's accident.

"You must go and sit with the body," she'd said firmly. Even then, she could barely bring herself to say Nicky's name. "It is expected. People will talk."

"They're talking anyway," I said. "It's bad enough that I have to go to the funeral at all. I will not parade my grief to satisfy Delphi."

"All the more reason for you to hold your head high. It's obvious that the two of us share an attraction to weak men," she said with a stiff, motherly pat on the shoulder.

The sisterhood ploy didn't fool me. I knew she was polishing up the big guns.

"I assume it's hereditary. Your father found it easy to avoid unpleasantness too," she said, taking aim and firing. "Do you honestly think you're the only one to face the public with something like this?"

I knew I wasn't. It could not have been easy for Mother either. But the fact that she stared down the tigers didn't mean that I should. Or could.

She wasn't the only one who found my reluctance puzzling.

"You can hide out all you want afterward," Del had said. "But you've got to make some decisions right now."

So I made a decision.

I decided that Del should handle all the arrangements. I let her duke it out with the priest. I skipped the rosary, insisted on a closed casket, and sat through the service in a daze. I've never been sorry that I took the easy out, spared myself the awful sight of my husband's lifeless body.

I would have made the same choice with Charles Winston. Unfortunately I had no warning he'd be crumpled and dead in the cafe mop closet.

Having no other frame of reference, I blithely accepted Agatha Christie's sterile drawing room descriptions as fact and believed Charlotte MacLeod's notion that there could be humor in murder.

I know better now.

Amazingly enough, I didn't faint or scream. A hard knot of pain in my stomach left me gasping for a moment but passed quickly. The light was sharp and bright. With senses on overdrive, I felt overwhelmingly alert, aware of swirling dust in the air, certain I could see the very molecules if I concentrated hard enough.

The smell of death was nearly submerged in an undertow of Lysol, an odor I had noticed earlier. Only then did it strike me that Charles had been in the closet, dead, all morning.

He'd been here, with his knees pushed under his chin, while Del and I searched for Eldon's flat bar.

He'd been here, tie loosened, shirt unbuttoned, lifeless eyes half-open, during the Anti-Santa show, while I was being swept off my feet.

He'd been here, like a child playing hide-and-seek in a closet.

Dried blood and dark blobs matted his hair around a gaping, horrible hole punched, torn, in his skull just behind his ear. His face was swollen and bruised, and the skin around the wound was gray and ragged, the bone caved in by a terrible force.

I could not, right then, picture Charles alive. Not his gentle religious banter or resistance to Del's flirtation, or his lovely brown eyes. All memories were superseded by the sight of this empty shell carelessly dumped on a closet floor.

Laughing, handsome, young Charles Winston, Mormon missionary, native of Memphis, was dead. Beaten, undignified, the life gone from his slack face. Hidden. Dead.

Murdered.

Obviously he didn't bash himself on the head and crawl into the cafe closet to die. On the floor around the body were several faint brown swirls.

Someone had tried to clean up the blood, I realized. A sudden memory flooded my brain and I jumped back and looked down.

Brownish stains swirled the linoleum in the rest of shed too, which was also littered with the crumbled remains of what had probably been distinct muddy shoe tracks, on which I had been squarely standing. Destroying evidence.

Another wave of pain washed over me. I pushed the bucket back in and quietly closed the door, not worrying about fingerprints, since I had already smudged whatever was on the knob.

The police would have to be notified, of course, which would involve Big Dick Albrecht. I remembered Lottie Kendall's telephone description of the argument between Charles and Big Dick yesterday.

Shouting, she had said. Red faces. Anger.

At least one of Del's paramours had required hospital care after a beating by mysterious attackers. All the hospital care in the world would not help Charles now.

Big Dick is a large and powerful man who enjoys exercising that power. Did that make him a murderer?

I hoped not. For Del's sake, for my sake, for Delphi's sake.

I was suddenly, terribly, tired. Tired and cold, on this hot, late June morning. I wanted nothing more than to find a warm corner, a place to curl up and sleep.

"Hey, you go to sleep back there?" Del shouted from the kitchen, her voice muffled through the door. "Let's step it up, we got ourselves a mess out here that needs to be cleaned."

Nothing compared to the mess back here, I thought. Del sounded impatient but happy and carefree. How long would it be before she felt that way again?

Before any of us felt that way again?

In the bright kitchen Del was sitting on the chopping block, smoking and laughing, swinging her legs like a girl. Aphrodite was filling the steamer with raw bratwurst sausages for today's dinner special—bratwurst and sauerkraut. Aphrodite called the dish Cook's Day Off since preparation involved only steaming the sausages and heating a five-pound can of sauerkraut.

Del called the dish Penis on a Plate.

She liked to wave a flaccid sausage suggestively under my nose and ask what it reminded me of.

Mostly it reminded me of Del asking what it reminded me of, though if you squinted just so, there *was* a certain anatomical resemblance.

She jumped off the table and picked up a sausage and jiggled it jauntily between her thumb and forefinger.

"What's this remind . . ." Her singsong voice trailed off. "Jesus Christ, Tory. You better lay off the booze completely if it makes you feel that bad."

Surprised into a multiple syllable, Aphrodite ordered my sorry ass home.

I stood in the center of the kitchen, eyes closed, absurdly thinking that the past could be undone, that Charles could still walk into the cafe, alive and smiling, if no one else knew he was dead. The terrible fact of his death could perhaps be reversed, like a magic spell, if the secret were kept.

But the magic had no chance to work. Even as the thought surfaced, I realized that I wasn't the only one who knew that Charles was dead. Whoever had put him in the closet knew.

Both Aphrodite and Del watched me closely as I marshaled my thoughts. How does one spring this kind of news? I doubt Emily Post has a rule for announcing the presence of an inconvenient dead body in a closet.

"We have to keep everyone calm and quiet," I said, beginning logically, I thought, marveling at the calm and quiet in my own voice. "Del, you better man the door and make sure no one leaves. I'm sure the sheriff will want to talk to everyone who ate here this morning."

Luckily, everyone seated in the cafe was a local. That would make keeping them in place easier.

"You might as well turn off the ovens," I said to Aphrodite. "Business is going to be a bit slow this afternoon.

I'm going over to Crystal's to use the phone. I'll be right back.''

Del and Aphrodite looked at each other, clearly puzzled, frozen by my strange behavior. I was nearly through the door before Del leaped and spun me around roughly.

"Do you mind telling us just what in the fuck you're talking about?" she asked, patronizingly fierce. "Or have you flipped entirely?"

Though she was exasperated and beginning to be angry, her eyes held a wary look, tinged with fear.

I didn't want to frighten Del, or anyone else, for that matter. It seemed I had no choice in the matter and there was no point in putting off the inevitable.

"You really don't want to see this," I said sincerely, giving them (and myself) one last chance to pretend that everything was normal. "But it'll be easier just to show you."

I crooked a finger for them to follow, which they did, though they were obviously considering calling the men in white coats.

"Stand over here, and don't touch anything," I said, arranging them in front of the mop closet. "What you're going to see is terribly upsetting. Unfortunately, I think that the upsetting part of our day has just begun."

I was making pretentious speeches. Delaying.

I swallowed hard and swung the closet door open.

And as I opened the door, a rogue thought formed. What they were about to see might not be such a surprise after all.

Someone had folded, spindled, and mutilated Charles Winston, and stashed him in the closet. Someone who knew the layout of the cafe, someone who could get in after hours and leave without being seen.

Someone, but not Del or Aphrodite. I would bet everything I owned that neither one could have done it. Almost everything, anyway.

Right then, the only innocence I knew for certain was my own.

For a moment, just a moment, nothing happened.

And for that instant, I thought a magic spell had been worked after all, that there was no dead Mormon missionary in the mop closet. That I had simply lost my mind. That Aphrodite and Del would laugh, I would convince them not to have me committed, and we would go about our day as though nothing happened.

Then Aphrodite slumped. The resignation in the motion made her older, shorter, and sadder.

Del gasped harshly, then grabbed my shoulders. "Is this some kind of a joke?" she shouted. "Because if it is, your sense of humor is out of whack. If you think it's funny to frighten us with a schoolboy prank, you can just get your shit and move out of my house. Go live with your sainted librarian. You can play fucking jokes on each other all day long."

Aphrodite laid a heavy hand on Del's shoulder and clucked. For a second I thought Del would fling the hand away. Instead she looked at both of us in turn, beseeching. Sadness made her younger, more vulnerable, the toughness washed from her face.

"He can't be dead," she said in a small voice, crying now, quietly. "He's too young. He's too gorgeous. He's too serious. Boys like that don't die. Do they?" she demanded of Aphrodite. "Do they?" she asked me.

She gazed at Charles for what seemed like a long time, though I don't suppose it was more than half a minute. Then the softness in her face solidified, she straightened, rolled her head on her neck, and grimaced in a parody of a smile. It was an acknowledgment and an acceptance, I think.

"Go use the phone next door at the store," Aphrodite said to me.

Gee, why didn't I think of that?

The pay phone by the front entrance was the only one in the cafe. It would be easier not to report this death in front of an enthralled audience of customers. They would demand, hear, repeat, and embroider the gory details soon enough.

"Can you keep things calm?" I asked Aphrodite.

"Sure, Del can flirt with the men till the cops come."
She put a companionable arm around Del's shoulders. "I'll
shut things down. Too bad we can't move him. Make less
of a mess that way."

She raised an inquisitive eyebrow. "He won't be less
dead out there." She pointed at the door.

She was calmly suggesting that we move the body outside, so that the investigation wouldn't involve her and the
cafe directly.

"Not a good idea," I said, though I understood her di-
lemma. Who would reimburse her for the lost business?
The notoriety would attract the worst sort of looky-loos for
a couple of weeks. But even locals might stay away once
the furor died down and the news crews left.

If we're really unlucky, we'll end up being one of those
Unsolved Mysteries on TV.

"The police'd know if we did that," I said, certain from
my vast knowledge of literary crime. "And then we'd be
prime suspects."

Del barked a short laugh. "Just who do you think *will*
be the prime suspects, Sherlock? Who do you suppose will
be the first one they haul in for questioning? His mother?
Your mother? My mother?"

Violet Bauer, old at thirty-nine and unable to face another day, had left thirteen-year-old Del to discover her
suicide and suffer four more years of paternal wrath before
escaping with the first in a series of exceptionally poor romantic choices.

Del rarely mentioned her own mother, and never mentioned mine. We didn't know if Charles even had a mother.
She was really rattled.

She was also frightened.

I didn't seriously think anyone would suspect Del though
clearly, she did.

"Why would they suspect you?" I asked her back as she
strode toward the kitchen.

She turned and gave me a look that I couldn't interpret,
then straightened and squared her shoulders and disappeared around the corner.

Aphrodite grunted, or maybe it was a sigh.

"Go call and get this show on the road." She chucked me roughly under the chin. "Buck up, kid. The worst is yet to come."

12

....

Psychic Barking

To block the vision of Charles slumped on the floor of the mop closet, I concentrated on muddy footprints as I stepped into the harsh sunlight, careful this time to tiptoe around the few remaining shoe tracks etched in mud next to the cafe doorway. I walked behind the combined grocery/insurance office, out to the sidewalk, and back to the storefront, mulling and sorting the few details I could put together.

In the first place, the doorway was an odd spot for muddy shoeprints. The few raindrops in last night's storm would have soaked into the parched ground without a trace, and the overhang would have protected the doorway from mud, in any case. No matter what the weather yesterday, the dirt there would have been dry and hard.

The mud must have been on the shoes already, tracked in from someplace else, I decided. That the shoeprints belonged to the murderer was a foregone conclusion. We had a body in a closet and mud where it shouldn't be—the two must be connected.

I had uncovered my first clue. Look out, Miss Marple.

A small spate of self-congratulation pushed the sight of Charles's body back a little further, and occupied the portion of my brain that should have been figuring out what to say to both Crystal and the sheriff.

Actually, calling the sheriff would be the easy part since I wouldn't talk to him directly. The dispatcher would take the message and she'd only want the specifics, the What and the Where. I doubted they'd be interested in speculations about the Who and the Why from me.

But what would I say to goofy, gentle Crystal, who was genuinely fond of Charles? She would be deeply saddened by his death, especially under such circumstances. I envisioned quiet tears and herbal teas and voluminous, suffocating hugs.

Hey, I thought, with an inappropriate smile, she's psychic, maybe she already knows.

In the end, I didn't have to say anything to her at all.

Jasper Singman, with a faint look of impatience, was behind the counter in the store, waiting for a small boy to decide whether he wanted a tin of sardines and a box of Hot Tamales, or Twinkles with a V-8 chaser.

After living with Presley, who likes chocolate sauce on bologna sandwiches and dips barbecue potato chips in milk, I'm no longer surprised by juvenile culinary weirdness. And anyway, no food or drink combination compares to snot and cheese on crackers, Boogerman's recommended appetizer.

Never eat an hors d'ouevre prepared by a giggling twelve-year-old boy.

The kid at the counter finally settled on Barq's and a dill pickle, paid, and raced out of the store. The look of faint disgust on Jasper's long, thin, face was replaced by a look of faint concern.

Spiritual and otherworldly, all of Jasper's earthly emotions registered low on the Richter scale.

"He's a burnout," Rhonda had declared. "Just look at his eyes."

Jasper's eyes were certainly mournfully vacant, and his

long thin torso had the emaciated look of a longtime druggie. He moved slowly and deliberately, as if his own motion would upset his equilibrium.

"Crystal said you'd be in this morning," he said ponderously, reaching into the pocket of his heavily embroidered chambray work shirt. "She told me to give you this. To say it's important."

He held out a pale blue envelope printed with rainbows and unicorns. My name was written in an upper corner. It was my day for notes, I guess.

"In a second," I said, tucking the envelope into my shirt pocket. "First, I need to use your phone, if that's all right."

"To call the sheriff," he said, nodding emphasis on his own words. "Yes, Crystal said you'd want to do that."

That one flummoxed me.

"Crystal knew?" I asked, incredulous. "She knew Charles Winston had been murdered? That I'd want to use your phone to call the sheriff? This morning?"

I ran my fingers through my hair, trying to squash the note of hysteria that had crept into my voice.

How did Crystal know? Is she really psychic, or did she witness something?

Worse yet, did she do it?

"Murder?" Jasper asked in dumb surprise. "Charles Winston?"

"That's what you just said, that Crystal knew I'd be in to call the sheriff and report a murder, right?" I demanded, wishing he would show some shock. Or horror. But he just stood, tall and mostly imperturbable.

"I know nothing about murder," he said, shaking his head slowly but emphatically. "I know only that Crystal said events of some importance had occurred and that *you* would come to the store early this morning to telephone the authorities."

Jasper was right, I had brought murder into the conversation, not him. And Crystal's supposedly psychic rumblings notwithstanding, I could not afford to waste any more time being sidetracked by hysterics. Or semantics. My own, or anyone else's.

Though it felt like a lifetime, barely fifteen minutes had passed since I discovered Charles's body. It would be another fifteen, at least, before the sheriff and coroner arrived, if I ever got around to making the damn call.

We'd have a restaurant full of restless natives by then.

"Perhaps you should take a moment to read what Crystal wrote," Jasper said gently, pointing at my shirt pocket. "In the soft fabric of the Universe, even small tears have a large consequence."

Oh good, a dollop of mystic bullshit to cap the morning. I weighed the envelope in my hand, balancing obligation and curiosity, and my ability to speed-read, against the ticking clock. Recognizing my own weakness, I tore open the note.

A ten-dollar bill that had been placed in the folded paper drifted slowly to the floor.

In a spidery-fine, closely written feminine hand, the note read:

> *With this, I entrust some information and evidence, dear Tory, which you will find disturbing and will almost certainly set in motion events which cannot be recalled. I would rather have talked directly to you, but I am called out of town on urgent business today, and I feel the need for you to know these things as soon as possible. And so, I write.*
>
> *I have mentioned to you the suspicious activities of the deputy, Delphine's friend. Last night, before going to bed, I saw him again take the keys and enter the cafe.*
>
> *He was inside for 10–15 minutes. When he came out, he replaced the keys. I sensed something fluttering from his pocket, but he apparently did not notice.*
>
> *I watched him walk away, around the back of the cafe, then dressed and went downstairs and outside.*
>
> *On the ground, near the drainpipe, I found a ten-dollar bill, lying where it had fallen from his pocket. That bill is enclosed in this envelope.*
>
> *The money came from inside the cafe, all of my*

senses tell me this. And it was stolen. Of this, I am absolutely certain.

The deputy is a thief, Tory, and possibly danger-ous. He has been stealing from your Goddess all this time. He must be stopped. It is not possible for myself or Jasper to report this crime, so we leave it to you and your good conscience.

You will not want to be overheard at the cafe or at home. Please use the telephone at our store to contact the sheriff, who I feel is an honest man. Do not trust this information or evidence to anyone else, especially Delphine, who may want to protect her deputy.

There are many currents swirling around you to-day, Tory, and there is great potential for change, but whether for good or evil, I cannot tell. Be ex-tremely careful, and consider carefully. Appearances are deceiving.

Jasper handed me the ten-dollar bill, which he had re-trieved while I read Crystal's note. In the center of the upper left zero was a small red dot.

Fingernail polish. The same bright red Aphrodite used to mark the Burglar Bait money.

However she had come to the conclusion, Crystal was right—the bill had come from inside the cafe.

And it *had* been stolen. The Burglar Bait was never cir-culated, never used in the till to make change or pay bills. It was kept in reserve as a decoy only.

It had already occurred to me that Big Dick Albrecht had the means and the motive to murder Charles Winston. A powerful body in a jealous rage is a formidable weapon.

But did I actually think Big Dick was capable of murder? I was surprised to find that the answer, instantly, was yes.

The midnight encounter in the bathroom, the hand on Del's head enforcing his own rhythm, the mimed pistol shot were all violently threatening.

I considered him at least capable of manslaughter, the

powerful bludgeoning of another human being, if not a carefully plotted and planned murder.

It was stealing that particular money that I didn't believe.

Big Dick is large and mean. He may well be evil. But he is not stupid.

Though Aphrodite usually handles the petty thefts without resorting to charges filed and official proceedings, all of the local police, including Big Dick, know how the bills are marked and have even helped round up a few strays for us when the offenders were enthusiastically careless in their spending.

Big Dick wouldn't steal, and then drop, evidence while leaving a crime scene of his own creating.

At least not accidentally.

At least I didn't think so.

I had made a career of avoiding unpleasantness. The woman who had not once confronted her husband with the evidence of his many infidelities, and who had not even looked in his coffin to make sure it was really him, and that he was really dead, was the woman who wanted to run home and bury herself in a book. Now.

Crystal was barking up the wrong waitress if she expected me to take charge. I did not want to report a theft, much less a murder. I did not want to unravel clues, to put myself in danger, to anger Del and her well-armed boyfriend, whatever he might be guilty of. I did not want to solve this mystery.

I just wanted to be left alone.

I stood for a moment, and thought how nice it would be to walk away, to let someone else handle the details. To let life go on as it had.

And then I sighed and held my hand out to Jasper for the phone.

"I've already dialed for you," he said quietly.

13

....

Violating the Prime Directive

If Andy Warhol had ever visited South Dakota, he'd have revised his notion of the whole fame/time-frame thing. These days a thirty-second sound bite, down about fourteen and a half minutes from earlier estimations, is all anyone can expect in the national eye.

But here in Delphi, even a brush with fame can be parlayed into a lifetime in the spotlight.

"Well, me and Fran thought Dallas and Pittsburgh was both riding for a long fall," Willard Hausvik said last football season. "But Fran, he knows they'll get their shit together sooner or later."

Not surprisingly, ex-Minnesota quarterback Fran Tarkenton also thinks that the modern-day Vikings don't hold a candle to the teams of yesteryear.

All of Fran's pronouncements, with frequent updates, were gleaned from the supper Willard and Iva shared with Tarkenton as the grand prize in a drawing held by KSDN radio out of Aberdeen. Twelve years ago.

So intimate and personal was their three-hour acquaintance, and so firmly etched is Tarkenton personality in the Hausvik mind, that Willard feels perfectly free to explain Fran's thoughts on any number of subjects.

"Fran, he hated that instant replay bullshit," Willard says with certainty. "And he's goddamn glad they didn't institute it until after he retired." Or "Fran don't believe in all that ozone stuff."

I couldn't wait for the official Tarkenton bulletin on dead missionaries in mop closets.

I was still at the grocery store, wrestling with decisions and phone calls, when Del made the initial announcement about Charles to the astonished crowd.

"It was weird at first," she said to me when I got back. "At first the place was so quiet you could hear a pin drop. Then everyone started in all at once, grumbling and accusing. They already know who did it, take your pick: hippies or drug gangs."

"What's Fran think?" I asked.

Del laughed. "Satanic cults."

Aphrodite's assessment was short and to the point, "Heidi puked, Clay preached, Eldon whined, and Ron blinked."

There was a good deal of whining and blinking when I passed on the sheriff's instructions too.

"I can't stay here all day. I got work to do."

"Who's gonna explain this to Renee? She ain't gonna care who died, she just wants her sliding door."

"A statement?" Blink, blink, blink. "What the fuck they want a statement for?"

"Hey, I didn't even know the guy."

"Fran thinks the world is going to hell in a handbasket, that's for sure."

"Fingerprints," Del said resignedly, "I knew it."

"No, it's not like that," I said. "They want fingerprints from everyone who works here to distinguish ours from any strange ones they might find. They'll want yours, mine, Aphrodite's, and the relief girls'. It's all routine."

"Sure it is," Del said. "Just wait and see."

"Here come the cops," someone said about five minutes later. "Lots of them."

Big Dick's cruiser and another sped in, followed by the coroner's van and a dark, unmarked car from which a tall man in an overcoat stepped.

"The Feds," Del said to my raised eyebrows.

I had forgotten that the DCI—the Department of Criminal Investigation—would be called in to investigate murder cases.

Everyone except Del, Aphrodite, and I was firmly but quietly ushered from the cafe out into the bright sunlight. As he squeezed through the door, Eldon noticed a white truck barreling toward the cafe.

"Hey everyone, it's the TV guys!"

The herd mood brightened immediately, fame was just an in-depth interview away.

"I figured they'd get here pretty soon."

"Suppose we'll make the nightly news?"

"Course we'll make the news. This ain't New York, murder is a big deal here."

"They won't *make* us talk to the cameras, will they?" Blink, blink.

"Hey, it's Crane Compton. He looks shorter in person."

I edged over to a window, watching the news crew unload cameras and microphones and set up shop. Crane Compton, the handsome anchor for the Channel 9 On the Spot News Team, barked orders that were obeyed laconically by blue-jeaned cameramen and assistants who were all a head taller than Compton, though not nearly so well barbered. They fashioned an outdoor set with the cafe framed in the background.

I wondered if Channel 3's Nancijean Montrose (Channel 3, We're There When It Happens) would arrive before the juicy quotes dried up. It looked as though Compton had the scoop on this hot story.

A sharp finger poked me between the shoulder blades.

"Go sit over there, out of the way, until we get a chance to take your statement," Big Dick growled, the sun glinting off his mirrored sunglasses as he pointed at the counter.

I wasn't about to argue with the man Crystal saw leaving the cafe last night, pockets stuffed with stolen petty cash, a man who just possibly had committed a crime much more serious than theft.

When had Crystal seen her intruder? How late last night?

Big Dick had canceled the Cities jaunt to escort a prisoner to Fargo—allowing four hours' driving time each way plus time for meals and official proceedings, a minimum ten-hour round trip.

Lottie Kendall had seen him arguing with Charles around one-forty-five P.M. If he'd left Delphi soon after the argument, he could have been back in town by three-ten A.M., when the storm broke and I saw him in our driveway.

But had he been in Delphi before Crystal's bedtime?

Not if Crystal's bedtime was before two A.M. Not if Big Dick really did go to Fargo.

How does one check on the comings and goings of a county deputy?

Carefully, I decided. Very carefully.

Outside, yellow plastic ''crime scene'' ribbons flapped in the wind, stretched between sawhorses on the sidewalk in front of the cafe. People gawked at the real live TV personalities and milled aimlessly around the knot of cafe patrons who were loosely corralled by a couple of uniforms patiently asking questions and jotting in small notebooks.

Quite a crowd had gathered. The whole town, and a few outsiders with police scanners, were busy enjoying the most exciting event since a twister deposited a prize heifer, unharmed, on the roof of the school.

Now with the irresistible lure of a real dead body, and actual famous TV people, everyone was unabashedly reveling in the spectacle. Even Mrs. Beiber came out into the street to disapprove.

In an assembly-line procedure, each person from the cafe was released after official questioning, only to be captured and questioned again by debonair Crane Compton, this time with cameras rolling. Then slightly dazed and highly gratified, they faced an eager crowd of locals who began the real questioning. In earnest.

Clay spoke seriously to the cameras for a few moments. Junior surprised me by refusing an interview altogether. Eldon had to be led away by a frazzled assistant director, and Ron Adler looked pale even from a distance.

The five-thirty news tonight would certainly be interesting.

"Tory!" Big Dick interrupted my train of thought with a barked command. "Come back here a minute, please." It was not a request.

I followed him through the kitchen where Del, arms crossed and leaning against the stainless-steel counter, was answering a question with a slight smile. A young deputy grinned in return.

"Nope, he came in and I served him his supper like usual," Del said to the officer. "He ate and then he left. Said he was going straight back to Aberdeen."

Her eyes flickered, but she didn't acknowledge us. Big Dick's jaws clenched and his lips tightened into a colorless line.

"Back here," he said, stepping aside, and for once did not touch me as I walked past him, into the back room.

There were more people squeezed into the shed than I would have thought possible. A photographer was rapidly snapping pictures of poor Charles in the closet, his flash lighting the room at regular intervals and odd angles. The coroner stood beside the photographer, talking softly into a hand-held tape recorder. Aphrodite was huddled in the far corner, and a tall man stood in the middle, directing the whole operation.

A gurney, front wheels rolled just over the sill, propped the outside door open. A black plastic zipper bag lay open on it, waiting for the men inside to finish their work. Waiting for Charles's body. Behind the gurney, the coroner's van had been backed up, its doors swung wide.

The tall man motioned Aphrodite out with a rumble, saying, "We'd appreciate it if you gave a full statement to an officer before you leave. Thanks for your help."

He turned to me, "Ah, Miss Bauer, isn't it?" he asked.

The fed. The G-man. The investigative officer from the Department of Criminal Investigation.

He held out his hand, "Agent John Ingstad. We'd like to ask you a few questions, if you feel up to it."

He was tall and bald with a fringe of dark hair around the ears.

"Actually, it's Mrs.," I said, making a distinction that didn't seem particularly important at that juncture. I tend to babble when I'm nervous. "Miss, Mrs., it doesn't really matter, does it? I mean, it doesn't make much difference as far as this is concerned . . ." I trailed off uncertainly.

"Well," he said with something that might have passed for a smile under ordinary circumstances, "we like to get these things straight right from the start. Mrs. Ferguson here tells us that you discovered the body."

Mrs. Ferguson? I had never pictured a Mr. Aphrodite. This would call for some follow-up snooping.

Agent Ingstad looked at me expectantly. I realized he was waiting for confirmation.

"Yes," I said, resolving to stick to simple declarative sentences. "I found the body. Ah, Charles. Ah, him. This morning. About an hour ago. Well, it was probably about an hour ago, I didn't look at my watch. But I think it was an hour. More or less."

My New Year's resolutions tend to go the same route.

"I understand you moved the body slightly, so that it is now sitting in an altered position," he said gravely.

Oh Lord. I had moved the body. I had broken the Murder Scene Prime Directive without even realizing it.

"Well, I, ah, yes, ah, I . . ." I mumbled. "Yes, I moved him a little. To get the bucket. There was this mess out front, you see, and I came back here to get the mop and stuff. I just didn't see him. I didn't realize, until after."

"You didn't realize he was dead or didn't realize who he was?" he asked gently.

"Both," I said, miserably. "Until it was too late."

"I see," he said, and then waited for me to continue.

"I also stepped on the footprints," I confessed in a rush. He waited for me to continue.

"There were dried mud footprints, boot tracks they looked like, here, in front of the door." I pointed at the floor. "I noticed them this morning when I came to work. But I just thought Jolene hadn't cleaned very well."

Agent Ingstad looked over at Big Dick, who was standing in the doorway sideways, probably keeping an eye on Del and the young officer.

"Jolene Bartelheimer, waitress on duty last night before closing," Big Dick said in a monotone.

"There are more footprints just outside the door," I said, trying to redeem myself. "I didn't step on those."

He raised an eyebrow at Big Dick, who reluctantly left his post and went outside to check.

"I know this may be upsetting to you, Mrs. Bauer, but I want you to look closely at the position of the body and tell us how it is different now from when you first saw it."

I took a deep breath and looked hard at Charles. "I don't know. I mean, I didn't really see him until afterward."

Agent Ingstad waited patiently while I tried to make sense of jumbled memories. I had shifted the body back to pull the bucket free, but I didn't actually move him.

"I think he must have been leaning forward more, with his arm over the top of the bucket. I sort of shoved and then pulled the bucket out."

Ingstad nodded to himself, forehead wrinkled in concentration.

"I'm all finished back here. Think I'll check up front and see if there's anything interesting there," said the photographer jauntily to the coroner, swinging through the door, camera in hand. "He's all yours now."

Big Dick came back in. "Most of the shoeprints were destroyed by the gurney and the van. There is one good one toward the back of the cafe, though. We'll get a picture and a cast made."

As he left, I noticed how dusty his boots were. As though he'd been kicking in the dirt, destroying footprints perhaps?

The coroner was on his knees, examining the hole in the back of Charles's head.

"In addition to a pretty thorough beating, he looks to

have been hit with something sharp edged and flat, about two to two-and-a-half inches wide,'' he said to Agent Ingstad. ''Nasty wound, certainly enough to have killed him, though we'll have to wait for the forensic pathologist's verdict before we know that for sure.''

I must have paled. The coroner's description fit the business end of a flat bar perfectly. And we had been handling a flat bar all morning. Probably smudging more fingerprints and destroying more evidence. Violating the Prime Directive even more thoroughly.

''Does that mean something to you, Mrs. Bauer?'' Agent Ingstad asked.

''My mother left a new flat bar here at the cafe for Eldon McKee to pick up this morning. It wasn't on the shelf where she said it'd be. We had to search before Delphine Bauer found it, beside the petty cash box.''

Which, I just now remembered, looked as though it had been jimmied. Which reminded me of Crystal's note.

Big Dick was guarding the doorway again, so I decided to keep Crystal's information to myself until I could sort out what should be told, and to whom.

I could just imagine Agent Ingstad's reaction to a tip accusing a county deputy of robbery and murder, made by a psychic hippie and relayed by a woman who had moved a dead body without realizing it.

''And did Eldon McKee take the flat bar from the cafe this morning?'' he asked.

''I don't think so,'' I said. ''He had it in his hand and was ready to leave, but we were distracted.'' I hesitated, embarrassed.

''Go ahead,'' he said.

''By Santa Claus.''

A pained look tightened Agent Ingstad's face. ''Why don't you tell all this to the officer out there in your statement. Make sure to include all the details.''

The coroner shook open a pair of small brown paper bags and slipped them over Charles's hands. He hummed lightly under his breath as he gathered the edges and wrapped them with red rubber bands at the wrists.

"Paper bags?" I asked. It seemed like the ultimate in-dignity, to be zipped in a body bag with your hands wrapped in brown paper mittens.

"To protect any evidence that may be under the finger-nails," the coroner said absently. "Hair, fiber samples, skin fragments, things of that sort."

Agent Ingstad nudged me gently toward the door.

"What happens to him now?" I asked.

"We contact his family for official identification, and then we ship him to Sioux Falls for an autopsy to be con-ducted by the forensic pathologist."

"Autopsy," I said dully, thinking of his family.

"Standard procedure," he said quietly as I left, "in sus-pected homicide cases."

Aphrodite had been busy in the kitchen. Apparently she had permission to put away the remains of today's uneaten dinner special.

She was conversing vehemently with the young officer through the opening between the kitchen and the cafe proper.

Beyond the kitchen I could see the Burglar Bait box open on the counter, with the blue flat bar beside it. The pho-tographer was busily snapping shots of both, and the whole interior of the cafe.

"Can you tell me when?" Aphrodite asked the officer, enunciating each word slowly and clearly. If he had been one of our relief girls, he'd have been quaking in his boots.

"I'm sorry, I can't," he said politely, holding his ground against her monumental disapproval. "It depends entirely on how quickly the investigation proceeds. This establish-ment is officially a crime scene, and as such, will be closed to the public until further notice."

"Well, girls," Aphrodite said loudly, her voice echoing through the nearly empty cafe, "thank the Men in Blue for the time off. With no pay."

Actually, these were Men in Khaki, but Aphrodite is not above making an occasional, inaccurate, theatrical scene.

"Get your stuff," she said to me, "And we'll leave these

boys to their work." She looked pointedly at the officer,
"We *can* take our stuff, can't we?"

"You may take your own personal belongings, but we'd
like to check them over first," he said.

She shrugged and handed her purse to him. He gave a
cursory glance to the contents and gave it back to her.

"Let's go," she said to me, "I'll buy you a beer. I need
one. Looks like you do."

It was tempting. God, was it tempting.

"Thanks," I said ruefully, "but they still want my statement. And fingerprints. And I need to get my stuff. I'll be
a while yet, unfortunately."

She waggled stained fingertips in the air. "At least I'm
done." She paused, watching Del and Big Dick seated at
the small table. They were deep in conversation, Big Dick
sat with notebook open, pen in hand, not writing.

Aphrodite pursed her lips for a moment. I wondered if
she'd offer a beer to Del too.

She didn't. "I'll call," she said over her shoulder as she
trundled out into the bright sunlight and was captured by
Crane Compton's minions.

"Why don't you sit in one of the booths," the young
officer suggested, "I'll be with you in just a second." He
joined the photographer for a conference.

"Is it okay if I get my things? There's some stuff I'd
like to take if we're going to be closed for a few days."

"Sure," he said, still conferring.

My purse was in the jumble on the shelf below the till.
In all likelihood I'd not be allowed back in until after the
investigation was complete. What else should I take?

Music, certainly. All the tapes in the box by the player
belonged to Del and me, and I didn't think there'd be any
objection to our taking them home.

Behind the counter, careful to step out of the photographer's way, I picked up the box of cassettes. I fished behind
the player for the tape that had overshot the box this morning.

I carried everything to a booth with an unimpeded view
of the melee. It was hot and bright, and close to dinnertime.

The crowd had thinned, though Willard and the Old Farts would stay rooted in order to report any interesting developments.

Crane Compton smoothed his perfect hair and squinted at his watch, determined to wait for an official statement. The Channel 3 News crew had not yet arrived, and the lure of an exclusive story was every bit as irresistible to him as he was to us.

"Sorry to make you wait," the young officer said as he slid in the booth, notebook in hand. "How about you just tell me what happened, from the very beginning."

14

....

Relativity

We don't deny that the sum of the squared sides of a right triangle equals the square of its own hypotenuse. It works out that way every time. And even though absolute proof might be hard to come by, E may very well equal mc squared.

We really don't care.

The only equation with any practical application to our lives is Neil Pascoe's Delphi Theory of Relatives.

"Let's just say that Willard Hausvik spots a flying saucer invasion from the Planet of the Liberals, here to take over the U.S. government," Neil said, explaining his theorem. "Who's the first person he contacts with this incredible news?"

"Fran Tarkenton," I said.

"No seriously, who would he tell?"

I thought for a second. "He'd call Iva at home."

"Right," Neil said. "If you got hold of a really juicy piece of news and had to tell someone right away. Who would you call?"

"I'd call you," I said.

"That doesn't count," he said with a smile. "Who would you contact if you were a normal person?"

"My mother, of course," I said.

"Absolutely, you'd call family," he said, warming to the subject. "We all would. So what does Iva do?"

"Well, Iva wouldn't have to call her sisters, because they hang out at her beauty parlor. She'd make the dramatic announcement in person."

"Boy you catch on fast," Neil said with mock admiration. "She'd tell the hair ladies that she just got the strangest call from Willard about a planeload of Democrats landing in Delphi for some kind of confrontation.

"And then?" he asked, waiting for me to continue.

"The hair ladies would disperse to the nearest bank of telephones to tell all their relatives that a bunch of extremists was on the way, looking for a fight."

"Yup. Now Willard has been mulling the situation over for a half-hour or so. He's called Iva already, so he figures he better drop in at the cafe to warn his buddies to sharpen up their conservatism in a last-ditch effort to save the country.

"He pops in, grabs a cup, and is all ready to make a speech when Eldon McKee taps him on the shoulder. 'Did you hear?' Eldon asks Willard, 'A bus full of commies is parked around the corner!' "

"And Willard scratches his head and says, 'They must be here to meet the flying saucer.' "

"Very clever." I laughed. "But what's your point?"

"There are three points actually. First, we're so inbred that even when we tell only relatives, the story still spreads. Second, we rarely recognize our own rumors when they circle back. And third, and most important, no matter how outlandish the story, there's always a kernel of truth embedded there somewhere."

It's that kernel that fascinates us, the delight we have in sorting and storing and discarding and comparing notes that keeps our ears glued to the telephone.

"So, was he shot or stabbed?" Mother asked after establishing that yes, I was okay, and yes, the police had treated me politely, and no, so far as I knew, they didn't have a suspect yet.

I had been forced to run the gauntlet of two news crews as I left the cafe. The folks from Channel 3 had finally arrived and were desperate to make up for lost time. A visibly irked Crane Compton tried to ask me a few cursory questions, which I tried to duck. Unlike every other United States citizen, I have no desire to see myself on television, or to know exactly how wide my rear end really is.

Del was still closeted with Big Dick, and I hoped for some peace and quiet at the trailer. A beer, perhaps, and a shower.

I was barely in the door when the phone rang.

I answered Mother's question with a silly question. "How did *you* hear about it so fast?"

"What a silly question, Tory. Junior was there too, remember?"

"I'll bet she broke a land speed record getting the news out. What's Aunt Juanita's verdict on the whole thing?"

"Aunt Juanita had several interesting theories. She thinks that biker fellow, the one in the trailer, did it. You can't ride a motorcycle and be a good person in Juanita's universe," Mother said. "She also thinks that none of this would have happened if we had stopped this missionary stuff to begin with. She wants to pass a city ordinance."

"Aunt Juanita always has a tendency to overlook the First Amendment," I said. "What else?"

"She especially thinks that I'm at fault for not insisting that you get a decent job and live a normal Christian life."

"Did you tell her to sit on it?" I asked.

"A tempting thought, dear, but it would serve no purpose to ruffle Aunt Juanita's feathers, especially when she really is thinking of your welfare." She got back to the main point, "So, again, bullet or knife wound?"

"Neither," I said. "You'll never believe this, they think he was killed with Eldon's flat bar. The one you left at the cafe! By the way," I demanded, "what was it doing there in the first place?"

Mother sighed, "I got home yesterday and sent Lottie scuttling with her ears burning for leaving Grandma with a stranger. Grandma was so agitated last night that I had to dose her."

Mother kept a small locked supply of mild sedatives, and was under doctor's orders to use them sparingly, but as necessary. Grandma must have been really upset.

"She finally calmed down, and the phone rang. It was Eldon. He said he couldn't come to the farm for a few days because his daughter-in-law wanted some work done on her house right away. He was sorry about the delay, and asked if I would please bring the flat bar in, because he'd need it in the morning."

"Why not just leave it at the feed store?" I asked.

"Eldon said that Stuart had already gone home, and that he was leaving too. Word is he sits in on Uncle Albert's five-card stud insurance meetings. So he told me to leave it at the cafe and he'd pick it up in the morning. Grandma was sleeping peacefully, so I took a chance and ran the flat bar back into town myself. Are they sure it's the murder weapon?" she asked.

I told her what the coroner said. "They think the murder is connected to a robbery, since the cash box was jimmied and some money taken."

"Oh?" she asked. "That's the first I've heard about any robbery."

"Junior doesn't know everything, does she?" I crowed. "We probably wouldn't have noticed the missing money either, except that we had to search everywhere for the flat bar this morning. We finally found it behind the cash box."

"Come again?" Mother said.

"We had to search for the flat bar," I repeated. "It wasn't where you had Jolene put it last night. Or maybe Jolene got your instructions wrong."

"I told her to put it on the shelf under the counter, and I watched her do it," Mother said.

"Well, the murderer found it, used it, and didn't put it back where it belonged," I said, sounding breezier than I felt.

"Apparently," Mother said slowly.

I think we just remembered what we were talking about. Charles Winston's death was not just an abstract puzzle, a piece of hot gossip to bandy about. I decided not to mention Crystal's notions about Big Dick, or her psychic rumblings. Mother already thinks the Singmans are flakes.

She hung up with an admonition to rest, to be careful, and to take a shower.

Good advice, even if I had already thought of it myself. Even if it came from a woman whose dual purpose in life was to care for her own mother and overprotect her daughter.

In the shower I concentrated on not thinking, my mind a total blank while the water beat a cool tattoo on my shoulders. Eyes closed and head rolled back, I let the icy water run down my face in rivulets. Delicious small shivers took me as I turned, and turned again, under the cascade.

The phone rang, a faint trill half a house away. I let it ring, in no hurry to move. The whole day washed away, leaving a mindless shell with wonderfully cool skin and tingling nerves.

I slipped into a floor-length silk wrapper, an unregretted extravagance worth two months of tips. Wearing it always made me feel rich and elegant, the smooth fabric creating a lovely friction on bare skin.

I spritzed myself with another extravagance, a wildly expensive perfume whose black-and-white ads featured pouting beauties of both sexes posturing in unlikely settings.

The illusion of wealth and glamour fractured when I realized I was drying my hair with Presley's Boogerman towel.

I padded barefoot into the living room, robe open and billowing, toweling my hair, thinking about that beer I'd promised myself. I tuned in the oldies station on the radio, the one I'm only allowed to listen to when I'm by myself. Pleased, after the awful morning, to be alone at last.

The doorbell rang.

15

....

Carpentry and Condolence Calls

We in South Dakota are famous for rallying around one another in times of crisis. But we wouldn't be human if we didn't mix in a little self-interest with the outstretched hand. A carpenter who was the first to arrive after a fire or hailstorm could be excused for mentally calculating a damage assessment and harboring fantasies of being hired for repair work as he raked and shoveled.

And certainly the ladies of our town might be forgiven for pumping the unfortunate victims for any new bits of gossip as they provided comfort.

So I wasn't really surprised to hear the doorbell chime. No one would be as much in need of comforting as, or be better able to provide juicy tidbits than, the person who actually discovered Charles's body.

Sighing, I tied the robe closed, dropped the damp Boogerman towel behind a chair, and opened the door, expecting a committee of casserole-laden church ladies ready to sympathize and suck up as much information as possible.

Stu McKee, his cap pushed back on his forehead, green eyes asparkle, stood in the doorway with a leather nail apron buckled around his hips and a toolbox in his hand.

My heart thundered wildly.

"Sorry to disturb you," he said with a smile. "I tried to call and see if you wanted to wait until later for this."

"Huh?" I asked, not understanding. Wait until later for what?

"The cupboard door," he said gently. "You asked me to fix a broken hinge, remember?"

Oh that.

A furious blush kept me from looking directly at him.

"You'll have to forgive me if I seem a bit fuzzy," I said to the floor. "It's been a tough day."

"No shit," Stu agreed amiably. "Dad's been babbling since I got back, but he always gets his stories garbled. Your version is bound to make more sense. Point me to your cupboard and tell me about it while I get started."

I pointed. His hand brushed my shoulder, warm fingers lingering a moment, tracing tiny circles on the silk. He strode across the kitchen. The touch had been fleeting, the urge to lean into it coming a beat too late.

I bit my lip, trying to control an out-of-control imagination. It was just a pat, I told myself sternly, a sort of condolence caress.

Stu put down his toolbox. With lips pursed, he examined the cupboard door, swinging it back and forth a couple of times. His short-sleeved shirt stretched agreeably across the span of his shoulders and was neatly tucked into the waistband of a pair of blue jeans faded honestly by hard work and long wear.

He bent over and rummaged in the toolbox at his feet. I didn't notice if the jeans stretched agreeably across any part of his anatomy because my attention was diverted by the sudden dawning horror that I had answered the door, and was now standing in the kitchen with Stu McKee, wearing only a filmy silk wrapper.

With nothing on underneath.

With wet hair and no makeup.

Damp and naked is not a good look for me, take my word for it.

One hand scrunched the neck of the robe together, and the other furtively tried to push some shape into my hair.

He must think I'm an absolute idiot. Or worse yet, that I entertain men wearing a silk robe, every day.

"Excuse me, would you?" I said. "I just got out of the shower and haven't had a chance to dress. I'll be just be a minute."

I was halfway to my bedroom door when Stu cleared his throat.

"Um, if you want to wait a second on that," he said quietly, "you could hold this door in place for me. And then I'll be done and out of your hair."

His eyes locked mine with a steadfast gaze. It was, on the surface, a logical suggestion—help him quickly and then he'd leave.

But I knew it meant exactly the opposite. Get dressed and help him in that order, and he would leave quickly. Nothing would be said. We'd still joke at the cafe, we'd still smile, carry on a low-level flirtation. But nothing would happen between us. Ever.

And he knew it.

And he knew that I knew.

The silent kitchen echoed as he waited patiently, looking directly into my eyes. The promise made earlier was still there.

Part of me exulted, gratified and amazed. Part of me was terrified. Remember Nicky, I thought. Remember Renee.

No, I said firmly to myself, forget everything.

I swallowed. Maybe I hesitated. Then again, maybe I didn't.

"Sure," I said brightly, "what do you want me to do?"

A small smile, concentrated mainly in his eyes, lit his face. "Well, grab a chair and stand on it," he said, "and hold the door level while I put some new screws in the hinge."

This didn't sound like a very good idea. What if I fell? What if the chair broke?

"I'm not very graceful at things like that," I said truthfully. "I get dizzy when I climb on things."

And when I stand nearly naked on a chair next to men who make me breathe funny.

"Don't worry, I'll catch you if you fall," he said semi-seriously.

"That's what you think," I amazed myself by saying out loud. "I'd squash you flat."

"I doubt it," he said softly, and held out a hand to help me up.

I was more aware of the difficulty in holding a robe closed while climbing onto a chair than I was of my hand in Stu's, which he squeezed briefly before getting an electric drill from his toolbox.

Standing safely on the chair, however, I was acutely aware of Stuart McKee. I wanted to reach out and touch the soft brown hair curling down over his collar. I found his lips, set firmly in concentration, fascinating.

He inhaled deeply. "You smell great," he said.

"It's a designer cologne," I said. "You know, expensive and hard to find. The only one I like." Wonderful, I thought, babble some more. Just thank the man for the compliment and shut up. "Thank you," I said and clamped my jaws together.

"Can't wear the cologne or smelly stuff myself. Makes me break out," he said conversationally. "There, hold the door steady, like so." He placed a large warm hand over mine for guidance.

"Okay," I said. At least I think I did.

I was on the wrong side of the door to watch the repair, but it involved the drill and a couple of swear words. Less than two minutes later, he was done.

"That's it," he said, closing the door. "Good as new."

He reached up and placed his hands on either side of my waist. Oh Lord, I thought, heart sinking, he wants me to jump.

An average-size woman could turn a move like this into a romantic bonanza, falling gracefully into the man's arms. Not me. Stu's hands would have to bury themselves in my marshmallow waistline just to lift me, and even then he'd stagger and fall and I'd smother him. Think of the *Enquirer* headlines: LARGE LADY KILLS MARRIED MAN IN BIZARRE TRAILER KITCHEN ACCIDENT.

"It's okay," he said, looking directly into my eyes as though he knew what I'd been thinking. "Trust me."

Hoping, for both our sakes, that he really did know his own strength, I stepped off the chair.

Stu's hands slipped slightly up the smooth silk on the slow downswing, fingers brushing the flesh beneath.

With every nerve screaming, breath catching in my throat, hands still on his shoulders, I gazed into his wonderful green eyes.

He smiled slowly and broadly, the most beautiful smile in the world. His arms tightened around my back and he leaned down to kiss me.

I closed my eyes, imprinting my memory with the sensation of his broad chest held against mine, the warmth of his hands through the silk, the lumps on his thighs pressing deeply into—

Lumps?

I opened my eyes and pulled back, dazed and confused.

"Oops," he said, with a little-boy grin. "Sorry." He unbuckled and dropped the nail apron to the floor, and tightened his arms again.

This time the kiss went according to fantasy, long and soft and warm and adult. No slurping or fumbling or nose bumping. It was firm and purposeful and perfect.

"I love this song," he whispered in my ear, warm breath sending shivers down my body. "Shall we?"

The radio, which I had forgotten, was now playing something torchy. By the Eagles, I think, though I was too befuddled to make out the lyrics.

Stu held out his left hand and smiled. We danced, circling the kitchen slowly, his lips pressed to my neck.

His pulse quickened and mine raced. It was all familiar somehow. The Eagles had finished and the radio played something with a rhythm too fast for slow dancing. We didn't care.

And we didn't stop until I took his hand and led him, wordlessly, into my bedroom.

My room, with the bright sunlight streaming in all the windows. With the rumpled bed. With a haphazard pile of dirty clothes filling a corner near the open closet door.

I had purposely invited Stu McKee into this pigpen of a room to make love. The first man I had desired since the death of my husband, indeed the only man I had ever desired who wasn't Nicky Bauer, and I expected him to want me amid the bright light and mess.

My favorite picture of Nicky was on the dresser, an old black-and-white shot of him at age fourteen, stocking cap pulled low on his forehead, muffler pulled up high on his neck, dark curls stuck damply to his forehead as he wound up a snowball pitch. His eyes in that photo had always looked young and innocent and happy to me. Now they looked accusing.

My euphoria evaporated, shriveled, and shrunk into nothing. Worse than nothing. Into despair.

"Let me just straighten this place up first," I said, pulling at the sheets, wondering if I could turn Nicky's photo facedown without Stu noticing.

"Don't worry about that," he said, smiling. "We have better things to do." He'd untucked and unbuttoned his shirt.

Stu lightly kissed my forehead and then fumbled a bit with the knotted tie of my robe.

"Here, I'll do that," I said, I hope gently.

He shrugged and continued to undress.

A terrible thought took me as I climbed into bed. What if he doesn't realize that I'm fat? What if he thinks that I'll be thin and beautiful under the covers?

I pulled the sheet up to my chin, closed my eyes, and waited miserably.

Unused to more than one body at a time, the bed creaked and groaned as Stu joined me. I clasped my arms around his neck as he covered my face, neck, and breasts with small, swift kisses.

A week ago, an hour ago, I would have been filled with

delight. Now I waited numbly, eyes closed, wanting to be anywhere else, doing anything else.

On me and in me now, he rasped in and out dryly. He shifted and probed, trying to find a position that would suit us both.

Gently unclasping my hands, he raised himself up on extended arms, an expanse of air and light now between us.

No, I thought, turning my head to the side. Not that way. Don't look at me, soft and flabby with no shadows to hide in, no darkness to make this first, and probably last, time easier.

I clenched my eyes tightly, willing the tears not to flow, and endured. Why couldn't it have been more like one of Mother's novels? Where were the throbs and quivers?

"Hey," he said softly, "this is supposed to be fun."

Warily, I opened my eyes, frightened I'd see ridicule or disgust in his face.

He was still thrusting slowly, his face had that loose look, the skin slightly slack, his lips soft and moist. But his eyes, heavy-lidded now, focused on mine with a smile.

Incredibly, I saw only acceptance in his face. An acceptance of us, of me, of what we were doing. And desire.

Like a great loosening, the tension inside me melted. I found myself moving with him, slowly at first, but easily, fluidly. Accommodating and returning the rhythm.

My hands, plunged finally into his hair, twined in the silky softness.

Bolder, I raised myself to circle, kiss, and taste with my tongue.

A small sound escaped with his ragged breath, a tiny noise for me alone. A supplication. A benediction.

Hands around his neck again, I pulled Stuart McKee down to me, and into me, and arched upward to meet him. My lips felt the pulse in the hollow of his shoulder, and I was lost. In him.

And with him.

Lost.

16

....

Cousins and Christmas Trees

I'm far from the first person to observe that sex is strange. For something we dream of having; scheme to accomplish; lie, cheat, and steal for, it is, on the surface, a ridiculous activity.

Not unenjoyable, mind you, just ridiculous.

As a spectator sport, it's sadly lacking. Del sometimes plays for me the X-rated videotapes she rents to share with Big Dick. I rarely watch more than ten minutes before boredom, tinged with nausea, sets in. What little erotic power they have is drowned in overkill by the third scene.

"These'd be great training flicks," Del said to me with a grin.

"For what?" I asked. "Examples of sexual practices to avoid at all costs? If some guy did that all over my face, I'd slug him."

Sex isn't even much good for comparative storytelling purposes. How do you know if your orgasms measure up against anyone else's? People of both sexes are perfectly capable of faking them to each other, and even better at fictionalizing encounters to rapt audiences.

It's hard enough to make comparisons among your own experiences. Orgasms are like Christmas trees: Each really good one seems like the best one ever, and the only one you can objectively examine is the one you have right now.

For what it's worth, the Christmas tree I'd just enjoyed was one of the best.

Unfortunately, sex is the easy part. It's getting undressed, and dressed again, that's hard.

I had been lying, my head cradled in Stu's arm, for about ten minutes, which meant his arm was completely dead.

We talked quietly, and laughed, I don't remember what about. We kissed lightly and sweetly and often.

We're neither of us teenagers. Nor are we characters in one of Mother's novels. We didn't try to relight the tree.

"As much as I hate to," Stu said, "I really have to go."

He was right, we didn't want to get caught.

And I didn't want to be reminded that we didn't want to get caught, or shatter the illusion that we were sharing a guilt-free, leisurely afternoon.

How would we handle the redressing stuff? I planned to shower again, so I could shrug on the robe.

It wouldn't be that simple for Stu. He had a numb arm, and shoes to tie. His pants had been kicked to the middle of the room. I considered turning my head, closing my eyes, averting my gaze in a ladylike manner. I didn't do any of those things, but I did consider them.

"Shameless, aren't you?" he asked while tucking his shirt in, amused.

"Yup." I grinned, sitting up with the sheet tucked primly under my arms.

His smile faded and he sat on the edge of the bed, looking away from me, fidgeting.

Here it comes, I thought. The Thanks-But-No-Thanks. The Good-bye. This is when we find out what kind of man you really are, Stuart McKee.

He sat for a moment, saying nothing. For once in my life I kept quiet, waiting for him to speak.

It was a long silence.

"Listen, Tory," he said to the floor, "I didn't mean for this to happen."

Oh shit. I looked straight ahead. Damn.

He faltered. "I mean, I've kinda been watching you for a long time. But I didn't know if you were interested. In me. I mean, it's hard to know what you think. You know?"

He glanced over his shoulder, hoping I'd say something to help him out.

I didn't.

"Jeez, I'm botching this," he said to himself.

I had to restrain an urge to comfort him. No sense, I decided, in making it any easier for him to dump me.

"Look." He turned toward me, fixing me with a steady gaze. "I'm going to be completely honest with you."

His eyes pleaded with me to believe him.

"This"—he looked at the ceiling—"this isn't the first time I've done something like . . . like this. It's not something I do often, but it's something I *have* done." He looked at me again. "You get the distinction?"

I nodded.

"Those other times, they just happened. There was no connection, no linking. When they were over, they were over.

"I might have thought it'd be that way with you. I mean, at least at first. But even before today, I knew you were different. That it'd be different with us, you and me."

Sure, I thought. Sure.

"I know, it sounds like a line," he said sadly, "but I don't know what happened here today. My marriage—" He stopped and swallowed. "My wife has threatened to leave me. I don't know if she will. I don't even know if I want her to."

He looked at me. "This is a complication neither of us bargained for, but if I know anything right now, it's that I want to see you again. I want to keep on seeing you. I'll give you all the time in the world to think and decide. I won't blame you if you tell me to go to hell.

"But I will promise you one thing, Tory Bauer. I promise that I'll never lie to you.

"Do you believe me?" he asked.

Lord help me, I did.

"Well, say something, then," he said.

"Kiss me," I said.

Lord help me, he did.

I used the Coors magnet to stick Stu's bill, $7.50 for hinge repair, to the fridge door. I'd insisted on the bill.

"Presley and Chainlink did the damage," I explained to a horrified Stu, "they can pay the bill. Be practical, you have to account for your time, don't you?"

"I guess you're right." He shuddered. "But it sure feels wrong."

"Pretty squeamish for a guy who switched trucks with his father, aren't you?" I asked with a snort. I'd noticed from the bedroom window that Eldon's beatup Ford was parked in the driveway, not Stu's shiny new Chevy.

"I thought it'd look better that way," he said uncomfortably.

"You know how people talk," I said, enjoying his discomfort, and then feeling bad about it. "Relax," I joshed. "Everyone would just think you were fooling around with Del."

A look of distaste tightened his face. "No thanks, once was more than enough."

A part of me collapsed. No wonder she disliked him. I had probably married the only man in Delphi who hadn't slept with Del, and that's only because they were first cousins.

"It's not like that," he hurried on miserably. "It happened a long time ago, before I left Delphi. When I moved back, she wanted to, um, well, you know Del."

I knew Del.

"But I wasn't even tempted," he said.

"I know, you only wanted me," I said sarcastically.

"Yes," he said quietly, "I only wanted you. I said I'd be honest and I meant it. You aren't making it easy, though."

"It's not supposed to be easy," I said quietly.

"It isn't," he said ruefully. "Can't you tell?"

That was worth a smile.

"Much better," he said from the door. "Think about us, and call me. Please."

That was an easy request. What else would I think about? Besides murder, I mean.

"Go," I said firmly.

Stu ducked back in and planted a soft kiss on my forehead, and then was gone.

I ran shaky fingers through my still damp hair. Was there ever a time when life was uncomplicated?

Sure, yesterday. When Charles Winston was still alive. When Stu McKee was just a married fantasy. When Del's romantic adventures seemed more amusing.

I didn't look for life to uncomplicate itself any time soon.

The second shower wasn't quite as mindlessly enjoyable as the first.

Del was sitting on the couch, watching TV when I padded back through the living room, drying my hair with a plain towel this time.

"I didn't hear you come in," I said carefully.

"I've been here for a while," she said flatly. "I see you got your hinge fixed."

I looked at her closely. Her face was rigid, with no expression in her eyes. Her body was stiff and tense.

"Did you have it oiled, too?" Del asked nastily. "You know old hinges get rusty if they're not used much."

"This one wasn't that old," I said, pretending to take her literally. "It still works just fine."

Had Del seen Stu driving Eldon's truck away from the trailer? She was pretty good at putting the sexual two and two together.

Worse yet, did she come home while Stu and I were still occupied? I wouldn't have heard a thing, being fairly engrossed at the time. Did she hear our last conversation at the door?

I found that I didn't care. Del could be vindictive, recklessly so. But she didn't frighten me. And I absolutely refused to discuss Stu McKee with her.

Long ago, Del suggested that I find a married boyfriend to occupy my afternoons. Unfortunately, I seem to have done just that. At least for today. She'd have to accept it, whether she liked it or not.

I marched past her into the kitchen, suppressing the memory of what had happened there, only an hour or so ago. I could replay the entire afternoon later, in my room, alone. In the dark. "Want a beer?" I called over the countertop.

"Sure," she said, "with olives."

"Let me just get dressed first," I said, not smiling. Definitely not thinking of Stu McKee.

"I was going to ask if you planned to float around half-naked all day," Del said, sounding more like herself.

"Listen, after the day we've had, nudity is the least of our worries."

"You got that right," she said with a sigh.

"So what happened after I left the cafe?" I asked, handing her a frozen mug after I finished dressing.

"Not much," she said, sipping gratefully. "I gave a statement to the cops. They were real curious about the Burglar Bait money, by the way. Wanted to know exact totals and the last time we checked the lock. Things like that. Stuff with no real answers. Then they closed the place down, sent the body off, gave an official statement to the TV cameras, and left."

"What did *you* do then?" I asked.

"I rode around with Big Dick for a while," she said, sucking air through her teeth. "Talking."

Yeah, right.

"And then I came home. What about you? What have *you* been doing this afternoon?" Del cast a sideways glance at me.

I sipped. "Not much. I came home, watched the hinge fixing, took a shower." I'm not good at lying, but since this was not technically a lie, I sounded convincing enough. Time to change the subject.

"I want to know what happened last night," seizing gratefully on the only other topic that came to mind. "Why were you so late, and why did you bring Junior here?"

Last night was a lifetime ago. I barely remembered it myself.

"It was no big deal, as you say. Jolene had a date and asked to go home early. I did the cleaning myself and locked up. I found Junior wandering the street like a lost puppy, so I did my good deed for the day and brought her home."

"And deliberately got her roaring drunk," I added.

"Yeah." Del smiled, evidently relishing the memory. "I'd do it again in a minute."

"I doubt you'll get the chance," I said. "Junior's on her guard now."

"I hope she chokes," Del said, with all apparent sincerity. "I'm glad you brought up the subject, though. The police asked me what time I got home last night. I told them around eight. Is that about right?"

"I think it was a little later, actually," closing one eye to concentrate. "Probably eight-thirty," I said. "Why do they want to know that?"

"Because Charles came into the cafe for supper last night and so far as the police know, that's the last time anyone in town saw him. I didn't look at the clock when he left, and I tried to work the time out backward from when I got home. As far as I can tell, he must have left the cafe before seven. That's what I told the police, anyway."

"You should probably add another half-hour to that," I said, calculating, "since you got home later than you thought."

"A half-hour either way doesn't really matter," Del said. "I got the distinct impression from Big Dick that they think the murder happened close to ten-thirty. They have a suspect in mind already, I gather, though he didn't tell me any of the details."

"What makes them think the murder occurred at ten-thirty? The official reports won't be back for a couple of weeks at least," I said, drawing on my vast experience of literary crime.

"They don't, really," Del said. "Big Dick said that the coroner, unofficially and off the record, narrowed the murder time to between eight-thirty and ten-thirty last night. They're going with the ten-thirty time frame because it fits in better with the robbery evidence."

"Such as?" I asked.

"I don't know," she said. "Big Dick won't say. He says I already know too much for my own good. And that he can't trust me not to blab everything to you over a couple of beers."

She raised her mug, "Here's to perceptive boyfriends and roommates who can keep secrets."

I wondered if Crystal saw a Big Dick–shaped intruder leaving the cafe somewhere around ten-thirty.

I realized that I had to talk to Crystal right away.

"Big changes," "swirling currents," she had written in her note.

No shit.

I still didn't believe in psychic powers, but Crystal's lucky guesses were uncomfortably coincidental.

"I'd like to know where Charles was during the time between supper and when he was killed, and why he didn't go back to Aberdeen on schedule," I said.

"I wouldn't have the foggiest notion," Del said pointedly. "And what's more, I don't give a shit. This subject is exceedingly boring."

"Don't you find the puzzle intriguing? I mean if you can forget about Charles, that we knew him and all, that we're sad that he's dead." At least I was sad that he was dead, this morning I would have sworn that Del was sad too. Now I wouldn't take any bets.

"I have a feeling that we already know everything we need to, if we could just put it together in the right order," I finished.

"Are you turning into a detective all of a sudden?" Del asked, looking straight at me. "I'd leave it be if I were you.

Let the big boys play with the clues. It's dangerous out there. A person could get killed.''

It wasn't a threat. At least I don't think so, just a statement of fact. Someone had already been killed.

How, why, and when had Charles been murdered? I couldn't shake the feeling that if we knew those three things, the *who* would become obvious.

The door banged open and Presley stormed in, duffel bag in one hand and objects made of wrinkled, poisonously green fabric bunched in the other.

"Jeez," he said disgustedly, "I live in this stupid town my whole life. Does anything ever happen? Noooo. Just the same old thing, every single stupid day. But I go away one night and miss the most fun this town has ever had."

He was genuinely disappointed, his Bauer brown eyes registering extreme indignation.

"Well, kiddo," I said, "I wouldn't call a murder fun, exactly."

"Yeah, but you found the body at least," he said. "What'd he look like? Gooshy?"

"Mostly he looked sad," I said, hoping to remind Pres that this wasn't a Boogerman adventure.

"How did you hear about it?" Del asked him.

"Mrs. Adler had the radio on, and we heard it on the way home. I bet you get to be on TV, don't you?" he said sadly, realizing he'd missed the chance to pick his nose on camera. "Boy, I'm going to kill John Adler. If it wasn't for his stupid birthday, I'd a been here for all the fun," Presley said dejectedly.

He brightened. "I saw him, though. The dead guy. Charles Whatshisname, yesterday as we were leaving town. He was walking across the street, away from the garage, you know, John Adler's dad's place. I'll bet that's a clue."

"Don't be ridiculous," said Del. "Give me a kiss and go put your things away."

"Wait'll you see what I bought in Aberdeen at the Surplus Store. You're gonna love it." He pecked his mother self-consciously on the cheek, then ran down the hall to his bedroom.

Del and I groaned. The Surplus Store was a boy's paradise, stocked from floor to ceiling with such irresistibles as slightly dented Ping Pong balls, one hundred for $2.95; stacks of plastic airline cups ("From a real live airplane, no kidding"); and go-cart kits complete except for the motor, wheels, and seat.

Once Presley came home with a flight suit and a set of harnesses.

"As soon as I get me a parachute," he'd said, "I'm gonna jump off the elevator."

"Close your eyes," Pres said theatrically from the hall, "and get ready."

With dread, we did.

"Ta da!" Encased in green, he bowed deeply.

"It's surgical guy stuff," he gloated. "And look, a real knife and everything!"

He was wearing a green hospital gown and pants rolled at the cuff. It was an operating room ensemble, complete with paper shoe covers and green skullcap. He held an untied mask up to his face with one hand and took practice swipes with what looked like a straight-edge razor in the other.

"What do you think?" he asked us. "Neat, huh?"

"Well," I said, "it's certainly authentic. Do you think you should be swinging that razor around in the house?"

"How much did this set you back?" Del asked tiredly.

"Only $7.50," Pres said. "What a bargain!"

"What a coincidence," I said. "That's just exactly the amount you and Chainlink owe the McKees for fixing the cupboard door you broke."

Even that didn't dampen his enthusiasm.

"Here, Tory." He backed up to me. He was almost my height now, having grown, apparently, overnight. "Tie up the back and the mask, would you?"

"Thanks," he said, voice muffled by cotton, fiddling with the TV knobs. He grinned, mouth and nose covered, brown eyes sparkling with delight.

I studied Presley's face, suddenly struck by something I couldn't quite grasp that danced just beyond my reach. A tantalizing fragment that stayed out of focus.

The door burst open without warning. Rhonda stumbled into the trailer, panting and sobbing incoherently.

"They took him!" she wailed, collapsing on the couch. Her hair was disheveled, mascara had run black streaks down her cheeks. "They came in a car and they took him. He didn't do it, I'd *know* it if he could do it." She wavered between Del and me, lips trembling, nose running. "*You* know he couldn't do it."

"We'd know who couldn't do what?" Del asked, not unkindly. "Pres," she said over her shoulder, "run and get some Kleenex."

Presley raced down the hall and back and stuffed a crumpled wad of tissues into Rhonda's hand. She wiped her face and made an even worse mascara mess.

"Michael," she said, as though we were imbeciles for not guessing. "They think Michael killed the missionary." Her voice rose in near hysteria. "They came and took him."

"Who took him?" Del asked.

"Why do they think he did it?" I asked at the same time.

"Did they arrest him?" we both asked together.

Rhonda sniffled and then blew her nose. "I don't think they actually arrested him. Big Dick said they were just taking him in for questioning. But they don't take people in unless they're going to arrest them, do they?"

Rhonda still hadn't answered my question.

"Why do they think Michael did it?" I asked gently.

"The cops found some money, marked dollar bills and stuff in the camper. They said something about mud and boot prints. I don't know what else," Rhonda said miserably.

Boot prints and money. Marked bills and muddy tracks. Cafe intruders in the dark.

"Hey you guys," Presley shouted excitedly. "Look, it's on TV. The cafe is on TV. Delphi is on TV!"

He'd pushed the green surgical cap back on his forehead. The mask was pulled down so he could talk, though it still covered his chin. His eyes were flashing, and happy, and young and innocent and excited.

The fragment danced into full view.

This time my heart really did stop. I looked at Presley. And I looked at Del. And I looked at Presley. And I looked back at Del.

And I could not stop seeing what I'd just seen.

"They're awfully fond of their own cousins, dear," Mother had said.

Did she know or was it a shot that accidentally hit the mark?

I remembered Nicky holding an infant Presley up to the mirror, searching and examining, studying and concentrating.

"Elvis," Del had declared firmly. "The father of my child is Elvis Presley."

I remembered being certain that I had married the only man in Delphi who hadn't slept with Del.

Silly me. Silly, stupid me.

17

....

Like Father, Like Son

South Dakota is Investigative Reporter Hell. Sure, there are occasional car thefts, bank embezzlements, and mysterious fires in well-insured buildings to report. And we expect breathless recounts of automobile fatalities involving alcohol, accidental shootings during hunting season, and satanist sightings.

But by and large, our area newscasts are made up of sports scores, the weather, and fillers about folks who sell designer doggie clothes, or who have collected twenty-five hundred penguin salt and pepper shakers, some dating from as far back as 1920.

Yes, we have our share of crazies, crooks, drug dealers, child abusers, and traffic code violators, but with a total state population less than that of the city of Seattle, and an average density of 3.3 persons per square mile, any crime wave is, by necessity, pretty widespread.

The most local excitement a reporter can expect is an improperly closed public meeting, to which any bewildered school board trying to fire a janitor in private can attest.

I sometimes think that the highways are spotted with roving bands of extremely bored, fresh-faced journalism majors sniffing the air for even a hint of a scandal.

What else could explain last summer's in-depth series probing the disturbing number of out-of-state owned Dairy Queens?

It stands to reason when a really meaty story pops up, reporters fall over themselves in a rush to find a unique perspective.

And in South Dakota, murder, any murder, is a meaty story.

"The twenty-third of June," a screen-size Crane Compton intoned from a handsomely framed shot in front of the cafe, "another sleepy, dusty, Delphi day. Some were out chopping silage, and others were baling hay."

"Oh my God," Del moaned, "he's going to sing 'Ode to Billy Joe.' "

"Yesterday, the twenty-third, all was normal in the small town of Delphi. But this morning in a back room of the Delphi Cafe," Compton continued, "one young waitress made a discovery that shocked this town from its sleepy, dusty mood."

Compton emphasized the statement with a sweep of his arm as the camera cut to a pan shot that traveled the length of our sleepy, dusty Main Street.

Del nudged me with an elbow. "Get that, now you're a *young* waitress."

I wished she'd shut up so I could concentrate. It was important to pay attention, if for no other reason than to quiet the tumult in my brain, to block any thoughts of Nicky and the awful discovery I'd just made.

Del was still hooting and heckling the TV.

"Shh!" I said so sharply that she actually did.

Del shot me a surprised look and flopped back on the couch beside Rhonda, who was now calm enough to lean forward and watch.

Compton droned on, explaining more or less accurately (if you discount the "young waitress" reference) how and where Charles's body had been discovered. And unfortunately, by whom.

Some researcher had done a quick synopsis of the Mormon missionary system, and Compton presented a short explanation of their pay-your-own-way philosophy.

"You mean, he had to save all his own money to do this? Nobody paid him anything?" Presley asked, incredulous, crossing missionary off his list of possible career choices.

Then the screen filled with a photograph of the Winston family in Memphis, a cluster of younger brothers and sisters proudly circled a smiling Charles in graduation gear.

How did they get that photo so quickly? Did the network call his family in Tennessee and ask them to fax the most heartbreaking picture they had? Did they explain that this young man's murder could be parlayed into a ratings bonanza?

Honorable though it was, I could not afford to be sidetracked by my own indignation. I focused on Compton again.

"The police have finished interviewing some of the cafe patrons who were present when the grisly murder was discovered. Sir, can we speak with you a minute?" he asked someone offscreen.

"Why sure," Eldon McKee said companionably, the words ELDON MCKEE, DELPHI CAFE PATRON strung in large white letters across the bottom of the screen. "I was over to the cafe this morning, like I always am, I come from across the street over there." He pointed. "I own and run the feed store with my son. Anyway, we was all in the cafe, yakking and yammering, when the gal, a purty thing let me tell you, came out and said she had some news that would be kinda shocking but we all had to sit still and stay calm."

Del smiled smugly.

"That's when"—Compton, with a wan smile, consulted a sheaf of notes in his hand—"Delphine Bauer announced there was an actual dead body in the back room. How did you feel when she made that announcement?"

"I thought to myself, whoa Eldon, we got us a dead body

right here in the cafe. Delphine, she don't want to say much about who it was, though I could see from her eyes that she knew him. There's lotsa husbands in this town whose wives might like to conk them on the head and stash them in a closet, so I was mighty curious to know who it was. Just in case it was anyone I knew, you see?'' Eldon paused and took a deep breath, which was a mistake.

"Yes, thank you for your insight," Compton said, turning to his left. "I understand you were also on duty as a waitress this morning when the body was discovered. It must have been quite a shock to know it had been in the closet all morning."

"I know I'm not looking in any closets by myself anymore, that's for sure," said HEIDI HELEN HALVORSON, DELPHI CAFE WAITRESS. "I mean, if there's gonna be dead bodies and all inside. At home, with my own clothes, I'm not gonna worry. I mean, I can't wear the same thing everyday. Like a person's gotta get in her own closet, you know."

"Thank you," Compton said in a small voice, turning to the much taller Clay, with a look of relief. "How did the discovery make you feel?"

"We are all saddened by the death of this young man and the terrible loss to his family, especially under such circumstances," said the PASTOR, ST. JOHN'S LUTHERAN CHURCH, DELPHI. "Though we had our religious differences, he was serious and studious and well liked. It is a tragedy for our whole town."

"Indeed, it is a loss for the whole community," Compton agreed. He turned again, "You, sir, were also in the cafe when the awful announcement was made, weren't you?"

ROB ADLER, GARAGE OWNER, looked at the ground, he looked in the air, he looked miserably back at the cafe. He swallowed, eyes wide open, and said, "Yeah, and I wish I had stayed at home. I mean, I didn't have nothing to do with the guy, I hardly knew him, and I certainly didn't have nothin' to do with any of this. I'm sorry he's dead and all, but I got to get back to work."

There was something odd about his face that I couldn't quite place.

"I always thought his name was Ron," Rhonda said, coming to life again.

"It is," I said. "They misspelled it."

"Gee, I thought they got everything right on TV," Rhonda said seriously. "Just look how nervous poor Mr. Adler is. He's not even blinking."

That was it. Ron had not blinked during that entire sequence. Not once.

Presley burst into laughter. "He looks just like John trying to tell us that Mardelle Jackson let him look up her sweater when Mardelle won't let John anywhere near her. He opens his eyes up wide like that, and nods and says, 'She did so let me see 'em.' And his dad looks just like him."

Pres was right.

Ron Adler blinks when he's telling jokes, he blinks when he's drinking coffee, and he blinks furiously when he's lusting after Del.

"He's lying," I said, realizing the truth as I said it. "He does know something and he's trying to cover it up. That's why he isn't blinking."

"This blinking–not blinking stuff is a bunch of bullshit," Del spat. "Ron is just a stupid son of a bitch who's so scared that he's about to faint. Ron doesn't know anything about anything. Why would he lie?"

A good question. I didn't know. But I bet that Del had a good idea.

"Oh look, it's Aphrodite." Rhonda pointed.

APHRODITE FERGUSON, OWNER, DELPHI CAFE highlighted the screen as Crane Compton turned to say, "It was in your place of business that the body of young Charles Winston was found, bringing about a day much different than you had envisioned, right?"

The sound went dead, but Aphrodite's lips unmistakably formed the words, "No shit," before she trundled out of camera range.

Compton faced the lens directly and said mournfully,

"Tory Bauer, the waitress who discovered the body, has declined to interview with us, but we know from stated reports that she discovered the young man's body in a mop closet, informed the owner and another waitress, and used a nearby phone to notify the authorities.

"We also know that she was detained and questioned by the police inside the cafe this morning, though no information about that questioning had been released to the press."

I was outraged. "They're trying to turn me into a suspect just because I wouldn't talk to them on camera!"

"I told you. See what happens when you try to play detective?" Del asked smugly, though her smile faded a bit when Big Dick stepped up next to Compton.

"As yet we have no lead on a motive," Big Dick said flat-voiced in answer to the first question, expressionless face unsmiling, eyes squinting in the sunlight. "We have gathered quite a bit of evidence, and though we can't be certain until the test results come back, we are looking very closely into the possibility that the murder was committed during a robbery somewhere around ten-thirty P.M., last night. We already have a suspect in mind, and expect to conclude our investigation quite soon."

The report ended with Compton's signoff and another long shot of the street across from the cafe. Delphi looked dusty and shabby and nearly uninhabited. From the feed store and post office, with Michael's camper parked between, past Clay's cramped cubicle of an office in the rear corner of the Lutheran church, to Adler's Garage where a beatup tan Chevy rested next to a rusty '79 Torino out front, the whole town looked dead and crumbling.

"Not much of a tourist spot, is it?" asked Del.

Back in the On the Spot News Room, coanchor Mary Ellen Dannemeyer turned to Compton and said, "I believe some more information has come to light since you taped that segment this afternoon, right Crane?"

"That's right, Mary Ellen. Channel 9 News has learned that an unidentified twenty-two-year-old male has been taken in for questioning in connection with this terrible crime, and that investigative officers believe that there is enough evidence to convene a grand jury to ask for an indictment.''

"Thanks for that update, Crane," said Mary Ellen to the camera. "It's been an interesting day all over. After this break, we'll check on tomorrow's forecast and then meet a couple from Canistota who have been making a splash with decorative sheep shearing."

I flipped over to Channel 3 to see if Nancijean Montrose had any luck with her interviews.

"Hey I want to see the sheep," Presley objected.

"You can have it back in a sec, I want to hear what these guys have to say about all this," I said.

The murder was also the top story on Channel 3, and we had already missed everything except Nancijean's wrapup.

The Channel 3 crew had arrived somewhat later than Crane Compton's and their interviews were shot later in the afternoon when the light was more forgiving and the shadows longer.

Just to be different, they'd assembled their equipment with the length of Main Street as a background, though they worked in frequent exterior shots of the cafe.

The softer light did nothing to round Delphi's harsh edges, the street still looked deserted, and the lone Torino in front of Adler's garage still looked rusty.

"One thing is certain," Nancijean concluded, sincerity oozing from her pores, "the tiny town of Delphi will never be the same again."

Neil kept a videotape file of all local news stories. I'd have to stop over and watch Nancijean's report in full, though probably I'd only hear Fran Tarkenton's viewpoint of the whole situation.

I flipped the channel back to the sheep for Presley and turned to a pale, dazed Rhonda.

"You heard him," she said, close to tears again, "they're going to get a jury and convict him."

"No, hon," I explained, "that's a grand jury. The grand jury has to decide if there is enough evidence to charge Michael, before anything else can happen."

She grabbed my arm fiercely, "You gotta help him, Tory. You're smart, you can figure it out."

"I don't know about that," I said, thinking there'd been no recent confirmation of the fact. Del was right, playing detective could be dangerous. Despite the intrigue of the puzzle, I had no real desire to Archie Goodwin myself into the middle of a murder investigation.

"Please, you're the only one who can help. Everyone else already thinks Michael did it," she said.

"Except for Crane Compton. He thinks I'm the culprit," I said. How would Archie proceed? At least thinking about Charles kept me from brooding about husbands, mine or anyone else's. "Okay. Tell me what happened yesterday, everything."

"Well, I was out at the farm with my mom, helping her make jam in the morning. I was supposed to work for Del at noon, but she called and told me to never mind. Michael called right after Del, to see if I needed a ride. I told him I didn't. He says he'll pick me up at about six-thirty on the Harley and we'll ride into Aberdeen to pick up some"— she hesitated, maybe just to inhale—"tapes and stuff, and have supper and all that."

"What did you do in Aberdeen?" I asked.

"Well, we rode around and stuff, and talked to some guys Michael knows, and got gas, went to the music store, and, um, mostly farted round, I guess."

I remembered Rhonda's wild giggles and huge appetite last night. She and Michael probably did more than just ride around with friends on motorcycles. I imagine there had also been some recreational drug use.

Most people think that all druggies are capable of murder and mayhem while under the influence.

It's my belief, from long-ago experience, let me add, that marijuana smokers are far too happy and sloppy and hungry and horny to wash the dishes properly, much less plan and carry out a murder.

But if the police found any evidence of drug use, however minimal, helping Michael would be that much more difficult.

"Did you come straight here from Aberdeen last night?"
I asked. It had been after ten when Michael left Rhonda at
the trailer with us, and roared back up the street on his
motorcycle. Toward the cafe.

If he didn't have a good alibi for that next hour, it was
not just going to be difficult to help him. It would be impossible.

"Yeah, Michael said his head felt fuzzy, that he needed
to ride around for a while before going to bed. We took a
swing down Main and I saw that your trailer lights were
on and I told Michael that he could let me off here.

"He was sound asleep when Reverend Deibert dropped
me off at the camper. This morning I went out to the farm
to help my mom some more. I didn't know anything about
a body until I heard it on the radio this afternoon. By the
time I got back into town, the police were already searching
the camper, looking for evidence."

"What kind of evidence?" I asked.

"Something about muddy shoeprints. An officer took
one of Michael's riding boots and ran across to the cafe.
He came back and said that the prints matched, then he put
the boots in a plastic bag and took them."

"What else?" I asked, though I thought I knew already.

"Big Dick found some money outside on the ground, by
the camper door. And they found a whole wad of cash
stuffed in the pockets of Michael's leather jacket." She
pleaded, "Honest, Tory, I don't know where the cash came
from. We spent all of our money in Aberdeen, we didn't
even have ten dollars left, and Big Dick said there was more
than two hundred dollars in the camper!"

"Is that all?" I figured there would be one more unfortunate bit of evidence.

"No," Rhonda said miserably. "I didn't want to tell
you, but you're going to find out anyway. They found some
marijuana too. That's what he went to Aberdeen for. That's
what he spent our money on. And that's why they're going
to believe Michael killed Charles, because now they have
a dope fiend who rides a Harley, and that's all the proof
they need.

"Michael has done some bad things," Rhonda continued quietly, "but I know he'd never hurt anyone. And I know that he didn't kill Charles."

"Think carefully, Rhonda," I said, kneeling on the rug in front of her, "Which officer found the marijuana?"

She closed her eyes. "I don't know him, he's a young guy."

"Now, which officer found the boots?"

"Big Dick saw them under the table."

"And who found the money in the jacket?" I asked.

Del shot me a sharp look, but didn't interrupt.

"Big Dick Albrecht," Rhonda said.

I rocked back on my heels to think.

"Are you getting at something here?" Del asked in dangerously quiet voice.

Del didn't know that Crystal had seen Big Dick leaving the cafe last night. She didn't know that he'd dropped marked money on the ground, a bill that matched the marked bills found in Michael's jacket. And if she did know these things, she didn't know that I knew them.

For the time being, it seemed safer to keep it that way.

I said carefully, "I'm just trying to catalog what happened. At least they can't tie Michael to the flat bar. He had no way of knowing it was even in the cafe, much less where to look for it."

"Oh jeez," Rhonda said to herself.

"Damn," I said.

"Jolene called me out at the farm before I left for Aberdeen with Michael. First she wanted to borrow my pink earrings, and then she spent ten minutes bitching about how your mom was such a crab and all. Sorry, Tory." Rhonda flashed a wobbly smile. "And how she had to interrupt her work and put that stupid flat bar away, and then write a note with your mom spelling every other word for her, like she was dumb or something."

Del snorted, "It was pretty inconsiderate of Fernice to interrupt Jolene's gum chewing all right. That's why I sent her home early, she's useless."

"Anyway," Rhonda continued, "I thought it was kinda

funny, so I told Michael. Big mistake, right?''

"Well it complicates things," I said, "But don't worry about that now. Do you know what Michael did after he left you here last night?"

"Huh-uh." She shook her head, "He was asleep when I got home and asleep when I left this morning. He rides around by himself a lot. That makes it even worse for him—he won't have an alibi."

"Yeah, that's the trouble with alibis, only guilty people know in advance when they'll need one," Pres said.

We had forgotten he was in the room, a fact he gleefully took advantage of by listening to every word.

"Why don't you ask Michael about all this stuff?" Pres asked.

"Because he's being held by the police, dipshit," Del said kindly.

"But in the murder stories on TV," Pres said, "they can only keep someone twenty-four hours for questioning and then they have to charge him or let him go. Besides, it sounds like they only have money and boot tracks. Those might tie Michael to a burglary, but not to the murder.

"Without an eyewitness or a confession, they'll have to wait for fingerprints, and stomach content analysis to determine the time of death, before they can charge anyone. Michael's not stupid enough to confess to a murder he didn't commit, is he?" Pres asked Rhonda.

Rhonda shook her head no, but didn't answer out loud. We were all a little taken aback by Presley's knowledge of official procedure.

"Well, then I bet you can talk to him in person, tomorrow morning at the latest." Presley crossed his arms with a smug smile.

"In case you hadn't noticed," Del said to her son, "TV isn't much like real life."

"Actually," I said, "Pres is probably pretty close to the mark. It works that way in all the books I read."

"If you two idiots think you can solve a murder by reading books and watching TV, go right ahead," Del said, disgusted.

"All right!" crowed Presley.

"Just a minute here," I said to Del, "no one said anything about solving any murder. I didn't ask to get involved in this, and I have no intention of *getting* involved."

Which was, of course, a lie.

"And you." I pointed at Pres. "This is not a TV show, or a comic book. A real young man, not too much older than yourself, is dead. He doesn't get to go home, find a nice girl, and get married. His skull was crushed and punctured by a severe blow made with a sharp instrument. He is dead. We don't know the killer, and whoever it is might just kill again to keep it that way.

"This isn't a game. You may be a pain in the ass, but we'd like to keep you alive long enough to learn the error of your ways and become a productive citizen. Got it?"

He leaned over with a lopsided smile and gave me a swift hug. "Why, Tory, I didn't know you cared." He grinned.

He looked so much like Nicky. Could Delphi survive two of them? Could I?

"Yeah, well, it's everyone's day for surprises, I guess," I said wearily.

18

Blink, Blink, Blink

The medical world has precise clinical terminology for obsessives who daily clean behind refrigerators or bleach dish towels and shoelaces on a regular basis.

The rest of society would certainly call crazy a woman from whose toilet bowl you could safely drink and whose freshly washed ceilings gleam over a spotless, nay microbeless, home where the Lysol fumes waft lazily through the dust-free air. Here, we just call it normal.

Generations of stern German and Nordic immigrants have inbred to produce an entire region of women who cannot sleep until the clothes are put away, the cushions fluffed, and the floor swept, and who are psychologically unable to let a crusty pan soak in the sink until morning.

I am an aberration. Except for that mindless period just after Nicky's death, I've always had a blind spot when it comes to dustballs, laundry baskets, and unevenly piled magazines.

"Honestly Tory," Mother says disgustedly, "how can you live like this?"

The rules of the game state that I am truly unable to spot the mess that so offends Mother. She then marches purposefully over and puts a half-dozen tape cassettes in their boxes and stacks them neatly on the shelf. Or she refolds a pile of towels so that their edges are even and all facing the same direction. Or she grabs the clean dry silverware from the drainer and rearranges them in the drawer, except for the ones that are still dirty.

"At least it's clean egg," I say, though she doesn't smile.

"I don't know where your sloppiness comes from," she'll say then. "You certainly weren't brought up that way."

No, I certainly wasn't. Midwest girls are early indoctrinated with regimental rows of underwear and perfectly folded socks that have been ironed if necessary.

It all seems too goofy to worry about, especially with a bowl of popcorn and a Dick Francis calling me. But the programming took Junior in a big way.

I have watched her in dress heels, spit-cleaned children already buckled in, with Clay impatiently tapping on the steering wheel, frown at a doorframe, run back for a broom, and sweep down an impolite cobweb.

"We have people coming over later," she'd explain. "I can't let them see that kind of mess."

She actually vacuums her garage.

Evidently so does Gina Adler, because Adler's Garage is possibly the cleanest mechanic shop in the United States.

The chrome shines, the tools are immediately replaced in their labeled red drawers, and piles of floor-dry cover the few unavoidable grease spots on the cement.

The only visible untidiness was the rusty Torino still parked by itself in front.

"Out for a walk, huh?" Ron blinked conversationally, the creases still sharp in his usual brown coveralls. The ones with "Ronnie" chainstitched in white over a breast pocket.

At six P.M., it was 93 degrees and the sun still beat down unbearably. I would much rather have been back in our relatively air-conditioned trailer, but I wanted to find out what had forced Ron into an unblinking stare during his interview.

"Yup," I said. "Just trying to compare Delphi to the TV version."

"How'd it look?" Ron asked, eyes wide. "I haven't been near a TV set all day."

"Mostly the same, empty and dusty," I said. "You're quite the star though. Too bad they spelled your name wrong, *Rob*." I emphasized the mistake, waiting for a reaction.

"They got Adler right, and that's all that counts." He blinked, falling into my trap.

No TV all day, huh?

He wiped his face with a neatly folded blue hanky from a back pocket. "They're sure as shit going to nail anyone withholding information. I'm glad I didn't even know the guy, I'm behind schedule as it is, without more police and questions and shit like that."

There it was again, that wide-eyed stare.

"You must have known Charles a little," I said to the air, rocking on my heels, "Presley saw him walking away from here on foot yesterday afternoon."

The hanky appeared and disappeared, this time in an untidy wad.

Ron swallowed, "Well I didn't mean that I didn't know him at all. He brought that beatup piece of shit of a car in for gas and it died on him." Blink, blink, blink, "He was pretty anxious to get out of town, so I sent him across to the cafe just to get him out of my hair and promised to see what I could do."

Blink, blink, blink.

I want to play poker with this guy.

"Oh?" I said, full of automotive curiosity. "What was wrong with his car?"

"What wasn't wrong with it?" Blink. "Fuel pump died, air cleaner clogged, fuel filter shot. It'd be easier to list the three things that did work." Blink, blink.

"So did you get it fixed right away?" I asked in a conversational voice, just killing time.

"No." Eyes wide. The hanky appeared and swiped the forehead. "We got busy and when he came back, I told him it'd be at least six before I'd be done with it."

"And did he come back at six then, and drive his car away?" I asked innocently.

"Well, we closed at six-thirty, and he hadn't come yet. I just put the keys in the cubbyhole and parked the car in front."

Blink, blink, blink, blink.

"But this morning the car was gone so he must have picked it up later," Ron said, eyes wide.

"Hey Ron," one of the mechanics called from around the corner. "Quit flirting. This you gotta see."

"Probably the new kid, letting the winter air out of some tourist's tires," he said to me, blinking a relieved smile, "and replacing it with summer air. Gotta run. Say hi to Del for me."

He trotted off with a wave.

Did I learn anything? Yes and no.

Ron had watched the TV newscasts, and Charles had car trouble, that was certain. Ron also repaired the car fairly easily and quickly. I could tell that by the blinks.

But Ron had put Charles off until at least six last night. Why lie to Charles about how long the repairs would take? And why keep lying about it?

Ron was hiding something. And he was dreadfully afraid that the police would find out.

I couldn't help feeling that Del had somehow set the whole thing in motion. That Del knew much more than she was telling.

19

....

The Little Gray Cells

I should have been home reading, purposely not thinking about the upsets and upheavals of the day—doing my best to forget both Charles Winston and Stuart McKee, and their impact on my life. Until today, that would have been my automatic response to events so confusing and complicated.

But for some reason I was seized with the inexplicable notion that I could help—not that I'd actually come up with anything constructive so far. All I'd done was work up a sweat and upset people. And confirm that Ron Adler lied, something I already knew.

The street was deserted as I crossed and walked the half-block from the garage to the grocery store. I thought I heard quick footsteps on the pavement behind me, but saw nothing when I turned.

Crystal was dusting the long wooden shelves, her body swaying slowly to an inner rhythm as she swished a cloth over neat rows of cans and boxes. Sunlight reflected off her glasses as she turned and smiled at me.

"I knew you would need more information, Tory," Crystal said while I closed the screen door.

It must be hell buying Christmas presents for her.

"I hope you can give me some," I said, looking around to make sure we were alone in the store. "Keep working, I can talk while you dust."

She nodded. "I did not look at my watch, but I know the deputy entered and left the cafe last night between ten and ten-forty-five. Enough time to commit more than just a small robbery."

"Now how did you know I was going to ask that?" I was exasperated with psychic parlor tricks.

Crystal smiled. "I listen to the radio. I heard our esteemed law enforcement official name a probable time of death, and then tie that death to a cafe robbery that just happened to occur at the exact time I saw the same officer leave that very establishment, dropping marked, stolen money.

"Common sense told me that you would be back with more questions."

"You got any answers?" I asked.

"First a question of my own." She squinted in the dim light. "Why didn't you tell the authorities what I saw, and give them the dropped bill?"

"Because it was the 'authorities' you were accusing of robbery, and because that robbery is now connected to a murder, and because the 'authority' you specifically mentioned leaving the scene of a very serious crime was within earshot all morning.

"I'd already ruined nice Agent Ingstad's day by moving the body and talking about Santa Claus. It would have given him a headache if I'd hinted that an ex-hippie told me that she was psychically certain that one of the investigative officers on the case had committed the crime."

Crystal's laughter rang heartily as she put a large arm around me.

"Poor Tory. I was right about today's swirling currents, wasn't I?" She pulled back and examined my face. "Some-

thing of great import has happened to you today, unrelated
to this crime. Yes?''

"A whole slew of somethings," I said, not willing to be
sidetracked. Or reminded. "But first, tell me, why didn't
you report the sighting and the robbery yourself? It would
have made my whole day much less complicated."

She shook the dust rag and sighed. "As you say, no
official will take seriously an accusation made by an ex-
hippie psychic. I thought coming from you, especially with
evidence in hand, the charge would have been more cred-
ible.

"And though I sometimes have great flashes of insight
and prediction, I cannot control their timing or content. I
knew something would happen to involve you. I did not
know that that something would be murder."

Sometimes I have flashes of insight too. "It's not that
you don't want to go to the police," I said, amazed. "You
can't go to them. Why?"

Crystal smiled ruefully. "The sixties were a tumultuous
time when young idealists were apt to make some very bad
choices for what seemed like very good reasons." She finished dusting the shelf, then slowly lowered herself onto a
stool behind the counter. "There was a group who thought
that blowing up a National Guard armory in a small Pacific
Northwest town was a poetic way to protest the war in
Vietnam.

"Unfortunately they didn't make absolutely sure that the
building was empty before detonation. This group of idealists, who only wanted to stop violent death, accidentally
killed a janitor who just happened to be mopping the office
where the bomb had been planted.

"The story splashed across headlines all over the country
and the members of this group were, for a time, included
on the FBI's Ten Most Wanted List."

"Did you plan it?" I asked quietly.

"No, Jasper and I were only on the periphery. We took
part in a noisy protest in another part of town as a diversionary tactic.

"We did not mean to hurt anyone, but good intentions

could not restore that young man to his family. We went underground for almost a decade, and only lately have we felt comfortable enough to resume a normal life.''

''Are they still looking for you?'' I asked. ''The authorities?'' The statute of limitations does not expire in murder cases, and surely this had been called murder.

''Not actively, I shouldn't imagine. But the files are still open, and I could not risk exciting any official curiosity.''

''So you asked *me* to report the robbery instead,'' I said, sitting on another stool next to the counter.

''And now we have evidence that links a county deputy to murder as well,'' Crystal said. ''What do we do?''

''First, we'd better sort out exactly what we know,'' I said.

That's what Hercule Poirot would do, though my ''leetle gray cells'' were on the brink of shutdown.

I ticked off on my fingers. ''We know that Charles Winston was killed in the cafe between eight-thirty and ten-thirty last night. We know that Big Dick Albrecht was seen leaving the cafe at about ten-thirty, dropping money stolen from the crime scene. We know that Michael is being questioned because he was found to have money taken from the cafe in his possession, and because boot prints outside the cafe exactly match boots he owns,'' I said.

''We know that Deputy Albrecht is framing young Michael for this murder, that's what we know,'' Crystal said decisively, summing up what I had been afraid to say.

''That's gotta be it,'' I said, amazed. ''I couldn't figure out why Big Dick would steal petty cash from Aphrodite. Committing a murder, I could picture. Robbery just seemed out of his league.''

''Oh, he's perfectly capable of robbery,'' Crystal said.

''Well, the police can question Michael all they want, but they won't be able to bring any charges against him until the tests come back, and they convene a grand jury. We have a few days yet to sort things out. If Michael is charged with this murder,'' I said to Crystal, ''you have to come forward with your story. You can't let an innocent man be convicted of a crime he didn't commit.''

"Yes," she said sadly. "I know."

I filled her in on the Adler angle.

"It'd be nice if we knew more about what Charles did yesterday," I said. "Especially where he was during the rest of the afternoon."

"I don't think that'd help you much," Crystal.

"Why not?" I asked, a bit testy, expecting another mystic revelation.

"Because he was here, sleeping upstairs until just about six-thirty," she said simply.

My jaw hung open in surprise. I didn't ask her for an explanation. I figured, she was psychic, she'd know it was necessary.

Crystal grinned. "He must have come straight here from Adler's Garage, because he stopped in a little after three-thirty, pale and very upset."

"Yes, because Ron had manipulated his car repair so that he couldn't leave town immediately," I said.

"He had no way of knowing that," Crystal said. "He was upset about your grandmother."

I'd forgotten about that incident. I repeated Lottie Kendall's version of the fight between Charles and Big Dick in my grandmother's driveway.

"The deputy must have threatened him," Crystal said. "Charles said that he wanted to stay out of sight until his car was running properly again.

"I suggested he go upstairs and lie down, which he did. I woke him just before six-thirty and sent him over to the cafe for supper." She paused, tears gleaming behind her glasses. "That was the last time I saw Charles."

"It's too bad Charles had to be subjected to my grandmother's lunacy," I said, mostly to myself.

"Your mother said that too," Crystal commented sadly.

"Huh?"

"She stopped in for light bulbs. For Lottie Kendall. Remember? She was quite angry that Lottie had left your grandmother alone with a stranger. Your mother's dedication to her family is overwhelming," Crystal said with admiration.

As a recipient of that dedication, I had to agree.

"You wouldn't happen to know where Charles went after he picked up his car, or why he came back to town?" I asked hopefully.

"No, I have tried to follow his timeline and I cannot even get a vibration during the evening hours. It's as though he disappeared completely."

She took off her glasses and wiped them on the voluminous folds of her dress. She sat them down on the counter. Her large soft eyes were red-rimmed and moist.

"If we could ask *him*"—she pointed across the street, squinting—"we'd probably get the whole story. Too bad it's simply not possible."

"Ask who?" I peered through the window, across the street, and could see only Michael, in front of the camper preparing to kick-start his Harley.

"The deputy," she said. "The large man across the street."

"Put your glasses back on," I said. "That's Michael."

It *was* Michael, evidently released from custody, preparing to roar off on his motorcycle.

After what I'd just learned about Big Dick and timelines, it was imperative that I talk to Michael immediately, to warn him to be careful.

"Go, catch him before he leaves," Crystal urged.

I ran through the door, almost bowling Presley down. He jumped back, a couple of bucks in an upraised hand.

"Give a guy a little warning," he complained.

I ignored him.

"Michael!" I shouted, waving to get his attention, feeling like an idiot. "Wait up, I need to talk to you!"

Thank goodness he was too dumb to wear a helmet, or he'd never have heard me.

He straddled the purring motorcycle and waited.

"Michael," I panted. I'm not used to running, even across the street. "Listen to me, I have to talk to you for a second."

"I didn't do it," he said flatly, a surly expression on his face, "and I don't want to answer any more questions."

"I know you didn't do it," I said, still panting. "I think you were framed."

He peered at me warily. "That's what I been trying to tell them. That I didn't commit no murder. Someone planted that stuff on me. But they already got their minds made up and they're set for a conviction. They won't listen."

"A witness"—I decided not to name Crystal—"saw Big Dick Albrecht come out of the cafe at about ten-thirty last night. He dropped some money, the same marked money they found in your camper this morning. We think that he put the wad in your jacket this morning and only pretended to discover it."

"Yeah," Michael said, beginning to grin. It wasn't a pleasant sight. "That musta been how it went. And then that asshole used my boots to make prints in the mud over to the cafe. And planted a baggie of pot to finish me off."

"Whoa," I said. "I already know that *you* bought the pot. You're gonna screw up your own defense if you lie."

"Pretty dumb, huh?" he asked.

"Absolutely," I said. I hoped it wasn't terminal.

"Okay, I won't lie anymore," Michael agreed happily. "I don't give a fuck about the pot anyway. That's small shit these days. I'm just glad someone saw him last night." He paused, eyes narrowed. "You're *sure* it's a positive ID, that your witness actually saw Albrecht?"

"Positive," I said.

He raced the motorcycle engine and hooted wildly.

"Hang on a minute," I said, trying to calm him down. "It'd help enormously if half a dozen people would swear you were with them at about ten-thirty last night."

"No such luck," he said, trying and failing to squash a nasty grin. "I dropped Rhonda off at your trailer and just rode around for about an hour by myself, to clear my head. I do that a lot. It's real peaceful, calming-like."

"Concentrate," I told him. "Did you see anybody at all who could confirm your whereabouts during that hour?"

"Yeah, I saw someone all right, but it won't do me a bit of good," he said.

"Why?"

"Because it was that pig Albrecht, parked with his lights off just up the street. Keeping an eye on your trailer, it looked like to me. He's sure as hell not going to come forward now and say, 'Oops, I guess we made a mistake, this young fella didn't do nothing wrong, sorry.' "

"It helps more than you think," I said, a little excited myself. "It independently confirms that Big Dick was in town last night at the right time." I thought things over quickly. "Listen, you better keep a low profile over the next couple of days. No more drug buys," I said sternly. "And don't tell anyone anything about this."

"Why?" he asked. "I'd like to nail the bastard and get it over with."

What does Rhonda see in this guy?

"First, because we don't have any proof," I said slowly, figuring I'd better explain in short, easy sentences. "If Big Dick really did plant evidence on you, and we let him know that we suspect him, he'll have plenty of time to work out an airtight alibi. And perhaps plant even more damning evidence. The second point should be obvious."

Michael looked bewildered.

"We don't say anything because the man has already killed once," I said. "Do you want to tempt him to repeat the crime?"

"I guess not," he said to the ground.

"All right then," I said. "You be a good, quiet, law-abiding citizen and you just might come out of this with nothing more than a misdemeanor possession charge. Got it?"

"Got it." He grinned and roared off toward the highway.

The headache that had started my day had returned and was now pounding dully.

For a lady who had spent this eventful day making some amazing decisions and sharp deductions, I was still confused. The facts seemed to be falling into place in an orderly fashion, and my little gray cells should have been satisfied. But I couldn't shake the uncomfortable notion that I had missed something along the way.

Something vital.

20

....

Anti-Santa

JUNE 25

South Dakotan youth have been raised in a safe, loving sphere of family unity and community support. They park their unlocked cars to attend classes staffed by the lowest-paid teachers in the country, and still produce some of the nation's highest SAT scores.

They wake in the morning to the grand expanse of rolling prairie and sleep at night with the twinkling stars undimmed by big city lights. They breathe unpolluted air and fearlessly open doors to strangers. They bask in the generous approval of friends and neighbors, and they share a unified goal: They can't wait to ditch this burg and go someplace with some excitement.

Anyplace, as long as it's far away.

"Why do you live here when you don't have to? Nothing ever happens," Rhonda said the day before yesterday, when that was still true. "You have to drive all the way to Sioux Falls just to see a rock concert. You have to fly east to Minneapolis to catch a plane to the West Coast! Pearl Jam wouldn't set foot in South Dakota,'' she finished, exasperated when I counted that a plus for the state.

Rhonda has a point, though. Shopping is impossible, the climate is horrid, and prices are a lot higher than you would expect in the nonindustrial, minimum-wage flatland.

She just doesn't understand the comfort in continuity, in knowing what to expect.

It's hotter than hell in the summer. It's colder than shit in the winter. Farm prices are always snarled by late spring or early fall frosts, embargoes or free trade agreements. There's never enough rain, except when there's too much. The wind always blows.

And families stay the same from generation to generation, easily identified by long acquaintance with inherited traits.

Female Engebretsons are bossy, Adlers have no chins, Bauers are unreliable, and Hausviks talk too much.

"If I hear the name Tarkenton just one more time, I'm going to dump this pot on Willard's head," Rhonda said, beaker of decaf in hand.

Saunderses are blond and crabby.

Thank goodness Pascoes are intelligent and faithful.

I'd spent a confused and restless night populated with dead bodies, menacing deputies, incestuous cousins, and naked feed dealers, though that last was rather more comforting than the rest. Except when his wife showed up, machete in hand.

I woke with the nagging thought that I had missed something important in last night's local newscasts. The only way to quiet the voice was to watch Neil's videos. I wanted to talk to him anyway, if for no other reason than to assure myself that the whole world hadn't turned upside down.

I needed calm, gentle Neil, whose books saved my sanity, whose friendship is an anchor, and whose quiet philanthropy and modest indulgence make it easy to forget his riches.

Of course, I wasn't going to discuss Stu McKee, or Del

and Nicky with him. But that still left a plethora of subjects open.

Yesterday was not exactly a slow news day.

I wanted to tell Neil about Crystal and Michael and Big Dick and the marked money. It seemed painfully obvious that Big Dick had set Michael up, but I wanted to hear his opinion. He had a way of cutting through the clutter.

Besides, after yesterday's confusions, I needed a laugh.

I rang the bell three times and hollered up the stairs. A muffled answer floated down from the next floor.

"Wait till you hear this, you are absolutely not gonna believe it," I said, coming up and around the corner into Neil's gleaming kitchen.

Neil, wearing only gray sweatpants, was cranking open a small can of cat food. Elizabeth Bennet and Mr. Darcy sat politely at his feet, waiting for him to empty the can into their dish.

Though it wasn't unusual to see Neil shirtless, I somehow had never noticed his broad shoulders and bulging biceps. Maybe he had a new weight machine stashed in one of the buildings. Or maybe he had always been muscular. I am more aware of Neil mentally than physically, I guess.

"I want you to listen and then tell me if you think I have it straight," I said, getting myself a Diet Coke from the fridge while he rinsed and flattened the empty can. There was an unopened bottle of champagne on the shelf. Dom Perignon.

"Celebrating something?" I asked, curious.

He mumbled noncommittally from the sink. I sat at the table and recounted the long story of yesterday's adventures, from discovering Charles's body to my talk with Michael last night. I left out the afternoon adultery, of course.

Neil was still standing, washing counters, polishing chrome.

"Well?" I asked. "Have I got it all wrong?"

"Probably not," he said quietly, pouring himself a cup of coffee. He pulled a chair out and sat, facing slightly away from the table, as though he were keeping a distance. Our relationship didn't involve much body contact, but neither did we avoid it. Especially by sitting half a room apart.

"What do you think, then?" I asked. I belatedly realized that I had breezed into his house, interrupted his morning, and raided his refrigerator without an invitation.

Of course, Neil had never made me feel as though I needed a invitation.

"First of all," he said, wrinkling his glasses up on his nose, "Big Dick would not have driven all the way to Fargo with a prisoner. He'd only drive to the state line, and a North Dakota patrolman would meet him and take the guy from there."

"So Big Dick would have had plenty of time to be back in Delphi by ten-thirty last night," I said.

"He could have been back here by six-thirty easily," Neil said.

"Why did he lie to Del about canceling their trip to the Cities? They could have left at suppertime and still had most of their weekend." I was thinking out loud.

"Are you sure he lied to her?" Neil asked. "Could they have set that scene up as a charade of some sort?"

"I don't think so. Del seemed genuinely upset at the cancellation. And Big Dick looked really furious. I don't think the scene was faked. So why would he bother to lie to Del?"

"To spy on her?" Neil suggested. "To catch her with someone else?"

"With who?" It was too early to worry about grammar.

"With our little missionary, who else?" Neil said. "With the guy who just happened to end up dead in a closet and ruin your day, remember?"

There was no trace of humor in his voice.

I had never seen Neil without a smile, or a sparkle in his eyes.

"That's not likely," I said, nettled. "Charles wasn't interested in Del. She'd been trying, and he'd been resisting all along. I doubt if he fell for her line after all that time."

"You might be surprised," he said flatly. "There's been a lot of that going on lately." He stood up and said, "Let's go watch last night's news, and see if we can catch any clues from the video."

He stalked past me, out of the kitchen. I had no choice but to follow, bewildered.

I perched on the arm of the couch while he rewound the proper tape, wondering what in the hell was wrong with him.

"There," he said, sitting at the far end of the couch, "we'll see Nancijean Montrose on Channel 3 first."

"Have you ever noticed how newsladies all have two first names and newsmen all have two last names?" I asked, hoping for a smile. "Nancijean Montrose, Mary Ellen Dannemeyer, Crane Compton."

There was a stony silence from the other end of the couch.

I shifted uncomfortably and tried to concentrate on the screen. The interviews and the long shot of Main, and Adler's Garage with the Torino parked all by itself out in front, were all essentially the same as Channel 9's version, except for a view of my own retreating back as I left the cafe.

"I don't think Bonny Bobby Burns had NBC in mind as 'the power the giftie gie us to see oursels as others see us,'" I said.

I don't remember much high school poetry, just that passage and "Look upon my works, ye Mighty and despair."

Only that and nothing more.

But I was desperate to make Neil smile. I'd be reciting limericks with Nantucket in the rhyme scheme soon.

His huge house was so quiet that I could hear the cats cleaning their bowl in the kitchen. Neil got up and ejected the tape from the VCR.

"Did you catch it?" he asked.

"Catch what?" I asked, starting to be annoyed with his manner.

"You didn't see it? Come on, Tory, think." There was an actual taunt in his voice.

That was it. I had been pushed and pulled and surprised and shocked and confused enough. I was not about to accept Neil Pascoe's condescension.

"Do you mind telling me just what is wrong with you this morning?" I asked icily.

"I don't know what you're talking about," he said, lips tight.

I realized, amazed, that Neil was angry, something I'd never seen before.

I realized something else.

"You're mad at *me*, aren't you?" I asked.

He just stared, finally looking me straight in the eye.

"What possible reason could you have for being mad at me?" I was hurt and totally confused. And starting to be angry myself.

He stood, arms crossed for a long minute. I thought he would refuse to answer. That he had no answer.

Finally he said quietly, "I thought you were coming over yesterday afternoon."

"What? You're mad about a stupid thing like that?" I was more amazed than angry now. "I'm sorry, I had one or two other things on my mind yesterday afternoon."

"I'll just bet you did." His words dripped acid.

I was flabbergasted by his statement. It meant that somehow Neil already knew about Stu, and he was angry with me. Furious.

"I can't believe it! I can't fucking believe that you would spy on me! I'm the one who should be angry!"

"I didn't spy," he said sharply. "It wouldn't take a genius to figure out when Stuart McKee drives up in his father's pickup and disappears in your trailer for a couple hours that more is going on than carpentry."

"Don't you have better things to do than put a clock on my visitors?" I asked.

"Not yesterday," he said. "I was waiting for company myself."

"What happened, didn't she show?" I asked nastily, knowing it was a mistake the minute the words left my mouth.

"As a matter of fact she didn't," Neil said with the first smile of the day, a chilling, parody of good humor. "She was too busy fucking Stuart McKee. The same Stuart

McKee who checks out ridiculous Desire McClain paperbacks to soften up his wife.''

I didn't want to hear anymore. And I certainly didn't want to lose Neil's friendship, especially this way. But I had to leave, to get out before one of us said something really terrible. Something that couldn't be smoothed over later on.

I spun on one heel, but he caught me by the elbow.

''I'm sorry,'' he said fiercely, ''I don't want to fight with you, not about this. Not about anything.''

I pulled but he didn't let go; the grip was painful. I looked at the floor, holding tears back by sheer force of will.

''Wait a minute, please.'' He loosened his hand. ''Please.''

I nodded.

He rummaged in a desk drawer and held out a small gray rectangle.

''Maybe this will help explain,'' he said quietly.

It was a cassette tape.

I took the tape and looked down at the label. It was marked, in Neil's neat handwriting, ''Brandenburg Concertos 4–6.''

It was my tape, the copy Neil had made for me.

I looked up again, thoroughly puzzled.

''Del gave it to me yesterday,'' he said.

I was still lost.

''It was in her pocket, remember? She was supposed to give me her Elvis tape? I have no idea what she was doing with your Brandenburg.''

''But she handed her Elvis tape to—'' I stopped, unable to finish the sentence.

''Anti-Santa,'' Neil said.

I would have thought that the nasty surprises of the last couple days had vaccinated me against more.

I was wrong.

''Anti-Santa,'' I repeated, head spinning. I reached back, found the couch, and sat in a daze.

I would like to have fainted, but I wasn't that lucky.

"You *really* didn't know." It was Neil's turn to be amazed. "I was so careful with the setup and the clues. I was so certain you were enjoying the joke.

"Until just this minute," he said bleakly.

"Quoting Dickens," I said to myself. "German saints. Christmas music."

Hundred-dollar bills.

Stu and I hadn't been the only ones to hear Christmas music.

I should have known.

Anti-Santa had smelled of some wonderful cologne, and Stu had told me, plainly, that he couldn't wear perfumes. "Makes me break out," he'd said in my kitchen.

But I'd wanted so badly to believe it was Stu that I fooled myself. When he'd looked at me with those marvelous green eyes, I'd been lost.

I looked at Neil's brown eyes, serious behind thick glasses.

"Green eyes?" I asked.

"Easy," he said. "Colored contact lenses."

"You asked me what my favorite eye color was," I remembered. "But that was only the day before yesterday. How did you get them so fast?"

"I didn't," he said matter-of-factly. "I had a pair in each color made up in my prescription so I'd have your favorite color on hand."

"Kind of expensive, wasn't it?" I asked.

He shrugged and rubbed his thumb and fingers together, "What does money matter to me? I wanted to surprise you."

"Why?" I asked.

"Don't you know?" he asked softly.

I remembered the warm kiss. The unopened bottle of champagne. His fury.

I knew.

I leaned my head back and closed my eyes. Neil sat on the couch next to me.

"Why do you think I started this library, Tory?" he asked softly. "Because a nice lady across the street had just lost her husband and was too sad to leave her house. Because the lady was smart and funny and too young to be widowed. Because I knew I couldn't attract her with money, that she wouldn't be impressed by gifts.

"So I bought the books I knew she'd like, did my best to make her laugh, and waited patiently for her to notice that I was in love with her."

Neil sighed. "And when I finally got brave enough to say so in the most romantic and amusing way I could, I discovered that I'd patiently waited exactly one day too long."

"Oh Neil," I said, leaning my head on his shoulder. "What are we going to do?"

"I don't know. Are you in love with Stu McKee?"

"I don't know," I said. "Can we still be friends?"

"I don't know," he said, sounding as miserable as I felt.

Should I have known? Del knew.

"You and your sainted librarian can play jokes on each other all day," Del had said. Del, ready to smuggle my Brandenburg 4–6 cassette out of the cafe in her pocket. Pretending it was Elvis.

Del who hated all classical music, who would never listen to Bach.

Everything was so confusing. I would like to have reeled my life back a few days, to when Stu was a dream and Del wasn't the mother of my late husband's child. Back to the time when I didn't suspect friends and neighbors, or even enemies, of murder.

Yesterday Neil was a wonderful friend whose passions were books and cars.

Today everything was different, and I didn't even have the satisfaction of being sure I made the right choices.

Why does change always involve loss?

A small voice spoke in my mind. Interrupting.

Cars, it said. Pay attention, Tory. Cars.

I sat bolt upright and knew what I had missed on the videotapes.

21

....

The Lone Torino

In South Dakota, we've adopted Thumper's mama's credo, with a small editorial change: If we can't say anything nicely, we don't say anything at all.

Visitors from either coast are often disarmed by our civility, mistaking a polite veneer for a solid virtue. As a group, we rarely fight in public, contradict our guests, berate salesmen, or heckle elected officials in anything but the most polite terms.

In fact, one can be appallingly rude without ever raising a voice or extending a middle finger.

Shortly before Nicky's death, Junior blindsided me while serving a group of her sales managers by commenting with a smile, "I saw your husband in Lila Pankratz's car yesterday. It must be wonderful being married to so charming and friendly a man."

We also use politeness as a dodge when the truth is too uncomfortable to bear.

"What an interesting hairdo, such a bright color," we often remark to Iva Hausvik's clientele.

And in a region famous for tight-lipped pioneer stoicism, we use politeness as a cover for anger.

"Self-control, Tory," Mother reminded me an endless number of times. "No good can come from words spoken in anger."

And of all the lessons she tried so desperately to instill, that one took.

I have spent my entire life avoiding confrontations, soft-soaping the truth, and disguising anger with detachment, politely avoiding sensitive subjects.

Like my husband's infidelities.

Unfortunately, that particular complaint is now beyond redress. But there were other topics ripe for consideration.

I had been lied to, and I didn't like it. I had been stupid, and I liked that even less.

It was time to face a few facts, and I was prepared to be impolite to get my point across.

"All right." I thumped a very surprised Ron Adler in the chest with an insistent forefinger. "I want the truth, and I want it now!"

He pulled a hanky from his pocket and wiped his face, with a sideways glance at the other smiling mechanics who had interrupted their work to watch.

"Tory." He swallowed. "How nice to see you. What seems to be the problem this morning?"

"You're the problem," I said. "Do you want to talk about it out here, or should we go into your office?"

I looked at the others significantly. They busied themselves in their assorted engines.

"I don't know what's upsetting you," Ron said nervously. "But why don't we go inside and see if we can work this out together. Probably just a disputed bill," he announced over his shoulder for the benefit of the room.

He had not blinked once during the entire conversation. He closed the door between the glassed-in office and the garage, and sat in the swivel chair behind his desk. That left me standing, which was fine. I was too agitated to sit anyway.

"Okay, now what's—" he started but I interrupted him.

"You have exactly one chance to tell me what happened with Charles and his car yesterday," I said.

I had been polite last night and it got me nothing. I would be forceful today.

Obnoxious if necessary.

"I *told* you what happened," Ron said, sounding a little forceful himself. "Charles left that broken-down piece of shit here. I fixed it. He took it. There's nothing else to say."

"Liar," I said quietly.

He swallowed and wiped his face again, staring.

"And I have proof," I said.

I waited. He waited.

I said, "It's amazing what you can learn about your town when you watch the evening news on both channels."

He sat back in his chair, deflated, swallowing. Blinking.

"Shit," he said. "I knew someone would notice. All right, where do you want me to start?"

"How about after you told Charles that you'd have his car fixed in half an hour," I suggested sweetly.

He wiped his face again. "The car just needed a new fuel pump and an air cleaner. Piece of cake. I finished 'er right up because I knew he wanted to leave town right away. Hell, I liked the kid. Strange religion, but he was okay otherwise."

"So what happened?" I asked.

"I finished working on it, and then I parked his Chevy in front there." He pointed out the window. "Next to that Torino, so he could just pay the bill and go. I seen him come out the front door of the cafe and start across the street this direction. Then the phone rang."

Ron looked off to the side, in the air, down at the floor and then at me. "It was Del, from the cafe," he said, "asking if I would do her a little favor."

I knew it would come to Del.

"I said sure, 'cause I'm always happy to do a favor for Del," Ron explained needlessly. Ron's crush on Del was huge and obvious.

He paused, blinking furiously.

"Well?" I said. There was no sense in easing the pressure now.

"Del asked real sweet if I would *please* delay Charles and tell him that something came up. That I couldn't get to his car until later. That it'd be after six-thirty before he could pick it up . . ." His voice trailed off for a moment. "She said that Charles could amuse himself for the rest of the afternoon and she'd amuse him for a while that night. All I had to do was say his car wasn't fixed and tell him he could get a free supper at the cafe for his trouble."

"What did you say to that?" I asked.

"I said, 'I don't like lying to customers,' which is true," Ron said flatly.

"What did she say then?"

Ron opened his mouth and nothing came out. He tried again. "She said, 'Gina's out of town tonight, isn't she? You'll be all alone and lonely. Maybe I'll stop over later, and keep you company.' "

Someone dropped a wrench in the garage. The clang startled Ron. He looked around furtively and continued. "You know Del, she always gets what she wants. I, uh, I told Charles what she wanted me to. I said I'd leave the keys in the car when I was done, and he could pick it up later. I didn't see no harm in it—it wasn't like a real lie or anything. His car got fixed, and I gave him a good deal on the parts and labor.

"He hadn't picked it up at closing time, so I stuck the keys in the ignition and left."

"And then you went home and waited for Del," I said, sighing. Ron was right, Del always got what she wanted.

"She didn't show." Blink, blink.

I knew that already, Del had been at the trailer all evening, vindictively getting Junior sozzled. And rendezvousing with Big Dick in the driveway.

Ron blinked miserably.

"So the next moring you get to work, and surprise, surprise, Charles's car is still parked in front of the garage, right?" I prodded.

"Yeah," he said, "I didn't worry about it too much. I

flagged Del over in the cafe in the morning and asked her if she knew where he was. She said that she called the date off last night, that Charles left the cafe and, as far as she knew, left town.

"I told her that he couldn't have gone very far because his car was still parked in front of my garage."

Right where it was in Crane Compton's early shot of Delphi—a tan Chevy parked next to a rusty Torino.

"Del was surprised, but she said, 'Don't worry about it, he probably got a ride with someone.' That didn't make much sense to me, but things got hectic just then. That Pascoe fella in the Christmas outfit came in."

Did everyone in Delphi know except me?

"I nearly shit when he said I was known for my honesty," Ron said quietly. "And right after that you found, uh, the body, and by the time they let us go, one news crew had already filmed and finished. And the other was just setting up shop."

"Where did you move the car?" I asked.

"Out back of the garage," he said. "I put it under a tarp. It's still there."

I had watched Nancijean Montrose's long shot of Main Street twice before I noticed the rusty Torino parked all by itself in front of the garage.

"So you lied to Charles," I said. "You kept him in Delphi, and now he's dead."

"That didn't have nothing to do with him dying," a trace of the forceful Ron returned, blinking. "That biker did it, they got evidence and everything. I feel bad about lying. And if I had to do it over again, I sure as hell wouldn't. But what's done is done."

"Why didn't you tell any of this to the police?" I asked.

"I wanted to," he said. "But Del said that I'd best keep quiet for everyone's sake."

For Del's sake mostly, I thought.

"You better polish up your excuses," I said. "If things turn out the way I'm starting to think they will, you're going to have to tell your story to the police after all."

"You think *Del* killed that poor kid?" he asked, paling.

"No, I don't think Del killed Charles," I said, though Ron plainly did. In a shortsighted panic, he'd hidden Charles's car to protect Del—and himself—from further suspicion.

I was filled with a sudden fury. For the first time in my life, I was mad enough to scream, to throw things. Mad enough to demand, and get, an explanation.

Del had manipulated poor Ron into lying the same way she manipulated everyone else. She used Ron, she used Charles, she used me. She probably even used Nicky.

Del had deliberately kept Charles in Delphi and at the cafe. And that knowledge brought the realization that I already had another key to the puzzle.

22

....

Brandenburg Overdub

Certain snatches of classical music have become indelibly intertwined in American popular culture—the 1812 Overture shot from cannons, Beethoven's fifth as a lead-in to the nightly news, Elmer Fudd atop a massive steed singing Wagner, and Mickey Mouse desperately trying to halt water-carrying broomsticks.

We recognize, without being able to name, generic musical snips used to hawk everything from dish soap to tampons. Tunes by Mozart, Vivaldi, and Tchaikovsky that we can all hum in five notes or less.

And then you have the Brandenburg Concertos, six Bach masterpieces that have themselves been sliced, diced, and served in small portions, an adagio here, an allegro there, as musical accompaniment for every conceivable advertising pitch.

Though they're not classical aficionados, Bach sets better with the regulars at the cafe than, say, the original cast album recording of the Broadway musical *Hair*.

"Jesus Christ, Tory, how do you expect a person to eat with that stuff playing?" Willard complained during the song "Sodomy." "Give us a break and play some of that flutey horn stuff, would you?"

He meant Brandenburg Concerto no. 2, though he didn't know it. To most of the regulars, the six are interchangeable, blending together into a stretch of musical mush.

I was counting on Del's inability to differentiate. And hoping that I wasn't too late to salvage what was probably a pivotal clue.

My anger had cooled and jelled by the time I got back to the trailer, and I was relieved to find that Del and Presley were already dressed and gone, though I took the precaution of checking all the rooms just to make sure.

I calmly contemplated the Brandenburg 4–6 cassette that Anti-Santa Neil had taken from Del. And then I tossed it into the box I'd brought home from the cafe yesterday.

That cassette didn't matter. Its significance lay in Del's attempt to smuggle it from the cafe. And her lack of musical knowledge.

She had taken the wrong one.

I had been surprised to find my Brandenburg 1–3 cassette in the cafe player, instead of Elvis, on the morning of June 24 but I was hung over and in need of down and dirty music for mental fuel so I plugged in Bonnie Raitt. And accidentally tossed the 1–3 cassette out of sight, behind the player.

Neil would buy music and then copy pieces I liked on cassettes for me. The sound quality wasn't very good, but then neither was my stereo. Or the tape player at the cafe.

Del liked to record her conquests. She kept a collection of audio and video sexual souvenirs. She had threatened to record Clay's seduction for Junior's benefit, and I knew she had saved several of Big Dick's epic moments for posterity.

On that particular recording of the Brandenburg Concertos, as with most of the other cassettes Neil recorded for me, I had forgotten to break the little tab off. The one that would make it impossible to record over the music.

What in the world would have happened if I had actually played that tape in the cafe?

I would bet everything that with Charles as more or less a captive audience, Del unobtrusively chose a Brandenburg cassette, loaded it into the player, and pushed the record button at an opportune moment.

And for some reason did not take the tape with her afterward. An oversight Del tried to remedy the next morning by saying she needed her Elvis badly enough to rush, disheveled, into town for a fix.

Had she listened to the cassette in her pocket, she'd have known her mistake immediately.

But Anti-Santa took it from her.

So she relaxed, thinking her soundbite was safe, not realizing that there were two Brandenburg cassettes, or that the incriminating one was still at large.

I did not expect to enjoy what I fully expected to hear. But I knew it'd be important.

I rewound Side One of Brandenburg 1–3, and for a long moment considered erasing or recording over it.

Instead, I sat on the floor, depressed PLAY, and listened.

I could hear the sound of the cafe air conditioner wheezing overhead, muffling but not smothering entirely the sound of footsteps walking away from the recorder. Then the scrape of moving furniture.

"Can you help me with this?" It was Del's voice, faint but recognizable.

"Sure," Charles Winston answered distractedly, in his soft drawl.

My heart contracted painfully to hear Charles alive still, on this tape.

A stool creaked as he swiveled around. He had to have been sitting on the stool at the end of the counter, the one almost under the air conditioner, for the recorder to have picked up that sound.

His footsteps receded, followed by heavy shuffling. Del who was strong as an ox, had asked Charles to help so she could mop.

"Thanks," Del said, walking across the room, followed

by the squeak of the mop bucket. "These tables are awfully hard to move by myself."

"I really should be goin', my car has to be finished by now," Charles said, back on the stool, sounding upset, plainly wishing to leave.

"Oh, please stay a couple more minutes," Del wheedled. "I really could use some help putting these things back in place. I'll be done in a jiff, honest." Her words were punctuated by the rhythm of swirling, wetting, wringing the mop.

Charles was a gentleman, and a Southern gentleman never refused a request from a lady, even one as unladylike as Del. Even when he was in a hurry.

"My, but it's hot in here," Del said, her voice slow and breathy. "Don't you wish we could just take our clothes off and run around naked? It'd feel so much cooler."

"I'm afraid our rules don't allow for that kind of cooling off," Charles said with a small laugh. Relaxing a little.

"Don't you ever break the rules?" Del asked, her voice closer now.

"I try not to," Charles said quietly. "I put a lot of effort into trying not to. You know I really do have to leave. Something happened today—"

Del interrupted, "Well, you should break the rules. I'd do you a world of good." She sounded very close to Charles.

"But I really must—"

"Excuse me," Del said. I could hear the reach in her voice. "I have to put this stuff in order."

She clinked some small objects, probably napkin holders and salt and pepper shakers. "Excuse me," she said again, "now for this side."

That was an old trick of Del's—firmly pressing her breasts into her victim's back (or front, or side—she wasn't picky) as she reached for the mustard or ketchup. I'd seen her do it a hundred times. It always got their attention.

Run, Charles, I thought. Get out while you still can.

But Charles sat on the stool, not moving. Not swiveling out of the way. Beginning to breathe heavily. I could picture Del pretending to clean, seductive smile on her face.

And still Charles didn't move away.

"And now for this side," she said so low that I could barely hear the words.

There was some shuffling, the soft *shh* of fabric. Charles gasped softly.

"I don't understand why you're doin' this," Charles said in genuine bewilderment, though his breath was ragged.

"Because you're beautiful," Del said. "And because"— she breathed deeply—"you want me to."

More shuffling, more breathing.

"This is wrong," Charles said desperately. "This is really wrong."

Poor Charles, he thought that good intentions and moral convictions would protect him against the juggernaut. Whatever had agitated him, whatever imperative he'd had for leaving Delphi, was lost in the sensual overload of Del's seduction.

"See," Del said with triumph, and perhaps just a little condescension in her voice. "See how much you want me to."

"This is *not* a good idea," Charles said, though the desperation in his voice was fading. "What about your boyfriend? The deputy?"

"Don't worry about him." Her words were punctuated with small wet sounds. "He's out of town. On business."

"He threatened me," Charles said, paused, and inhaled sharply. "I tried to tell him . . ."

His protests were muffled.

"Don't talk now," Del commanded quietly. "Just close your eyes and feel."

"But . . ." Charles protested weakly.

"Quiet," Del said, her voice muffled now.

The room echoed with the sound of liquid, rhythmic slurping, and soft moans.

I ran my fingers through my hair. Poor Charles never had a chance.

"Shit! Listen!" Del said suddenly, over Charles's protests.

"No, don't stop," he whispered, panting.

"Shut up and listen," Del said sharply. "Shit, there it is again. Someone's coming."

"What?" Charles's voice rose in panic.

"Someone's unlocking the back door," she whispered. "Duck down behind the counter and stay put! Just be quiet and wait for whoever it is to leave. It's probably only Aphrodite."

There were scrambling, fumbling, and panting sounds.

"Hurry," Del said with a laugh. "And zip up. It's been fun, sweetie. Catch you later."

Her footsteps pittered across the floor and out the door.

No wonder she hadn't taken the tape with her. No wonder she'd insisted that Junior about-face to the trailer with her.

On the tape there were a few moments of silence accented by the air conditioner rattle.

And then there were footsteps.

Heavy footsteps coming from the kitchen, walking toward the counter.

"I know you're in here." A deep singsong voice.

Big Dick's taunting voice.

"I told you to stay away from her," Big Dick said, wandering around the room. "But did you listen?" he asked, voice closer now.

Stay down, Charles, I thought. Stay quiet.

"I gave you that advice man to man. But did you take my very good advice?" Big Dick's voice was close, loud and menacing. He answered his own question. "No, you certainly didn't."

Silence. Tense, expectant silence.

"So," Big Dick said, followed by a sudden lunging sound, scattering small metal objects to the floor. "I hope it was good for you because it's the last you're going to get for a while."

I heard struggling, but no sounds of escaping footsteps. Big Dick must have pinned Charles in.

"I don't know what you're talkin' about," Charles said, defiant, voice strangled.

"Missionaries aren't supposed to lie," Big Dick said calmly. "Don't you know that?"

A soft thud followed, and the whoof of sudden exhalation. Then panting, either Charles or Big Dick. I couldn't tell.

"Where is she?" The words were flat.

"I don't know what you're talkin' about," Charles repeated slowly, with more courage than I would ever have.

"Again with the lies," Big Dick said sorrowfully, punctuating the sentence with more blows. "I can smell her on you."

Charles was breathing raggedly, his words were disjointed. "You can't do this."

"Wanna bet?" I could hear the smile.

I wanted to cover my ears, to block out the squelch of fists, the protests that became cries and then whimpers.

I don't think Charles had even a chance to defend himself. He took that beating without ever betraying Del, a favor she would never be able to return.

There was the heavy thud of a falling body, and the sound of that body being raised and hit yet again.

And worse, terrible quiet when the cries stopped but the beating continued.

And finally the last crumpling thud of a body hitting the counter and falling to the floor.

Then nothing but the sound of panting, of heavy breathing. The exhaustion a large man might feel after having beaten senseless a boy whose only mistake was being caught in the wrong place with the wrong person at the wrong time.

Gradually Big Dick's breathing returned to normal but he did not move. "Let's see what they think when they find you tomorrow," he said, quietly satisfied.

Grunting slightly, I heard him place Charles's unconscious body on the same stool where he'd sat earlier, with Del. The stool creaked as it spun.

Then the footsteps retreated back through the swinging gate to the kitchen, and the cafe was quiet.

I swallowed several times, nauseous. The silent seconds on the tape lengthened to minutes.

Del had been home just before eight-thirty that night, right about the time this beating was taking place. Big Dick had definitely been back in Delphi early.

Spying, as Neil had said.

I reached out to eject the tape.

But there was the faint sound of movement again. I cocked my head and listened closely.

Footsteps walked through the kitchen, through the swinging gate. Coming closer.

Walking purposefully over to Charles, propped at the counter.

Big Dick had returned.

He stood briefly still, then retreated. Across the cafe, but not back through the kitchen. There was no sound of a swinging gate.

He stopped and I heard rummaging. He was searching under the counter, I realized, behind the empty ketchup bottles.

No, I thought.

But what had been recorded could not be changed. What was done could not be undone.

He walked back to Charles. I heard small swooshes as something metallic and flat repeatedly struck the palm of his hand, each tap harder than the last.

There was a barely audible grunt followed by a huge swoosh and the horrible splot of Eldon McKee's shiny blue flat bar shattering Charles Winston's skull.

I had just heard Charles Winston die.

I had just heard Big Dick Albrecht, County Deputy Albrecht, kill Charles Winston.

On the tape there was another nearly inaudible grunt and the sound of something inert and heavy being dragged across the floor and through the kitchen.

The sounds faded and the tape ended.

I didn't need to hear any more to know the chronology. Big Dick had put Charles in the mop closet, and haphazardly rearranged and straightened the tables, chairs, and napkin holders. Then he mopped in a rudimentary fashion with the equipment Del had, in her haste, left out.

And later that night, while Crystal looked out her upstairs window, he returned, stole the Burglar Bait money, and used it to implicate Michael.

Charles Winston had died earlier than the official ten-thirty P.M. estimate. Big Dick's official estimate.

Big Dick Albrecht killed Charles Winston and I had proof.

Del thought Neil had safely taken her recording. Did she know what was on that tape? I didn't think so, but I couldn't afford to find out.

I could not turn the cassette over to the authorities since Big Dick was assigned to investigate the very crime I now knew he had committed.

I needed time to think, and the insurance of having some-one else hear what I had just heard.

Someone strong.

Any other day, I would have run to Neil, asked his ad-vice, and trusted his judgment. But our relationship was suddenly too raw and uncomfortable. The easy friendship was gone, perhaps forever.

I could not, and would not, involve Stu. I didn't know, yet, if he was going to be a part of my life. I did not want him to be a part of this death.

There was only one person to whom I could turn.

23

....

Motherly Advice

The only Midwest citizens who routinely remove car keys are high school principals, disgruntled students having a finely honed taste for revenge coupled with a vindictive imagination.

Everyone else leaves doors open and keys hanging in ignitions, and trusts to good fortune and the basic honesty of the general public. That and the fact that no one would want to steal the rolling junk most of us own anyway.

Not that we want to drive such ill-begotten cars. The weather and economy wither most auto-erotic fantasies on the vine.

When I was fourteen and first had my driver's license, a system that made more sense to me then than now, I had modest dreams: a dependable car with fair gas mileage, a functional air conditioner and heater, and a good radio.

I finally bought one, just a week before Nicky killed himself in it. The same week in which we entirely forgot about auto insurance.

The last of those bills is nearly paid now, and soon I can think about buying another car. Being without wheels hasn't been as inconvenient as it sounds, I stay home most of the time and walk the rest.

On those rare occasions when I need to leave the Delphi city limits, I borrow Del's Plymouth, a heap that meets my only automotive requirement these days—it runs.

There were Butterfinger wrappers in the open ashtray and the radio had been tuned to the hard rock station and cranked up full blast. Evidence that Presley, who turns fourteen in a little over a year, has been air-driving.

He doesn't actually start the car, he just runs the battery down pretending.

"I'd like a Porsche when I get a car," he said seriously. "Or one of those Mercedes. Maybe a Beamer. What do you think?"

"I think you'll be lucky if we let you drive a tractor," I answered equally seriously.

That's how I learned driving's finer points, dodging gopher holes in the pasture with Grandpa's H Farmall.

And that's probably how we'll start Presley, if I can talk Mother into trusting the farm equipment and outbuildings to his eye–steering wheel coordination.

I scribbled a note to Del, as per our loose agreement re car borrowing. "Running errand, took car. Back soon."

I didn't know how much detail to put in the note. The less hard info on paper, the better, it seemed. Certainly it wouldn't be wise to leave in plain sight a note saying, "I know your boyfriend killed Charles, and I'm off to ask my Mom what to do now." Though that's exactly what I had in mind.

If Del thought about the tape at all, she expected only a replay of her interrupted encounter with Charles, though she must, by now, wonder if the interruption had anything to do with his murder.

Big Dick did not even know there *was* a recording, much less the damning evidence it held.

It was time to consult Mother, and for once, to welcome her advice. For all that she drives me crazy, she has the

ability to see through things. I hoped she would offer me
a magic solution.

Her house, the one where I grew up, was dark and cool
in the way of all old farmhouses. The drapes had been
drawn early in the morning to cut the searing sunshine, the
windows closed to block the hot wind. The upstairs door
opened so the heated air could rise.

The second floor and the attic would be unbearably hot
and sticky, but the ground-floor temperature was tolerable.
The warmth was somehow neutralized by the dim quiet.

Mother was sitting at a desk recently moved into
Grandma Nillie's bedroom. The drapes were closed, dark-
ening the room entirely except for the bright lamplight shining over her shoulder.

She was bent over a yellow legal pad, scribbling in pen-
cil. Working on the latest novel.

Grandma was asleep in bed, covered by a sheet and blan-
ket, her skin waxy and yellow. Her chest rose and fell in
shallow, labored breaths. She was very thin, and for the
first time, I realized that she was dying.

"Shh," Mother motioned with a whisper. "She's finally
resting. Let's go out into the kitchen."

"What does the doctor say?" I asked, seated now at the
table. A tall glass of Diet Coke had been placed on a coaster
in front of me. There was no drinking from cans in my
mother's house, even in the kitchen.

"He says she's failing," Mother said matter-of-factly.
She sat down with a steaming cup of coffee. "She's been
so upset and agitated lately that it's weakened her system.
It won't be long now."

I squeezed Mother's hand. I'm not Aunt Juanita, I don't
believe in platitudes. That my grandmother's death will free
my mother from decades of round-the-clock caregiving was
not much of a consolation to her.

She looked worn and drawn, but she smiled softly, and
then peered closely at my face.

"What in the world has happened to you? You look terrible."

Trust Mom to hit the nail on the head with the first swing.

"Believe it or not," I said, "I'm here to ask your advice."

She smiled. "Will wonders never cease?"

I swallowed. "You're not going to like it as much as you think," I said. "I know who killed Charles Winston, and I have proof. And I don't know what to do about it."

Her eyes widened, but she said nothing. Mother is a wise woman sometimes.

I had no idea where to start; the past couple of days were a minefield. Though I wanted the insurance of having her hear the tape, I had no intention of discussing my involvement with Stu McKee. I didn't need Crystal Singman's psychic powers to know Mother's opinion on affairs with married men. My revelation about Del and Nicky and Presley could also wait for another day. Perhaps forever.

So very carefully, I told Mother what I knew about Charles's death. I told her about Crystal and Jasper, about Rhonda and Michael, about Anti-Santa and the tape mixup, and about Ron Adler and Del. I told her about the footprints, and the money, and the coroner's opinion, and Agent Ingstad. And I told her about Big Dick and the recording.

"My God, you make things difficult Tory," she said finally. "When you said you wanted advice, I thought maybe you'd decided to move from the trailer, or change your hairstyle."

"It's worse than that," I said with a small laugh. "I think you should actually listen to the recording. Just in case, you know, anything happens to me, or it . . ." I faltered.

Mother sat for a minute, face drawn, and then she nodded. So we sat together at the kitchen table and listened, hypnotized by the awful inevitability of what we were hearing.

Afterward the minutes ticked off silently. I'd heard the recording before, and still I was shaken. Mother was pale, the color drained from her handsome face.

She cupped my chin gently. "Tory, my dear, you've always been so stubbornly independent. You married when you wanted to, and salvaged some happiness from what seemed to be a bad choice. Life has treated you badly, but you managed to survive on your own.'' She looked out the window, then continued. ''I used to think that I could make your life easier, if only you would unbend enough to ask. Now, when you finally come to me, you have a problem I can't fix.''

''Come on,'' I said, covering a sinking heart with a weak smile. ''Can't you just wave your Mother Wand and make it all go away?''

Inside, I guess I actually thought that was possible.

''I wish I could,'' she said sadly. ''I do have some advice, though.''

''Anything,'' I said gratefully.

''I wouldn't tell anyone about this tape for a while,'' she said, pouring more coffee. ''The forensics report will narrow the time of Charles's death more precisely. Michael has Rhonda to back him up, and surely he can find at least one other person to swear he was in Aberdeen at eight-thirty.''

''What about Del?'' I asked. ''Shouldn't I warn her? She knows that Big Dick is violent, but I doubt she thinks he's a killer.''

''It might be more dangerous for her, and you, if you do,'' Mother said.

I thought about that. Would Del be frightened and careful, or would she tell Big Dick?

''Who do I contact, then? We can't keep this to ourselves. That's dangerous too, especially since this is the only copy of the tape,'' I said.

''The investigation is still proceeding,'' Mother said slowly, thinking it out as she spoke. ''It's entirely possible that they'll uncover proper evidence without this recording. The case may be resolved without ever needing to publicize the terrible things we've heard,'' she finished.

''Why delay?'' I asked, confused. ''Del's habits aren't secret and Big Dick deserves to fry.''

''Consider Charles and his family. Isn't it enough for

them to know that he was killed, without having to listen as it happened?'' Mother said softly. ''What about the episode with Delphine? Charles's Mormon congregation would be shamed, and we should avoid adding that to their sorrow if possible.

''Think about it, Tory. Something this sensational would be transcribed and spread on the front pages of every tabloid in the country, not to mention those awful TV shows. The damage would not just involve the Winston family. There are those in Delphi who could be hurt too.''

She was talking about Presley. Being Elvis's son would be nothing compared to having your friends hear your mother give a blow job to a Mormon missionary minutes before his murder.

''But what if they never catch Big Dick, or they arrest the wrong person?'' I asked.

''Then we do what we have to do,'' Mother said firmly.

She has always been good at that. I wish I had inherited her core of strength.

''You make a copy of the recording and mail it anonymously and directly to Agent Ingstad,'' she said.

''What do we do with it in the meantime?''

''Leave it with me,'' Mother said. ''No one will think to look here for something they don't even know exists, right? With Grandma so ill, I'm not leaving the house. It will be safe, and so will you, if you're smart and careful.''

''I have to tell Del *something*,'' I said, chewing my lip. ''She'll wonder where her recording is.''

''Let her wonder,'' Mother said harshly. ''If she says anything at all, just give her the tape Neil returned to you. Officially, you don't know anything about any cafe tryst, and you certainly don't know anything about any tape-recorded romantic encounters. It would serve no purpose to tell Delphine about the rest of that tape,'' she said.

Except, perhaps, save her life, I thought. I had asked for Mother's advice and had listened to it gladly. Whether I would take it remained to be seen.

''I think you're probably right about all this,'' I said.

"At least about leaving the tape here. I'll have to think about the rest."

"Can't ask for more than that," she said, still pale. The strain of all this, on top of caring for her own dying mother, had taken a toll.

"One more thing." I paused on the way out the door. Might as well make her day. "Change hairstyles, huh?"

"Please," she said with a wan smile.

24

....

Relative Indiscretions

There was a time, early in my marriage, when I mourned my inability to bear children. Those feelings, intense at first, faded rather more quickly than one would have expected. Any maternal leanings I might have had were exhausted by a relationship in which I was the mommy and Nicky was my very bad little boy.

I have no doubt that Nick loved me in his own nonexclusive way. The fact that I never sat him down and explained that it wasn't nice to screw other women, in my bed, car, or anywhere else, might have led him to believe that I really didn't care.

Like the child who thought it was okay to shove navy beans up his nose just because his mother didn't tell him not to, Nick barreled through his short life with his pants unzipped and a smile on his face.

I remember quite distinctly thinking, after his funeral, how lucky I was not to have to raise Nicky's child.

Maybe the Chinese have another curse: Be careful what

you congratulate yourself for, you may have to eat your words.

If I had known earlier about Presley's parentage, I probably would have blamed him for his own existence, the way I blamed Lila Pankratz for being tied up with my pantyhose.

And even without knowing, I sat on my maternal tendencies when I moved into the trailer. At first, anyway.

Pres was Del's son and I was not going to interfere or accept responsibility for him. But Del's irresponsibility made it tough to keep that vow. And Presley's charm made it more difficult. And my own loneliness made it impossible.

It's good that I didn't know Pres's lineage until after I loved him, since neither fact could be changed.

So now, preparing for a conflict of perhaps epic proportions with Del, I was astonished to discover that my overriding goal was not to avenge my own hurt feelings, but to protect Presley from the bad judgment of his mother and biological father.

"Where's Pres?" Del demanded before I got in the door, the same question I was going to ask her.

She looked genuinely concerned, worry lines marking her face.

"I haven't seen him this morning," I said. "It's just as well that he's not here. We need to talk now. Privately."

"Jesus, I thought he was with you," Del said, ignoring the rest of my sentence. "Where could he be?"

"He's probably farting around with Chainlink," I said. Pres rarely checked in except at meals. And Del never worried about him. "What difference does it make?"

She shoved a piece of paper at me. "Read this."

It was the note I had written earlier, but across the bottom, scrawled in a childish hand, was:

You guys are just too slow. Wait till everyone finds out that Presley Bauer, Boy Genius, solved the mystery! Too cool!

I looked at Del, confused.

"This was stuck in the phone book, marking the page with the sheriff's phone number, circled in felt pen," Del said, handing me Crystal's note, from which no marked bill fell.

"How did he find this?" I hadn't actually hidden the note, but I had put it in the top drawer of my dresser where it could not have been uncovered accidentally. I remembered hearing footsteps behind me on the street and then bumping into Presley just outside the grocery screen door. "Shit. He must have overheard my conversation with Crystal."

"Accusing Big Dick of robbery, no doubt," Del said nastily. "So what do you think the dumbshit kid did about it?"

"Looks like he called the sheriff," I said, my insides solidifying.

I tapped the circled number, thinking, then picked up the phone and dialed.

"Spink County Sheriff's Office," the nasal voice of the dispatcher answered.

"Yes," I said, swallowing, willing my voice to sound normal, "I'd like to speak to Deputy Albrecht if I could."

"Deputy Albrecht is out on a call just this moment, may I take a message?"

"No," I said, "it'll keep. Can you tell me when he left?"

"About twenty minutes ago. He's on his way north, up to Delphi. Someone called in with a lead on that robbery/ murder there, though you didn't hear that from me of course," she said conversationally.

I mumbled, "Thanks" and hung up.

"What's this all about, anyway?" Del asked, pointing to Presley's note.

I told her about Crystal, and Michael, and the Burglar Bait money.

"Don't you know it's not nice to keep secrets from your roomie?" she asked angrily.

"Oho, look who's talking about keeping secrets," I said,

though this was not the best time to broach that subject.

The old me would have let it go. But the old me was gone.

"And what's that supposed to mean?" Del countered.

"I'm talking about twelve years of 'me and Elvis' stories, Del. I'm talking about twelve years of lying. I'm talking about you and Nick. How could you do it?"

Her blank shock was swiftly replaced by a hard smile.

"That's a silly question, considering you recently rediscovered the process yourself," she said. "Right here in this very trailer, if I'm not mistaken. With a married man, no less."

"That's not what I mean, and you know it!" I shouted. "You were my friend. How could you have sex with my husband? How could you invite me to move in with you after you gave birth to his child?"

"Well what was I supposed to do? Say, 'Come live with me, oh by the way, I fucked your husband once, hope that doesn't bother you too much'?"

"I thought you were my friend," I repeated.

"I was. I am. What happened between Nick and me didn't have anything to do with you. I don't owe you, or anyone else, any apologies. I paid plenty for that particular mistake."

She lit a cigarette and dragged on it furiously. "Nicky spread himself pretty thin while you were married, and you never seemed to mind. What's one more or less on his record?"

The difference between fifty-six and fifty-seven wasn't very much, even measured in tears. But the difference between this one and all the other indiscretions was enormous.

"You were cousins. First cousins," I said, more sad than angry now. More tired than anything.

"Listen, babe," Del said, inhaling wearily, "be forced to suck your drunken father's dick every other night for a couple of years, and then get beat because he thought the devil in you made him do it, and see how picky *you* are about partners."

Her father? I was stunned. And nauseated.

"And those were the good days," she said with a hard laugh. "He was an imaginative man, my father. You'd be amazed at what he could do with common household objects. A jolly evening with just you and your dad and a broom handle would make even a brother look good."

"And Nicky was just trying to help?" I asked quietly.

Del snorted. "Nicky didn't know. That's my own dirty little secret." Her eyes narrowed. "And it's going to stay that way."

I nodded.

"I just caught Nicky on a night when his brains were shut off, that's all. A few too many beers and a very determined Delphine," she said. "Don't worry, he was absolutely horrified afterward. It never happened again. Unfortunately once was enough."

"Did he know about Presley?" I asked.

"Hell no. The kid was my problem. Nick was so ashamed, he convinced himself that nothing really happened between us."

I thought she was wrong about that. Nicky might have tried to tell himself otherwise, but I remembered him holding an infant Presley up to the mirror, gazing and searching.

He knew, I think. He just didn't want to. A problem with which I am intimately familiar.

"I'd pretty well forgotten it myself," she said with a very small laugh. "It never occurred to me that you would figure it out. Everyone assumed the family resemblance was natural. How *did* you know, by the way?"

"I don't know. I looked at him yesterday and I knew."

"Great, just what we need," she said, "more psychics."

Which reminded me of Crystal. And of Presley's note.

"We could use one right now," I said, "to tell us what Pres is up to."

"That's easy. He's out solving a fucking robbery. Impressing the shit out of himself," Del said.

"Oh my God, Del," I said, panicked. "Pres is going to confront Big Dick!"

"Yeah, it'd be funny if it wasn't so ridiculous. Big Dick always has more cash than the two of us can spend together.

What in the hell would he do with marked petty cash from the cafe?'' Del asked. "He's going to be pissed."

"It's worse than that," I said, heart pounding.

I had discovered the dead, bludgeoned body of a young Mormon missionary. I had been questioned by the police, and I'd listened to a tape recording of that death.

Through it all, I'd maintained a detachment, an aloofness. None of it touched me. Not really.

Until the son of my husband, a boy I loved, went to meet a burglar.

He would find a murderer instead.

For the first time I was frightened.

"What are you so worried about?" Del asked over her shoulder, going into my room to look out the window. "It's not that big a deal."

"You don't understand," I said, discarding Mother's advice. Del had to know. Her son was in grave danger. "Big Dick killed—"

"Looks like the shit is about to hit the fan," she interrupted from my room. "They're here."

"Who?" I was afraid to know.

"Big Dick and Presley," she said. "They just drove up. And boy does he look unhappy."

Blood thundered in my ears. I was no longer frightened. I was terrified.

25

....

Realizations

I've spent a good portion of my life being bored. An equal chunk was entirely occupied by sadness. I've had lots of uncertainty, a little happiness, a dollop of lust, and a fair amount of confusion.

But I haven't had much fear, I mean the real thing. I've been unsettled by *The Shining*, and intimidated by my dentist, and nervous about declaring tips to the IRS. I won't ride a roller coaster, and heights make me dizzy.

But I have never been physically afraid for myself, or anyone close to me. Until now.

And if this is the kind of rush that soldiers and policemen and parachuters crave, then I'm relieved to have been a sad, bored, small-town waitress.

You can read about blood turning to ice but the words mean nothing until you stand face to face with a murderer. Especially one who is holding a small, frightened boy.

The door slammed open and Big Dick strode in, dragging Presley in one viselike hand, the skin whitened around fingers dug deep into skinny arm muscle.

Big Dick stood, tall and terrible, and glared at both of us.

"You," Big Dick said flatly, pointing at Del, "keep this fucking kid out of my sight."

He threw Presley across the room like a rag doll.

"You son of a bitch!" Del shrieked and launched herself at Big Dick.

His backhand slap connected just under the chin and knocked her to the floor.

"Mom!" Pres doubled his fist into an angry ball.

"Not a wise thought, little man." Big Dick laughed. And then he turned to me. "You, come with me." He gestured at the door.

I was afraid, more afraid than I had ever been in my life. But I was thinking clearly, through the fear. Big Dick's way was to attack in the dark, to catch the unwary in deserted cafes, to ambush in bathrooms. If his intention was to kill us all, he would have done it already.

If his intention was to kill only me, he would not allow Del and Presley to know I had gone with him.

He could not intimidate them both into permanent silence.

I sincerely hoped.

But I had insurance. Proof that Big Dick had killed once already. It might not save my life, but it would surely complicate his.

As long as I didn't give myself away too soon, I would be relatively safe.

"Don't go, Tory," Pres pleaded.

"It'll be okay, sweetie, you just help your mom," I said, looking Big Dick directly in the eye. "I'll be right back in."

I followed him out into the hot afternoon sunshine. He indicated the front passenger seat of the cruiser.

I opened the door and got in, heart pounding. He sat in the driver's seat, looking straight ahead.

"I should beat the shit out of you," he said quietly. "But first I want some answers."

He leaned over, close enough for me to see the pores on

his face. Close enough to smell sour breath. Close enough to be frightened nearly out of my wits. "Now what is this bullshit about robbing the cafe and planting money on the biker? Frame-up, I believe, is the term you used?"

"It's not bullshit, and you know it," I said, forcing the waver from my voice. "You were seen leaving the side entrance of Aphrodite's at ten-thirty P.M. on June 23. You accidentally dropped some of the marked money you stole. The rest you put in Michael's jacket."

"Hippie," he mumbled to himself, shaking his head. "Long time ago I should have—" He recollected himself. "Do you want to tell me just why in the fuck I would frame our motorcycle friend? A young man with a record, I might add, and who was also found with a substantial amount of an illegal substance in his possession. Or do you think I planted the drugs too?"

"No. But they're convenient for your purpose," I said.

"Which is?" he asked.

"To cover what you did to Charles Winston," I said. The words hung in the air.

"And what exactly did I do to poor Charles Winston?" Big Dick asked, with a horrible smile.

"You beat him unconscious," I said. That was enough for a start.

"Don't be ridiculous, I was nowhere near Charles Winston on the night in question," he said with a sneer.

It was time to trot out some careful proof.

" 'Missionaries aren't supposed to lie. Don't you know that?' " I said, giving the best impression of my life. It wasn't very good, but it didn't have to be.

Big Dick pulled back suddenly, as if burned.

" 'Let's see what they think when they find you tomorrow,' " I said in a smug, satisfied voice.

He flinched and paled.

"Oh you beat him up all right," I said.

I was going to continue, to tell Big Dick that he then left the cafe, changed his mind and returned, gazed at the unconscious Charles, retrieved the flat bar, and calmly delivered the killing blow.

I was going to deliver a killing blow myself, and enjoy doing it.

But I realized, suddenly and horribly, that I couldn't.

Big Dick *had* savagely beaten Charles Winston.

But he did not kill him.

I knew this because, suddenly and horribly, I realized who did kill Charles Winston.

My fear, which had been replaced by a smug satisfaction, was now replaced by an enveloping sadness.

I knew who killed Charles Winston, and I did not want to know.

I struggled to keep this knowledge out of my face.

"I have proof," I said quietly.

"All right," he said, defeated. "All right. But I did not steal from Aphroditc or plant evidence on the biker."

I realized that he was telling the truth.

I also realized that I had the upper hand. I might as well use it.

"I have the proof and others know of its existence," I said calmly. "It can stay in a safe place, out of the public eye forever, if you like."

"What do you want?" he asked the windshield. "Money?"

"Just a guarantee against future mysterious beatings. No more, ever. No more shakedowns either. And most importantly, you stay away from Presley."

"Get out," he shouted. "Get out of my fucking car and out of my fucking life."

I took that as an agreement.

I did so, gladly.

It was apt to be the last glad thing I did for a while.

26

Loose Ends

I want to meet Jim Chee and Steve Carella and Adam Dalgleish and Hercule Poirot and Gervase Fen and Fletch and Nero Wolfe and Francis Pettigrew. I'd like to talk with Sarah Kelling Bittersohn and Jane Marple and V.I. Warshawski and Eileen Burke and Jemima Shore and Cordelia Gray and Judith Singer (whose detecting career was cut short by the commercial success of her creator).

If they were alive and breathing off the printed page, I'd ask them how they survived the crushing knowledge of death, and the terrible weight of murder.

I'd want to know how they reconciled everyday life with the awful business of dying.

Once, when Charles's murder was mostly an intellectual puzzle, I reasoned that if I knew the *why* and the *when*, I'd know the *who*.

I was wrong. I know the *who* but I still don't know the *why*. And if I do learn the *why*, will I ever understand?

Maybe, maybe not. But first there were a few loose ends to tie off.

Del was sitting on the couch when I went back into the trailer. Her face was tired, her arms crossed. She had been ambushed by a maternal instinct of her own, I think.

"Thanks for balling up the best sex I ever had," she said, a weak smile playing on her lips.

"Ah well," I said, "there's always Ron." Blink, blink, blink.

I knocked on Presley's door. He mumbled something. Possibly not "Come in," but I did it anyway.

He was curled on his bed, a ball of twelve-year-old misery.

My heart tightened for him.

"That was pretty brave," I said. "Stupid, but brave."

He snorted. I sat next to him on the bed, rubbing his bony back.

"Tory," he asked quietly, "do you like my mom?"

"Not always," I said truthfully. Though I thought that might change.

"Me neither," he said.

"Don't worry about it," I said. "You don't have to like your mom all the time, you just have to love her."

He sat up and snuggled under my arm. Something he hadn't done for ages. Something I hadn't realized that I missed.

"Can I ask you something else?" He looked up at me. "Something important."

"Sure, kiddo," I said.

"Do you think Elvis is really my father?"

I looked at his brown eyes and smoothed his dark hair back off his forehead.

"No, hon, I kinda doubt it."

"Do you know who he is then?" he asked.

"No." I told the most important lie of my life to the boy who was, for all intents and purposes, my son. Nicky's last, and perhaps only, gift.

"Do you think my real father would have liked me?" he asked in a small voice.

"Presley, your father would have adored you," I said.

And that was the truth.

Tonight, when the house is dark. I am going to tear that photo of Nicky into little pieces. Then I will burn those pieces and run the ashes down the drain.

And maybe, finally, I will put Nicky to rest.

Crystal was counting money at the till when I opened the door.

She didn't smile when she saw me.

"It is sad, Tory. I know," she said. "We have made a terrible mistake, yes?"

"Yes," I said. "Singman isn't your real name is it?"

"We have made it our name," she said.

"When did Big Dick discover your real identity?" I asked.

"Almost immediately. And almost immediately, he began demanding payment in exchange for his silence," Crystal said.

He always had cash, more than he and Del could spend together.

"How could you afford to pay his price?"

"Tory, a sad fact of the sixties is that the poor could not be part of the counterculture. They were too busy surviving to worry about marching and demonstrating. Both Jasper and I come from old money. My family disowned me long ago, but Jasper's people have helped us to stay hidden all this time, and they have funneled money into your deputy's pockets for nearly a year."

"You didn't *deliberately* accuse him of robbing the cafe, did you?"

"Of course not," she said, finally smiling. "I had seen him several times enter the cafe late at night. It was natural to assume that he was the same man who committed the burglary, though I admit to a certain satisfaction at the thought."

"You realized your mistake before I did, though," I said. "Would you have let Big Dick be jailed for a robbery, and perhaps a murder, that he didn't commit?"

"With absolute pleasure," she said, beaming. "Minutes after I mistook Michael for Big Dick without my glasses, I knew what must have happened that night."

"You were ready for bed, right?" I asked. She'd had to dress again before going downstairs to pick money up off the ground. It hadn't occurred to me to ask about the glasses.

"Yes," she said sadly, "And now you know about our poor dear Charles."

"When you sent him over to the cafe for supper," I asked, "which door did he use?"

"The side door. He wanted to avoid being seen by the deputy."

I thought so.

"One last thing, are you really a psychic?"

She laughed. "Some of it is close observation. Some of it is instinct. Some is guesswork. But some"—she tapped her own head—"is real."

Through the screen door, and across the street, I saw Stu leave the feed store and drive off in his pickup.

My heart flip-flopped.

I don't think I am quite finished with Stuart McKee.

"Got any predictions for me?" I asked over my shoulder.

"Only that you'll survive," Crystal said.

And that's no small thing.

With Stu out of the way, I had a detail to straighten out with Eldon.

"Well, if it isn't the cutie from the cafe." Eldon beamed. "You should come across more often. Liven up the joint a little."

"I might just do that," I said. Unfortunately, I just might. "I'm here to ask you something for Mother." It was an excusable lie.

"Fire away, honey," he said.

"She wants to know when you'll be out to finish tearing down the chicken coop," I said. It was the only way I could lead to my real question.

"I can go out there any time now," he said. "I finished installing Renee's door for her and I'm free again."

"Too bad Renee insisted that you interrupt your work

schedule. You could have been done out at Mother's by now,'' I said, getting to the meat.

''That may be,'' he said, smiling, ''But it was Stuart who interrupted my work, not his wife. It was him who insisted I drop what I was doin' and start on that damn door.''

''He's pretty busy around town,'' Stu had said of his father. That's because Stu had arranged for his father to be busy around town.

So that Stu himself could fix my cupboard door.

It was a small but important distinction.

Ever since Neil had revealed that he was the Anti-Santa, I had been afraid that I'd manufactured Stu's attraction to me out of thin air. That I had thrown myself at him. That I had fooled myself again.

It was a small consolation to know otherwise.

Michael was in his camper, with Rhonda.

''I have Good News and Bad News,'' I said cheerily.

''The Good News is that you're off the hook for Charles's murder,'' I cuffed Michael heartily on the shoulder. ''The lab reports will show that he died around eight-thirty in the evening, and you can prove you were in Aberdeen around eight-thirty in the evening, can't you?''

''Damn right,'' he said, grinning. Rhonda nodded.

''The bad news is that they're going to nail you for the burglary at Aphrodite's,'' I said.

''Why is that?'' he asked.

''Because you did it,'' I said simply.

Crystal had seen a large blurry man leave the cafe with money in his pocket. That man had been Michael.

''But you said the deputy planted the money on me and made the footprints with my boots,'' Michael protested.

''No, I said the deputy planted the money on you. You said he'd made the footprints and planted the drugs.''

Rhonda's mouth hung open in astonishment.

I continued. ''But that's a silly notion. The boot prints matched. Did Big Dick sneak in here while you were asleep, steal a boot, make prints in the mud, and then bring it back without waking you?

''Not very likely. It's much less complicated to believe

that you dropped Rhonda off at our trailer around ten, buzzed back here, snuck around the far end of the cafe, tromped through the mud under the air conditioner, tracked it around to the back door and into the cafe.

"You knew where the flat bar was because Rhonda had told you. You also knew about the keys, didn't you?"

Rhonda colored.

I thought so. Just try to keep a secret in Delphi.

"You entered the cafe, pried the box open, and took the money," I explained to Michael. "It was just your bad luck that there was already a dead body on the premises.

"I'll bet the lab reports will also indicate that your fingerprints were all over, inside the cafe. It's your good luck that they will know that the murder was committed earlier. If you'd put the flat bar back where it belonged, we probably wouldn't have discovered the theft until next week. You could have covered your trail by then. Sloppy." I tched.

I wondered how Rhonda would react to the news that her boyfriend had robbed her employer, using information he'd gleaned from Rhonda herself. I'll bet she spends a lot more time out at the farm from now on.

I had a farm visit to make myself.

27

....

The Missionary Position

This is the place in mystery novels where the triumphant detective marshals all the facts, confronts an overconfident suspect, trots out the damning evidence, and savors the enormous satisfaction of solving a murder.

Problem was, I still had a loose end to tie up before trotting out anything. And my knowledge of Charles Winston's death left me feeling far from triumphant.

"So, did you *know* that Nicky was Presley's father?" I asked Mother, who was much less surprised at two visits in one day than I had expected.

"I surmised as much," she said softly. "I hoped you'd never know. The pair of them made you suffer enough already."

"So you kept the secret to protect me."

"That's what mothers do," she said simply. "There's still no need to burden Presley with the knowledge. At one time it was not such a stigma—cousins married, and no one blinked. Unfortunately, attitudes have changed, and knowing would only make his difficult life even more so.''

She poured another cup of coffee for herself. "He's lucky to have you around. It will help counter his deplorable genes. And you will do what you must to protect him." She smiled. "The young man is not without charm, you know.''

"I know." I examined my fingers, looked out the window, chewed my lip, unsure how to proceed.

"What's the matter, dear?" She stood in the kitchen, partly in shadow.

"I'm trying to figure it out, but I can't," I said quietly. Sadly.

"Trying to figure out what?" she asked, not moving.

"What secret you were protecting"—I stopped, inhaled, and continued—"when you killed Charles Winston.''

She was steady, except for a small tremor as she set the coffee cup down. A tiny sound that echoed through the house. "What about the tape?" she asked. "We both heard Deputy Albrecht kill Charles.''

"I thought so at first. But a couple of odd facts snagged in my mind." I looked at her. "No wonder you didn't want that recording released.''

"It's not what you think, Tory. My reasons were valid. I *don't* want innocent people hurt. The tape would do more than implicate Big Dick, though I doubt if anyone would look any further for a suspect.''

"You know, I nearly ignored your advice and blurted the whole thing out to him," I said, remembering the awful scene in the patrol cruiser. "I was all ready to confront him with a step-by-step recount of his heinous crime when I realized that he couldn't have done it.''

Mother waited.

"He didn't know about the flat bar," I said simply. "He didn't know it was at the cafe, he didn't know where to find it, he didn't know it existed.''

On the tape, after the savage beating, after Big Dick had left the scene, footsteps had walked back through the cafe, over to Charles's unconscious body. They stopped, and then purposefully strode to the proper shelf. No hesitation, no fumbling under the counter. Directly to the weapon because the murderer knew exactly where to find it.

And how to use it.

My strong, agile mother was perfectly capable of swinging a flat bar on target.

And emotionally able to clean up the mess afterward.

"Other people knew where to find the flat bar," she said quietly.

"Ah, but they all have alibis. Del was at the trailer, getting Junior drunk. Rhonda was in Aberdeen buying drugs with Michael. Jolene was on a date, and Eldon McKee was playing poker with Uncle Albert." I spread my hands. "Neat as a pin. You're the only other person who knew about it."

"Aphrodite?" she asked.

"Del had already sent her home, so that it would be just her and Charles at the cafe. Just Del, Charles, and a tape recorder."

"Is that all?" She still stood in the shadows.

"No, the rest is little stuff but it adds up. Eldon said you *offered* to drive the flat bar back into town. You said *he* asked *you*. You were extremely surprised to hear that the flat bar wasn't where we expected to find it the next morning.

"I don't know how it ties in, but I know that this all has something to do with Grandma," I finished.

Mother sighed. "Tell me what you know, and I'll fill in the blanks if I can," she said sadly.

"After Lottie's phone call, I had thought that Charles was unsettled by his confrontation with Big Dick in your driveway. I assumed that Big Dick threatened him about Del. And he did, but I realized later that Charles was already upset. Lottie said that he was in a hurry to go when she got back after fixing Hubert's lunch. That was *before* Big Dick arrived.

"You were furious that Lottie had left Grandma with a stranger. At the time, I thought it was just overprotectiveness.

"Charles *told* Crystal he was upset about Grandma, but

we still thought he was talking about Big Dick's threat because it occurred in Grandma's driveway.

"And finally, Crystal told you about Charles. Where he was, and when he was leaving, and by what door."

I wanted her to contradict me, to laugh and give me a logical explanation for everything.

She exhaled softly. "You know, I have always had more empathy for you than you realize. Love is more than blind, it can make you crazy as well. And stupid."

She paused and tilted her head back, searching for words. "I loved your father. He was my first and only love and I wanted him so badly that I made a deal with the devil just to have him.

"I *knew* he was married, you see. I knew he had a family when I met him, and I didn't care.

"He was a traveling preacher, he probably had women in every town. I wanted him enough to settle for his terms. We married here, just to keep people from talking. We thought Delphi was far enough away from Sioux City that no one would ever make the connection.

"Then we had you, and believe me, Tory, I have never regretted it, though watching you make my same mistakes has been terrible.

"I kept your father's secret from Grandma and Grandpa. Grandma had always been unstable; giving birth to all those babies, just to have them die was more than she could bear. She watched over Juanita and me, and hovered and worried every minute that we were going to die too.

"When she accidentally discovered that your father was already married, she went berserk. I think she might have caught him"—she paused—"with Juanita. It drove her over the edge."

I considered this. The passion in her novels came from her own life. My mother had been so wildly in love that she would share her man, even with her sister.

There had been a rumor about Juanita with a married man, long ago. Furiously denied, and then ignored, the rumor had quieted eventually. And Juanita became a Christian fanatic, and married a man she could control completely.

"So Grandma ran Dad off the property, and he was never heard from again," I said.

"Not exactly, Tory," Mother said. "She killed him."

Of course.

Charles had uncovered a murder of his own during his little chat with Grandma. And he tried to report it to Big Dick, who was interested only in his own threats and accusations.

"Then she chopped him up in little pieces," Mother continued in a monotone, "and buried them around the farmyard."

"Under the chicken coop," I said.

Grandma's poultry fixation explained at last.

"Unfortunately, I didn't know about that until after I hired Eldon to tear it down. In the first couple months after, uh, your father's death, Grandpa and I found most of . . . him . . . and disposed of the . . . pieces. When we stopped finding any, we thought we were finished."

She smoothed her hair back from her forehead. "It killed Grandpa, you know, that knowledge. He died less than a year later.

"It was actually handy for all of Delphi to *know* that your father was a bigamist. It took their attention away from his disappearance. They felt smugly sorry for me, and never questioned why he didn't come back."

"So you spent your life raising me and protecting Grandma from her own craziness," I said.

"And protecting you from her craziness too," she said quietly.

" 'That's what mothers do,' " I quoted. "I take it Aunt Juanita doesn't know."

Mother had lived with this for more than thirty years, the only small-town person ever to keep a secret.

"Somehow, Grandpa and I kept her from finding out. She went on with her life."

"That's why no one else was ever allowed to care for Grandma," I realized. "You lived in terror that she'd blurt it out to someone. You gave up your own chance for a new life to protect your mother.''

"Don't feel sorry for me. Who should have paid the price? I've been busy and content. Until lately Grandma was manageable. Most of the time, she forgot entirely about your father. I could leave her for short periods without worrying.''

"Why Lottie?'' I had always wondered why Lottie was the only one allowed to stay with Grandma.

"Because Lottie is kind and partially deaf and completely stupid. She rambles on and on and never actually listens to anyone else,'' Mother said. "Unfortunately, I gambled everything on her, and lost.''

"So what happened?'' I asked. "Two days ago, I mean.''

She sat opposite me at the table and rubbed her eyes.

"I left Lottie here and ran my errands in Aberdeen, which included buying a flat bar for Eldon. Back in Delphi, I stopped to see you on the way home, as I always do.''

"I reported Lottie's telephone conversation,'' I remembered. "And asked you to buy light bulbs for her.''

"At the store, Crystal told me about Charles being upset, and his car troubles. She said that he was sleeping upstairs and that she was going to send him over to the cafe for supper.'' Mother smiled for the first time. A small one. "Psychics should know better than to talk so much.''

She inhaled, and continued. "Then I drove home, scolded Lottie, and assessed the damage. I knew that Grandma had told Charles something. Lottie said that he was quite upset *before* Big Dick arrived.

"Grandma herself was very agitated. She had been ever since we started that blasted chicken coop job. I gave her a tranquilizer and she quieted. I had already decided that I must speak to Charles, to beg him not to bring this old horror out into the open, that he would only damage a dying old woman. Then Eldon called, saying he needed the flat bar in town.''

Which Eldon wouldn't have needed if Stu had not arranged for him to install a sliding door at his own house to appease his wife. So that he could visit me.

"Grandma was finally sleeping peacefully, and Eldon had given me the perfect excuse to drive back to town.

"I want you to know, Tory, that I had no intention of killing Charles. I left the flat bar at the cafe, with explicit instructions so that you could find it and hand it over to Eldon the next morning. That's all."

She stood again, gazing out the kitchen window, and said quietly, "I parked my car on a side street, walked to the side door of the cafe, and waited for Crystal to send Charles over to supper. I thought I could convince him that no good could come from bringing this to light now."

"And Charles refused to be reasonable," I said.

"He was adamant. This was murder, it had to be reported. What difference if an old woman would be shattered and a young woman hurt? It was his position on the subject, and he was very clear about it.

"So I left him. He went into the cafe, and I walked across the street and sat in the office at the church. I wanted to talk to Clay. To hear his opinion. Maybe it *was* time to let it all come out in the open, to stop cowering.

"And I would have told Clay everything, then and there. But he was out on a counseling call. I peeked at his appointment book, he was meeting Lila Pankratz."

She raised an eyebrow. Clay and Lila?

Doing more than counseling?

Nah.

"I sat at Clay's desk for over an hour, waiting for him to come back, rehearsing what to say. I looked out the window occasionally, watching for Clay, but the only person I saw was Deputy Albrecht, skulking around. I finally realized that I had to go home and check on Grandma. I was going to write a note asking Clay to call me when I looked out the window of his office, across the street at the cafe."

"And saw Del rushing out the front door, buttoning her blouse, grinning like an idiot," I completed for her.

"Yes, and she joined Junior, who was kicking her car door in front of the grocery."

Mother took a deep breath. "From around the corner, Deputy Albrecht saw Delphine leave, and shortly after, I could just make out some kind of commotion through the cafe window. I knew Charles had gone into the cafe, and I had not seen him come out. It was easy to assume he was still inside. And it was easier yet to assume that Big Dick was in there with him.

"I hurried out of the church, walking around the back because Delphine and Junior were crossing the street toward me. I hid behind the cafe and waited."

Junior had left a note for Clay on the desk in his office, I remembered.

"Soon Big Dick came out the cafe side door. He carefully locked up and tucked the keys next to the downspout, and left. Smiling."

"So you unlocked the door and went in," I said.

"Yes. Of course, I had no idea that there was a tape recorder going. I quietly surveyed the scene—the disorder, the blood. I walked to where Charles was draped across the counter. He was unconscious and had been beaten very badly, he might even have died from his injuries. The lab reports will tell us that."

"So you decided to finish it up?" I asked.

"Not in so many words," Mother said. "I don't remember making a decision. I just looked at him and did what I had to do. I simply could not let my mother go to jail."

Could I?

"And then you cleaned up," I said. "I should have realized that Big Dick had no reason to move Charles."

"I only wanted to spare you. I'm so sorry you were the one to find him, Tory. And I'm so sorry that you had to know any of this," she said sadly.

"What are you going to do now?" I asked, afraid to hear her answer. Afraid to have to make an awful decision of my own.

"I'm going to wait for Grandma to die, peacefully and with dignity, in her own home, and then I will turn myself in."

She looked straight into my eyes as she said it. I searched her face.

With incredible relief, I believed her.

"But I'm not going to tell them why," she said, determined.

"They're going to wonder," I said.

"Let 'em," she said, smiling.

"What about the tape?" I asked.

"Gone already," she said, shrugging. "You read murder mysteries, Tory. Don't you know better than to trust the evidence to anyone?"

Amazingly, we laughed.

Epilogue

I drove through town on the way back home.

Aphrodite was standing by herself on the sidewalk in front of the cafe, outside the flapping yellow ribbon perimeter.

She looked burly and forlorn.

I parked and stood next to her, and squinted at our wavery reflections in the cafe window.

"I miss the old joint," she said.

"Me too," I said. "But they should let you open up soon, and after a while things'll be back to normal. It won't be easy though."

"Who said it would be?" she snorted. "Who said it could be?"

She was right. Life was never easy, a fact not likely to change in the near future.

Would Del make a new peace with her son? With me? With herself?

Could I mend fences with Neil? I needed him, at least as a friend.

Would I continue to see Stu? He was married and I wanted him. A bad combination.

For the moment, I was glad I didn't have the answers to any of those questions. I'd had more than enough answers for one day.

There was a new 87th Precinct novel waiting for me at home. I intended to bury myself in it.

Not forever. That was no longer possible.

Just for a while.

I threw an arm around Aphrodite's broad shoulders.

"We'll survive," I said, meaning it.

I remembered something Agent Ingstad had said—Mrs. Ferguson.

"Now what's this I hear about a husband?" I asked. "You got one stashed somewhere that we don't know about?"

Aphrodite grinned.

E. J. Pugh Mysteries by
SUSAN ROGERS COOPER

"One of today's finest mystery writers"
Carolyn Hart

HOME AGAIN, HOME AGAIN
78156-5/$5.50 US/$7.50 Can
Romance author and amateur sleuth E. J. Pugh finds the latest
murderous mystery strikes much too close to home when her
husband Willis disappears.

HICKORY DICKORY STALK
78155-7/$5.50 US/$7.50 Can
An invisible, high-tech prankster is wreaking havoc with E. J.'s
computer, phone lines and bank account. She suspects a creepy
neighbor kid—until he turns up dead in the Pugh family car.

ONE, TWO, WHAT DID DADDY DO?
78417-3/$5.50 US/$7.50 Can
Everyone in town is stunned by the apparent murder-suicide of the
well-liked Lester family. But E. J. may be the only one in Black
Cat Ridge who believes the murderer still walks among them.

JILL CHURCHILL

"JANE JEFFREY IS IRRESISTIBLE!"
Alfred Hitchcock's Mystery Magazine

Delightful Mysteries Featuring
Suburban Mom Jane Jeffry

GRIME AND PUNISHMENT
76400-8/$5.99 US/$7.99 CAN

A FAREWELL TO YARNS
76399-0/$5.99 US/$7.99 CAN

A QUICHE BEFORE DYING
76932-8/$5.50 US/$7.50 CAN

THE CLASS MENAGERIE
77380-5/$5.99 US/$7.99 CAN

A KNIFE TO REMEMBER
77381-3/$5.99 US/$7.99 CAN

FROM HERE TO PATERNITY
77715-0/$5.99 US/$7.99 CAN

SILENCE OF THE HAMS
77716-9/$5.99 US/$7.99 CAN

WAR AND PEAS
78706-7/$5.99 US/$7.99 CAN

Murder Is on the Menu at the Hillside Manor Inn

Bed-and-Breakfast Mysteries by

MARY DAHEIM

featuring Judith McMonigle

BANTAM OF THE OPERA
76934-4/ $5.99 US/ $7.99 Can

JUST DESSERTS 76295-1/ $5.99 US/ $7.99 Can

FOWL PREY 76296-X/ $5.99 US/ $7.99 Can

HOLY TERRORS 76297-8/ $5.99 US/ $7.99 Can

DUNE TO DEATH 76933-6/ $5.99 US/ $7.99 Can

A FIT OF TEMPERA 77490-9/ $5.99 US/ $7.99 Can

MAJOR VICES 77491-7/ $5.99 US/ $7.99 Can

MURDER, MY SUITE
77877-7/ $5.99 US/ $7.99 Can

AUNTIE MAYHEM 77878-5/ $5.99 US/ $7.99 Can

NUTTY AS A FRUITCAKE
77879-3/ $5.99 US/ $7.99 Can

SEPTEMBER MOURN
78518-8/ $5.99 US/ $7.99 Can

CHECK OUT MISS ZUKAS

Librarian and Sleuth Extraordinaire

by
JO DERESKE

MISS ZUKAS AND THE LIBRARY MURDERS
77030-X/$5.99 US/$7.99 Can
A dead body stashed in the fiction stacks is most improper.

MISS ZUKAS AND THE ISLAND MURDERS
77031-8/$5.99 US/$7.99 Can
A class reunion brings back old friends, old enemies...
and a new murder.

MISS ZUKAS AND THE STROKE OF DEATH
77033-4/$4.99 US/$6.99 Can

MISS ZUKAS AND THE RAVEN'S DANCE
78243-X/$5.99 US/$7.99 Can

OUT OF CIRCULATION
78244-8/$5.99 US/$7.99 Can